Duchess
If You
Dare

Also by Anabelle Bryant

The Midnight Secrets Series

London's Wicked Affair

London's Best Kept Secret

London's Late Night Scandal

London's Most Elusive Earl

Duchess If You Dare

ANABELLE BRYANT

ZEBRA BOOKS
Kensington Publishing Corp.
www.kensingtonbooks.com

ZEBRA BOOKS are published by

Kensington Publishing Corp.
119 West 40th Street
New York, NY 10018

All Kensington titles, imprints, and distributed lines are available at special quantity discounts for bulk purchases for sales promotion, premiums, fund-raising, educational, or institutional use.

Special book excerpts or customized printings can also be created to fit specific needs. For details, write or phone the office of the Kensington Sales Manager: Attn.: Sales Department. Kensington Publishing Corp., 119 West 40th Street, New York, NY 10018. Phone: 1-800-221-2647.

Zebra and the Z logo Reg. U.S. Pat. & TM Off.

First Zebra Trade Printing: April 2021
ISBN-13: 978-1-4201-5269-2
ISBN-10: 1-4201-5269-6

ISBN-13: 978-1-4201-5270-8 (ebook)
ISBN-10: 1-4201-5270-X (ebook)

10 9 8 7 6 5 4 3 2 1

Printed in the United States of America

For Beth-Ann, Kerri and Ellen, who always have my back

For David and Nicholas, who always have my heart

CHAPTER I

Scarlett wasn't alone. The dull scratch of pebbles against roof shingles revealed that fact. A heartbeat later a disturbing shift rippled through the dank air to confirm her suspicion. The soot-covered bricks of the alleyway offered few choices for escape.

No matter. Scarlett welcomed danger as an exercise to measure her skill. Nevertheless, she remained vigilant to the perils in wait for a woman out alone at first light, most especially in a neighborhood regarded as London's worst slum. Seven Dials was nothing more than a nest of narrow alleys and squalid tenements.

She glanced backward as a shadow arrowed across her path. She hurried her steps as behind her the stranger gave chase, appearing in the darkness as if dropped from the sky. Scarlett had surmised her enemy watched from above, slinking across the slates and down the eaves with the soundless grace of a falling star because she'd often moved in a similar manner. Except she'd never exposed her position as carelessly as the stranger who hunted her now.

Prepared for the inevitable attack, she pivoted and crouched low in a defensive pose, a motion so swift her black cloak wrapped around her body like a tight cocoon, quick to disguise her trousers and the long silver blade she'd drawn silently from her boot.

Women were expected to wear endless layers and cumbersome skirts, squeal and faint in the face of danger, to need the strength and courage of an able-bodied male, but not Scarlett Wynn. She refused to be categorized by a separate standard. She was an independent entity, capable beyond common belief and undoubtably lethal when the situation warranted violence.

Apparently, this moment warranted it.

Her foe remained in the shadows; his lean form unmistakably male. He held no weapon she could discern and when he lurched, she reacted with a honed agility that usually startled her attacker into momentary pause. But this man didn't hesitate, his arm a band of muscle as he caught the fluttering edge of her cloak and with a sharp yank pulled her closer. In the past, she'd employed the same method on the offensive, binding the cloth around an assailant's neck or body, the lightweight wool effective to choke or subdue as needed.

It appeared someone was knowledgeable to her technique—or worse, able to anticipate her reaction and counteract with skill.

Very well. The process would offer further opportunity to improve her dexterity.

Bringing her gloved fingers to the tie at her throat, she released the strings and shrugged free of the garment, twisting loose in the process before kicking her attacker in the rib cage with a sharp jab of her heel. He took the hit easily, only jarring backward slightly with a huffed exhalation before he came at her again, the blue-black light lending few clues to the most vulnerable parts of his body, her blade at the ready to pierce skin. She might have aimed her foot lower and crippled the fool with a strike to his ballocks—but then where was the adventure in getting right down to it? Unless necessary, an attack of that nature was inequitable, similar to when an assailant used her hair as a point of weakness. Scarlett refused to allow such an advantage and always pinned the lengths into a tight bun at her nape, no longer offering anyone easy access. She considered herself an equal if not superior fighter. Gender remained irrelevant.

The stranger dropped the cloak to the cobbles and whipped it outward in a far-reaching arc meant to entangle but she expected the trap and leapt neatly aside. Gaining momentum, she leveraged use of the right wall, turned against it and scissored her legs, her arm pointed straight at her assailant, her palm tight on the hilt of her knife. This was a fight easily won and she might have sliced into him were it not for a betraying slant of sunlight that spared a glimpse of her attacker's profile.

Recognition was quick and she lowered the blade at the last moment.

"You'll need to do better than that." Her statement, absent of fear, evoked laughter in response. "Or you may find my blade sunk deep into your neck."

"When did you know it was me?"

"Your identity?" Scarlett leaned down and slid her weapon into the concealed sheath in her boot. "Only now. But your presence . . ." She scoffed softly with a hint of indignant mockery. "You're too noisy on the eaves. I was aware of someone for twenty paces already."

"Duly noted." Felix Howell, friend more than foe, clenched his gloves together as if to lock the advice up tight.

Scarlett retrieved her cloak, snapped the fabric lengthwise to rid the wool of unwanted vermin and quickly reassembled. Then the two fell into step as if they hadn't just fought viciously in a confined alleyway in the wee hours of dawn.

"What brings you here?"

"The last time we spoke, you invited me to test your skill."

"To test *your* skill," she corrected with a shake of her head.

"Either way, my curiosity was piqued. How could I resist a rare invitation from a Maiden of Mayhem, a beautiful and vigilant fighter against crime? I'd be a fool."

"Things must be slow on Bow Street." Scarlett underscored her tone with annoyance though she wondered if Felix noticed. "You shouldn't speak so carelessly."

"We are out at an ungodly hour in Seven Dials where everyone is either pursuing cheap gin or how to rid oneself of the headache caused by the overconsumption of cheap gin."

"It's not the ape-drunk and befogged who would find that information useful."

"Agreed." He swiped the pad of his thumb against the side of his nose twice in a habit she'd come to recognize and when he spoke again his tone had sobered. "The shadows are always listening. Still, your identity is safe with me."

They exited the mouth of the alley and turned right on Suffolk Street. Scarlett meant to reach her seamstress's apartment before daybreak. The hired girl, Linie, fitted Scarlett's trousers, gloves, and every other article of clothing that couldn't be purchased forthright from a modiste because of its uncommon requirements. Moving about before most of London peeled open an eyelid was second nature to Scarlett and she preferred to conduct business under the cover of darkness, blending seamlessly into the newly awakened commercial bustle of the area without notice once her errands were completed.

Ordinarily, Linie worked in Madame Ivory's Emporium, a respected shop located on Bond Street where Scarlett first made her acquaintance. Linie was a sweet, young girl with nimble fingers and a flair for creative designs often unappreciated by her employer. When Scarlett had inquired casually about adapting a dress to include a split skirt for better mobility, Linie eyed her with genuine enthusiasm. Their relationship had progressed from there.

Since then, Scarlett brought her wardrobe requirements directly to Linie's single-room apartment and simultaneously advanced the girl's skillful experience, financial security and hopeful dream of becoming a lead designer in female fashion. Linie envisioned keeping her own shop someday, a place where customers could see her talent displayed through a variety of garments, the fashion designs au courant.

The early hour assured Linie wouldn't be late for work and, aside from her quick attention in producing the garments, the girl possessed an even more valuable trait. Linie didn't ask questions, often too anxious to explore a new idea to ponder why Scarlett required a hidden pocket sewn into the calf section of her breeches or two layers of leather on the palms of her gloves.

"As always, it is a pleasure." Felix bowed low as he prepared to leave, his pretense of chivalry somewhat comical. "Until next time."

"Next time don't make so much noise if you intend on surprising me. Appear when I least expect it if you'd like to test *your* skill." Scarlett spared him a smile and then turned on her heel. Linie's apartment was still four blocks to the east and she wanted to reach the address without further delay.

Ambrose Cross, fourth Duke of Aylesford, brought his fist down on the ornately carved mahogany desk and glared at his brother seated before him. "This can't continue."

"It's just a loan, Ambrose. A minor sum to tide me over until—"

"That's what you said last week." Forcing out a breath composed of equal parts frustration and exhaustion, Aylesford reclaimed his chair in an attempt to gain a better leash on his temper. "Much to my dismay you still possess no purposeful aim and while it's your right to dally with women, drink to excess and gamble foolishly, you've taken privilege too far. Worse yet, the people you surround yourself with are leeches and sycophants who will take your money and muddy your good name."

Martin appeared disgruntled but Ambrose noticed his brother didn't disagree.

"You won't get another farthing from me, never mind two thousand pounds, until you show you're more accountable with your spending."

"You'd force me to heel?" Martin eyed his brother with an incredulous expression. "*That's* taking privilege too far. Were our parents alive to hear this conversation, you'd be the one in the wrong, abusing your power simply because you were born first and hold the ledger books hostage. It should be noted I would have won at the tables last night if I'd had enough in my pocket to play longer."

"Come now, Martin. I was born at night, but it wasn't last night." Aylesford refused to have this argument yet again. He wouldn't defend his stance. Nor would he insist their father, if not mother as well, understood the responsibility of the title and the unending effort it took to keep the dukedom solvent and productive. He was tired of watching his hard work and dedication get tossed away on a shake of dice or squandered on ladybirds and liquor.

Yet Martin persisted. "You'd deny me recreation?"

This question burned through Aylesford's last nerve like a cobweb strung over a flame. "Yes, considering your entire adult life has been composed of nothing but the same." He stood, his temper ramped another notch, and shoved his chair backward to round the desk and approach his brother. "But I won't deny you purposeful work. You could oversee the swath of land to the north of our property in Oxford. Once established, you'd confer with the farmers about their upcoming harvest."

"I don't know a thing about farming—"

"Neither did I until Father taught me. A steward will educate and guide you until you understand the undertaking. It's meaningful work instead of the reckless way you while away your days on fanciful amusement and extravagant idleness."

"What would you know about either? You're always locked away in your study." Martin heaved a breath. "That's a deuced dull way to live."

"It's called responsibility. You should introduce yourself to the concept," Ambrose countered. "While you're out cavorting and wasting valuable time, I'm answering correspondence concerning the family holdings, providing for our tenants, and reviewing parliamentary matters."

"You say." Martin pinched his lips twice as if he couldn't decide which words to allow out. "But you've managed so well, I wouldn't wish to interfere with whatever system you have in place. Besides, it sounds as if you're attempting to shirk your duties and put some of that *meaningful work* on my shoulders. With the title comes the toil. I've perfected my purpose and have always considered my expertise to lie in the role of second son. The expendable male. It's better that way, for both of us."

Ambrose was too intelligent not to recognize these compliments as excuses, but if Martin believed he could continue to draw on the finances with careless haste, then his brother was about to receive an education nonetheless. "I'm reducing your funds."

"Reducing? I came in to see you today because I need more." Martin inflected the final word so determinedly even a bootjack would understand his meaning. "I'm requesting your help. That's what you do, Ambrose. You help. You help everyone and now I need you to help me."

"I have helped you. Again, and again, and again to no end. But be assured this is indeed the end. There will be no more expendable cash at your disposal. You'll need to learn how to live on a budget."

"A budget?" Martin's face screwed into a look of abject horror. "But you're Aylesford. You're a duke. One of the most powerful men in all England. I'm your brother. We don't . . . budget." The last word was tainted by a note of revulsion.

Ambrose waited patiently; however, when his brother remained silent with that same expression of shock etched on his pale features, he continued. "Your funds are being reduced by two thirds, one third of which will repay the woeful debt you've already accrued. The other third will be placed into savings for your future. I regret having to treat you like a child, but you've left me few choices. You'll need to make do with one third of what you're accustomed."

"One third?"

"One third." Ambrose couldn't resist the opportunity to deliver a final lecture replete with sarcasm. "Instead of your nightly entertainment of prostitutes, dice and brandy, from now on it will have to be prostitutes, dice *or* brandy."

"Truly, Ambrose?"

"Definitely, Martin. Do you understand and agree? Keep in mind a man is only as honorable as his word."

"I do." Martin's expression fell further. "Deuced. Life will be dull and uneventful."

"I don't doubt that it will and that's exactly what you need."

CHAPTER 2

Scarlett reached Linie's room on Earnshaw Street at dawn. She took the front steps of the tenement at one with the shadows and claimed the key left under the empty clay pot on the sill. She slipped it into the lock and eased the door open. This building housed three additional apartments and while Scarlett noted the occupants as was her habit of information inventory, she hadn't crossed anyone's path. The sooner she collected and paid for her clothing the better. Linie would undoubtably need to leave for Madame Ivory's soon.

Upon entering the narrow hall, the first thing Scarlett noticed was the absolute quiet. Not that any of her early visits were met with conversation or other ambient noises of life, but the eerie silence struck her as a foreboding sign that either Linie wasn't at home or remained abed, both suggestions unlikely. Never had the girl shown a disregard for her responsibilities and more than once Scarlett had encouraged her to slow down. Working toward a goal was one thing, but exhausting oneself in a race against the clock was quite another.

Entering Linie's room confirmed Scarlett's initial misgiving and simultaneously created several more concerns. No lantern burned and the fire lay dead in the grate. It appeared Linie hadn't spent the night at home. Any presumption she'd stepped out this morning for fresh bread was swiftly dashed. Scarlett lit the lantern so she could see the interior with ease.

Articles of clothing were strewn across the bed as if considered and discarded. None appeared designed for sale. The skirts were part of Linie's simple, serviceable wardrobe although Scarlett suspected the seamstress tried on all designs, whether intended for herself or others. That would be a temptation too difficult to resist.

A peek into the narrow closet on the opposite wall revealed three satin gowns, all of which showed signs of wear but were so unexpected they forced Scarlett to pause. The necklines were low, the colors and styles garish, and not at all in keeping with Linie's distinctive appreciation of fashion. But then, what did Scarlett know of the girl other than her talent with a needle and ambitious desire to become London's most innovative modiste? Perhaps the dresses didn't belong to her and were hung there in wait of a paying client.

The single window that faced the alley was partially opened, wide enough for Stitches, Linie's adopted stray, to come and go as she pleased, although the cat's water bowl was dry and food bowl empty with only a few crumbs crusted around the rim. Further proof Linie hadn't returned to her rooms for a good length of time. Certainly not since last evening. But then where had she gone? And where was she now? It wasn't like the girl to neglect her pet or shirk her responsibilities, most especially on a day when Scarlett would retrieve her commissioned garments and pay a handsome sum.

Despite these abnormalities, near the footboard atop an old wooden trunk where Linie often kept Scarlett's order, the wrapped package waited. What should she make of this? Linie must have expected her visit. What happened to disrupt their planned appointment? Scarlett wasn't comfortable leaving the payment in the room. The open window as well as an easily picked door latch were all invitations to theft. She would return this evening to pay and confirm everything was as it should be. While Scarlett thrived by balancing on the razor's edge of danger, she wouldn't wish for anything untoward to befall her young friend.

"Come now, Martin, your brother is behaving downright priggish." Kenneth Kilbaren, fellow second son and general ne'er-do-well, leaned his chair back on its rear legs and raised his brandy for another swallow. "It's easy for those with power and money to be cruel to the lot of us without."

"I dare say that isn't exactly accurate, KK, although I know you understand my problem, being in damned low water yourself." Martin downed the last of his drink, his mind busy in an attempt to rationalize this unexpected upset to his finances. "My brother takes great pride in reputation, opinion and appearance. I suppose all I can do is compromise."

"In which way exactly?" Kenneth shifted forward and dropped the chair to the floor in a thud loud enough to cause other patrons of Cribb's Parlor to glance in their direction.

Had his friend paid attention? Kenneth's mind was known to wander if one went on too long in conversation.

"The way I see it, as a nobleman but not an heir, it's generally expected I fritter away my time in various forms of excess. Being a second son works to my benefit, KK, as it should to yours. We have the chance to embrace an indulgent life without all the brainwork and paper shuffling that accompanies a musty old title, yet this sudden change of heart by my brother makes that impossible."

"We'll just need to be more innovative, won't we?" Kenneth added, equally invested in the outcome since he so often relied upon Martin to fund their escapades.

"I'm up for the challenge." Martin nodded with surety. "Aylesford suggested I economize my pleasure and choose one source of nightly entertainment instead of three."

"Choose between gambling, liquor or women? An interesting proposition that, if I may be so bold."

"You may." Martin paused, the seed of a new idea taking root. "Regardless, I still have a few feathers to fly, enough for us to celebrate this newfangled notion with a bang-up evening."

"I bet we'll manage brilliantly."

"I'll accept that wager." Martin drew an X in the air. "Now, we've gambled, haven't we?"

Kenneth knocked on the scarred tabletop beside his glass. "And we've already imbibed."

"True, quite true. So, what do you say we treat ourselves to a little bubble and squeak tonight?" Martin grinned, his usual carefree disposition restored. "And I'm not talking about beef and cabbage, my friend."

"The Scarlet Rose?"

"Only London's finest brothel for London's finest second sons."

"Let me check my schedule." Kenneth pantomimed donning spectacles as he withdrew an imaginary book from his breast pocket to open and review. "As I suspected, I've no sessions to attend in the lofty House of Lords being I don't hold a seat in Parliament."

They raised their glasses in celebration of their evening plans. It didn't matter Martin's was already empty.

Scarlett made her way to Mortimer Street along Cavendish Square and up the steps into Wycombe and Company, the squat building of sandy limestone and rectangular grid windows unremarkable in comparison to the other fine shops in the vicinity. This establishment was a poky little premise, modest at best, and overshadowed by the adjacent haberdashery. Wycombe's didn't sell fashionable trinkets or offer necessary services to its customers because it had no customers and no wares to sell.

On the lower level there was everything one would expect to find within a merchant's place of business, though it rarely if ever was used. In contrast, abovestairs there were several rooms, a working kitchen, bath chamber and drawing room.

In essence, to all passersby the property was innocuous, but if you happened to be a member of its exclusive population, then the building was indispensable. And so, it was that the nondescript structure of Wycombe and Company existed in plain sight for all of London and no one was the wiser for its importance.

Scarlett entered, cheered to see Julia Wycombe at the writing desk near the far window. Out of necessity Scarlett had kept her cloak drawn around her unconventional narrow-fit trousers as she bustled through London's busy streets, but the action often left her overheated and now she couldn't wait to shed the garment.

Julia Wycombe was a widow whose husband, a viscount, had acquired considerable wealth through wise investment. Upon his passing he left everything to his younger brother who had since relocated to America, content to gift the Mortimer Street address and London town house property to Julia. The arrangement smoothed away most every wrinkle when Julia, Scarlett and the other Maidens of Mayhem realized they needed a centrally located and specific meeting place away from their individual homes in order to accommodate their uncommon lifestyle. With society disinclined to allow females to conduct business, own property or invest finances without the consent or participation of a male, the Wycombe building became their fortress of secrets.

"Scarlett, how are you?" Julia turned to glance over her shoulder and then after a swift smile reorganized the papers she'd attended and stood to approach.

"Well enough considering I had my knife drawn before sunrise." Scarlett draped her cloak over the chair back and dropped into the cushion with a sigh.

"Not your usual morning?" Julia took the chair across from Scarlett. "Seeing you're in one piece with a sparkle in your eye, I suspect it wasn't anything serious."

"Nothing to worry over."

"Who was it?" Julia's slender brows rose with the question.

"Howell."

"Your thief taker acquaintance?"

"Acquaintance." Scarlett deliberated the word. "Now there's an interesting descriptor."

"It sounds like there's more to tell."

"Perhaps." Scarlett abandoned the subject, unsure how she'd categorize her relationship with the Bow Street Runner. "I'm concerned about Linie."

"Your seamstress? Why so?" Julia didn't miss a beat, accustomed to Scarlett's tendency to speak candidly and to the point.

"When I stopped by to collect my recent order, she wasn't there despite the early hour and our previous agreement. Additionally, it didn't appear she'd slept at home."

"That is strange. Have you noticed the habit before?"

"No, though I daresay I don't know her well enough to understand her routines." Scarlett only knew the seamstress in one capacity, although an innate sense of understanding frequently offered her insight in regard to people. "Still, something about the scene struck me as unplanned."

"Your intuition is your greatest strength." Julia nodded thoughtfully. "One of many, in truth."

"Thank you." Scarlett continued, "I purposely disturbed a few items in her room to help indicate whether or not she or anyone else visits through the day. I'll stop by again later this evening and pay for my order. I hope she's there and this all has a logical explanation."

"I'd chance it's a misunderstanding. She may have gone to see family and stayed the night. Or kept the company of a beau."

"Yes, very plausible suggestions, and yet . . ." Scarlett couldn't explain why she doubted either of these reasons would prove true. "I'll know soon enough when I return. How are things with you? Have you spoken to Phoebe or Diana lately? The last few times I've come by they haven't been here." When the four ladies had banded together with a vow to right wrongs in London and fight for women who had no voice against male harassment or otherwise unjust travesties thrust upon their gender, they'd labelled themselves the Maidens of Mayhem. Perhaps it was a fanciful thought at first, but their intention was soon realized. London had more nefarious secrets than anyone imagined. And while they could never correct all of the city's multitude of heinous sins, if they righted one wrong or bettered one female's situation, they'd succeeded.

"No, and I suppose that's good news. Less need for the four of us reflects well on London, doesn't it?"

"I wouldn't go that far," Scarlett said with a short laugh. "You're more optimistic than I. If we aren't hearing reports of offenses then I'd assume the miscreants are becoming adept at concealing their crimes. It causes me to feel *more* wary than usual. Like we're on the verge of something calamitous. All this quiet makes me twitchy."

"I hope not, Scarlett, but if you're correct, we're here to support each other through all circumstances. We joined together to right wrongs and fight for justice no matter the cause."

"Yes, I know, and I wouldn't have it any other way." Her words were spoken sincerely though she couldn't dismiss the lingering pulse of uncertainty that insisted her sense of impending danger held true.

Much to Scarlett's disappointment, when she returned to Earnshaw Street later that evening, Linie's room remained empty with no trace of the seamstress having come or gone. Things appeared exactly as Scarlett had left them. She took a minute to right the dressing table stool left in front of the doorway and return the emptied tinderbox to the mantelpiece. She regretted not visiting Madame Ivory's shop to check on Linie's whereabouts when she'd had the time this afternoon. Now a visit to the modiste would have to wait until morning.

Collecting her package from the trunk at the foot of the mattress, she gave the room a final glance, extinguished the lantern and opened the door to leave, startled by a petite woman who entered the hall.

"Pardon me." Scarlett's split skirt gave the impression of a traditional day gown and she was thankful for it as she hadn't planned on meeting anyone. A woman wearing trousers was memorable and she wished to be anything but. "Are you here to visit Linie?"

"Yes. She's repairing one of my gowns. I'm Sally." The woman offered a genuine smile. "I live across the hall." She gestured over her shoulder to the opposite doorway.

"Linie isn't here but I doubt she'd mind if you retrieved your dress. I picked up my order as well." Scarlett indicated the package she held and stepped back into the room. Sally was a connection to Linie and might have information of her whereabouts or habits. With no clues to pursue, Scarlett couldn't let the neighbor slip away without first asking a few questions.

Scarlett relit the lantern she'd only just extinguished moments before. Sally moved to the narrow closet and rifled through the handful of dresses there.

"That's strange."

"What is it?"

"My gown isn't here and yet we just had my final fitting yesterday morning."

"Perhaps Linie brought it to Madame Ivory's."

"No, she would never do that. Madame Ivory already complains Linie spends too much time daydreaming about new designs instead of stitching the commissions ordered in the shop. There's no way she'd have brought outside work into the modiste."

"And none of these are yours?"

"No." Sally grimaced as she spared another look at the gowns. "Linie wears these to work."

"Work?" The thought of Linie wearing any of the gaudy designs at Madame Ivory's Emporium made not one whit of sense. "At the modiste?"

"Not there." Sally's voice dropped to a whisper although there was no one to overhear their conversation. "Her other job . . . in the evening."

"I see." Though Scarlett didn't. "She's still working there then."

Assumption of understanding would go far if Sally believed she wasn't revealing secrets.

"Oh yes. With Linie's wanting to start her own business and that pitiful wage Madame Ivory pays, there's no way she can afford this room, eat, and save for the future. That's why Linie's always appreciative when I have a gown in need of repair." Sally pointed to the package Scarlett held at her side. "I'm sure she welcomes your commissions too."

"But I don't think Linie has returned since yesterday. The cat hasn't been fed and her bed doesn't appear to be slept in." Scarlett paused to let this information sink in as Sally eyed the room. "Does she have a gentleman caller? Or family nearby? Somewhere she might stay the night?"

"I suppose if it grew too late, she may have stayed at The Scarlet Rose, although I've never known her to do that. She works there because it's a reliable source of income, but I can't say she enjoys it."

"The Scarlet Rose." Scarlett knew of the brothel and this information was both enlightening and troubling all the same. The popular locale was situated near Vauxhall and catered to proper gentlemen with loose morals and too much time to waste. A refined place where sin was welcomed and discretion was paramount, if one tolerated the contradiction.

A brothel offered legitimacy and pride not found by the gels who accepted coins for a quick bang up against the bricks of a slum alley. The Scarlet Rose conducted business as a place where women exchanged innocence for payment. That fact pierced Scarlett's heart for no other reason than her personal experience with the practice. Nevertheless, her conversation with Sally proved advantageous and offered further clues to Linie's disappearance.

CHAPTER 3

Ambrose settled into a familiar time-worn leather chair in a corner of his club and exhaled a resounding sigh. He didn't understand his brother. Martin was only three years younger and yet his carefree approach to life proved baffling. Didn't he wish to live with purpose and meaning? Didn't the distinguished Aylesford legacy evoke a sense of duty? It was certainly that way for Ambrose. He'd inherited the title, its responsibility and the daily, sometimes suffocating weight of preserving his pristine heritage. It composed the core of his being.

He'd hardly organized these thoughts when his closest friend, Roger Ellis, Viscount Galway, sauntered across the threshold. Ambrose beckoned him over with a wag of his chin, content to silence his mental considerations. He needed distraction. *Fast.*

"Your company is exactly what I desire this evening."

"Me?" Galway made a show of looking back over each shoulder. "Is there a fetching blonde behind me? A beautiful brunette tagging along?"

"A woman? Not here at White's and definitely not the answer to my misery." Another sigh escaped, much like the first one.

"You'd be surprised how many troubles can be forgotten once you're buried inside a willing female. We're hot-blooded bachelors, aren't we?" Galway claimed the leather chair across from Ambrose.

"Honestly, an ungodly chill runs through me whenever you open your mouth and Martin's mentality comes out."

"Oh, so we're to be serious this evening," Galway muttered as he signaled for a brandy. "Brother troubles?" he asked, his voice returning to normal.

"More than you can imagine."

"Come now, Aylesford. If Martin prefers to spend most evenings foxed and otherwise distracted, it's because you're damned intimidating. He believes he can't be seen in the shadow cast by your radiant glow."

"I'd prefer to think I lead by example." Aylesford accepted a brandy and waited until the footman served Galway before he continued. "I need my brother to realize London is not his play yard, the family coffers are not bottomless, and my patience isn't endless."

"Indeed." Galway took a sip of his liquor.

Ambrose quickly relayed the specifics of his conversation with Martin earlier in the day.

"So with this tightening of the purse strings, you think he'll suddenly understand his sense of responsibility when nothing has been expected of him for twenty-five years?"

"I know." Ambrose groaned, pressing his mouth into a firm line to stop an oncoming scowl. "I have only myself to blame. When my parents left us early, I worried for his youth. For a time after their death he lost the light in his eyes." Ambrose averted his attention to a nondescript corner. "And then I became too busy, enmeshed in assuming the title and learning the tasks needed to oversee the duchy. I shouldn't complain when it's my negligence that led us to this juncture, but I worry on his behalf. How soon will it be before he finds himself mixed up in something I can't easily put to rights?"

Galway nodded. "I know you value your privacy above all else and prefer a quiet life, at times almost reclusive, while Martin is the opposite. It's in your protective nature to keep the peace, amend mistakes and smooth out problems, but eventually your brother will need to stand on his own two feet. You must let slip the leading strings."

"That's why I've decreased his funds, to force some sense of responsibility. I believe this time more than any other, he knows how serious I am."

"I hope so. For your sake."

"Your Grace." A footman approached, his arm outstretched with a folded note in hand. "A messenger left this at the front. He implored me to find you at once and stated it to be a matter of utmost urgency."

Ambrose set down his drink and stood. With a curt nod he dismissed the footman and read over the missive before he cursed a string of words not often heard within polite company and definitely not from His Grace's mouth. Then Ambrose headed for the door.

Scarlett paid the hackney driver and melted into the darkness without a sound. No matter her bold nature, she couldn't walk up to the brothel's front door, drop the brass and ask questions concerning Linie's whereabouts. She hadn't decided yet how she'd go about addressing the situation, but first and foremost she needed to get inside The Scarlet Rose.

Keeping her hood drawn and cloak securely wrapped around her, she skirted the building and blended into the shrubbery at the rear, finding a place to observe before she ventured inside.

A makeshift roadway of crushed oyster shells angled to the back door where gentlemen concerned with discretion gained entry. The contradiction rankled. While everyone was entitled to privacy, if one had to hide a practice, perhaps one should cease the habit. Proper gentlemen and their need to preserve a pristine reputation among the *ton* while secretly consorting with women forced to earn money out of necessity were worthless in her opinion. If those same gentlemen realigned their efforts in Parliament to fight for better laws and equality within the workforce, they'd hold a chance at earning her respect.

She'd hardly completed the thought when a hired hack rolled to the back door, the occupant in such a hurry to exit he didn't wait for the wheels to stop their revolution. And just as she'd surmised only an exhale earlier, beneath the sallow light of two box lanterns a toplofty gentleman appeared, one who likely had a wife at home, a mistress tucked away and an appetite for *more*. Simply because he could. He was titled and *en*titled. Gentlemen such as he had wealth, freedom and abundant advantage.

Scarlett was of opposite thinking. If only she could liberate and educate every woman who was forced without choice to exchange dignity for coin. But that wasn't possible and she understood the necessity of the trade despite the fact that it had claimed her lovely mother.

Biting back a curse, she curled her gloved hands into fists beneath her cloak. This man was no different, no better than the dandy who led her mother on a merry chase, stole her happiness and ultimately ended her life. She watched him knock on the door insistently, the pathetic sinner in an unholy rush to get inside.

She hoped someday, in an irrational but understandable lament, he'd be discovered for his loose morals and made to accept the consequences of his choices. Life seemed terribly disproportionate.

Of course, there was always the pox.

Amused, she enjoyed a soft laugh. Unexpectedly the gentleman ceased his knocking, glanced over his right shoulder and stared in a direct line to her location. Oh, he couldn't see her protected by the black shadowed shrubbery of her surround, but had he heard her? That seemed doubtful as well. The hack had left long ago; however, the area was hardly quiet. Scarlett's attention didn't waver. The gentleman was a combination of innate elegance and rugged good looks. His face was illuminated now that he'd turned and with his eyes pinned to hers unknowingly, a strange fission passed through her, straight to the soles of her feet.

His classic features composed a handsome profile; dark eyes, straight nose and noble chin, quick to prove her earlier assumption correct. Yet something else held her captive. Something unfamiliar and unsettling, and that aspect of his visage disturbed her most of all. Mayhap he couldn't see her in the brush, but he'd sensed her. He'd perceived her somehow.

A looming hulk of a man appeared in the doorframe to address the stranger and with a final quirk of his brow he pivoted and entered the brothel. Scarlett waited. She needed a moment to steady her pulse.

"Stay here." The brusque command of the man who'd allowed Ambrose entry brooked no protest. Ambrose nodded, his irritation at having to rescue Martin yet again drove him to pace a hard line within the confining quarters. The vestibule only accommodated five strides before he was forced to reverse his direction. Time stretched to wear his patience thinner. What had Martin done this time?

A slight jiggling of the latch on the door behind him drew his attention and he watched as the lock released and the panel cracked open a narrow width, just far enough for a cloaked woman to slip through. She hadn't knocked and could only be one of the working girls with her key coming in for late hours. He surmised she'd want to keep her identity concealed though in the small interior it would be a difficult task.

Nevertheless, he turned away wishing for anonymity in equal measure. It proved difficult enough holding the gossipmonger populace at bay regarding Martin's escapades. The last thing Ambrose desired was for it to be reported the Duke of Aylesford frequented The Scarlet Rose. Brothels weren't a place he chose to visit, not even in the green years of his youth.

Damn Martin.

He closed his eyes and inhaled deeply. Why hadn't anyone shown to address his concern? He wasn't accustomed to being made to wait and yet he couldn't wield the power of his title without inviting conjecture. Frustration lit another flame of anger within him. The cloaked woman still hovered in the space behind him. Shouldn't she have gone off to attend her evening's business? Was it expected he acknowledge her? Was there such a thing as flash house etiquette?

The enforcer returned, heavy steps announcing his approach before his wide shoulders crowded the room.

"Madam will see you shortly." The worker glanced briefly to the woman behind Ambrose and back again before he continued. "She's with you?"

"No!" Ambrose's immediate objection sounded stark in the quiet room. "I mean to say . . ." He lowered his voice. "I've come alone."

But his answer didn't seem to matter as the man had already left. Ambrose waited with the silent stranger and the suffocating result of his disconcerting reaction. He eyed the cramped room, the only piece of furniture a single chair. The walls were polished plaster imprinted with a floral design and the floor tiles gleamed. The expensive décor indicated a lucrative business, yet the plush fabrics and decadent accessories did little to disguise the truth for Ambrose. By God, he was a duke, one of the Prince Regent's trusted advisors. What was he doing here in a Vauxhall brothel?

Rescuing his brother.

Still, he wouldn't be made to feel lowly by a woman of questionable morals. A proper lady would fall on her fan and pierce her heart before entering a disreputable establishment.

"Not to worry." Her silky voice reached for him and he jerked around to view her fully for the first time. "I'm immune to your disparaging opinion although a long look in your gilt-framed mirror might offer his lordship a modicum of enlightened humility."

She lowered her hood as she finished speaking and for a moment he couldn't respond. Her face was best described as . . . unexpected. She was young and quite lovely, although only a fool would mistake the hard gleam in her eyes as flirtation and not astute cunning. Why a woman with dulcet speech and remarkable appearance would lower her values to enter a brothel added more confusion to the current situation.

"Pardon." At last he found his voice. He always behaved with honor and courtesy. Respectability composed a pillar of his moral integrity. "I have an appointment." Belatedly, he realized the error of his statement.

"I've no doubt you do." Her lips curved in a sly smile, a bit of deviltry in her expression. "You seemed in a great hurry to enter, my lord."

Your Grace. But he wouldn't correct her. The less anyone knew of his attendance here, the better.

He slid his gaze to her mouth, concerned with her mistaken assumption though he became distracted soon after. She had full lips, deep pink in color, and his attention lingered before ingrained propriety forced his focus upward. Damn, but that was another trap. Her eyes flickered with challenge, their soft gray hue a contradiction to the steely strength of her demeanor. He fought against a misplaced twist of lust.

"I'm here to meet someone." Why he continued to explain his presence was a cursed mystery.

"No one to your liking in the ballroom tonight?"

"No, you misunderstand." Not that it mattered.

But it did. For reputation sake, he supposed. Due to his innate veracity. And another reason too. One he couldn't decipher at the moment and shouldn't have a care about.

However, he wouldn't have her judge *him*. He summoned an expression meant to convey *You have insulted a peer*.

She returned one of her own that declared *I know, and what of it?*

Their facial battle was interrupted by the entrance of an older, imposing woman, dressed in a lavish gown of aubergine satin ruffles.

Excellent. Now they could get on with things. The situation needed to be handled delicately. He'd resolve the problem, extract his brother, and leave with no one the wiser to his identity.

"Aylesford."

So much for anonymity.

"I am Madam Violet." The proprietor eyed him pointedly.

"I'm here for Martin," he replied quickly.

"Of course." Madam Violet nodded. "He's waiting for you in a private room."

Behind him Ambrose heard a distinct murmur that sounded too much like *Not what I expected.* He clenched his teeth to keep from explaining further.

The burly enforcer could only have indicated to Madam Violet that Ambrose and the cloaked woman were together. It would explain the proprietor's indifference though it set match to tinder at the gossip it could incite. If he'd learned anything about the tongue-wags anxious to spread invidious rumors during tea it was that no one, not servant, aristocrat or doxy accomplished discretion when offered the proper incentive. How many times had he been privy to some braggart at White's bemoaning a tale of private troubles as confessed to a courtesan or mistress?

Against his better judgment Ambrose slanted another glance over his shoulder but this time the cloaked woman averted her gaze. He looked to Madam Violet and drew a deep breath, ready to face whatever calamity Martin had caused this time. "We should speak in private."

"Right this way."

Scarlett didn't follow Madam Violet and the condescending *although intriguing* Lord Aylesford farther than the hall. Instead she scurried up the nearest staircase to the second floor and began her exploration. She needed to speak to one of the girls and inquire of Linie's well-being.

She advanced down the long corridor, passed closed doors from which a variety of sounds emanated and decidedly didn't consider the activities within, intent on her purpose. Eventually she neared a narrow alcove where two girls huddled in conversation, one almost completely obscured by the shadow of the other.

Scarlett smiled as she approached, hoping their curious surprise would lend them to answer a few questions before Madam Violet ordered her brawny enforcer to throw her out on her ear. Scarlett knew enough of this business to realize if she wasn't a paying customer she wouldn't be welcomed on the premises.

"Hello." She stepped up to the pair. "I'm looking for a friend."

"You'll need to see Madam Violet downstairs." The taller girl spoke first. "She arranges all the appointments."

Scarlett nodded, her attention drawn to the other girl, the one who hadn't raised her eyes in greeting. She appeared visibly shaken and perhaps Scarlett had interrupted at a time when her friend offered comfort. "I'm sorry. I didn't mean to bother you." She began to back away and then thought better of it. "I'm looking for Linie. I'm concerned because I haven't been able to locate her." She gave just enough information to invite a reaction. Scarlett didn't know the extent to which Linie was involved at the brothel or her relationship with the girls in the hall.

"Linie? You mean Daisy. Linie is her real name. You must be a friend if you know that." The shorter girl who wore a lacy white gown turned as she spoke. Her cheeks were tearstained and lips pressed tight, but she composed herself after a deep sniffle. "Madam Violet names us after flowers and we give those names to the customers. It offers us a degree of privacy. Is Daisy missing? Is something wrong?"

"I hope not, but that's what I'm trying to understand. I only just learned of her employment here and I thought someone might know of her whereabouts. We had an arranged meeting and she never showed up. It doesn't look like she's been at home either." Scarlett hesitated.

The girl in the white gown looked toward her friend, her brow furrowed with worry.

Scarlett couldn't dismiss it. "Are you all right?"

"Well enough." She wiped her hands over her cheeks and drew a deep breath.

"Darla's fine." The taller girl angled her body closer to her friend. Scarlett didn't miss how the girl reached for Darla's hand and offered a reassuring squeeze as if to affirm her answer.

Over the next few minutes the girls were willing to share what they knew of Linie but unfortunately their information amounted to little. Apparently, Linie recently had begun to talk of leaving the brothel. It would explain the garish dresses in her closet. Otherwise the girls kept their lives separate, the clothing used for their trade here at The Scarlet Rose and their personal belongings safe at home.

Like so many bawdy houses, girls came and went with frequency. Variety was a desirable aspect of any profitable establishment and while some girls had regular visitors, most paired up with the random guests who arrived on any given evening. Prostitution was a transient business. Girls aged out quickly. Some entered and left as needed, at times disappearing for long stretches until necessity forced them back into service. Other times the girls vanished forever and it was that aspect that concerned Scarlett most of all. She knew firsthand a level of brutality accompanied the risk of employment.

From what she'd witnessed this evening, the entire scene troubled Scarlett. Something wasn't right. The furtive manner of the girls she'd met reminded her too closely of her mother's fate. Scarlett needed to talk to Madam Violet.

CHAPTER 4

"Tell me what happened and include every detail no matter how insignificant you believe it to be." Ambrose stared at his brother so intently he was surprised Martin didn't complain of a headache. His brother looked pale, his eyes wide and expression strained. When he remained silent, Madam Violet became impatient.

"I wouldn't want to summon a runner."

"You won't summon anyone." *Except me because I have a fat purse.* Ambrose shook his head in the negative, full knowing the proprietress would never invite the law into her establishment. Places such as this clung dearly to confidentiality, otherwise the elite clientele would take their business elsewhere.

"I wouldn't want to spread a rumor." She was quick to retort.

To this, Ambrose had no reply. His reputation was precious indeed.

"What's important is that we aim to achieve the same result and resolve this problem." He returned his attention to where Martin sat in a chair near the wall. "Let's hear it. Start talking."

Martin shifted his gaze to each person in the room, his eyes resting the longest on the trusty enforcer who shadowed Madam Violet. After a sigh of resignation, he began to speak.

"KK . . ." Martin paused and began again. "A friend and I thought to celebrate our new plan for stability with a visit to this fine institution." When Ambrose cleared his throat, Martin offered him a wan grimace but without further pause picked up the thread and kept speaking. "We were having a jolly time. My friend went upstairs right away but it took me a few extra minutes to decide. My usual girl wasn't here so I—"

Again, Ambrose cleared his throat to hurry along the retelling. Mercy spare him the intricacies of Martin and Kilbaren's disregard for good character.

"Once upstairs I commenced with the planned activities. I mean to say, not my friend and myself but—"

"We understand." This from Madam Violet in an annoyed tone. "Get to the point."

Ambrose's expression sobered and he suddenly looked weary. Why was it his brother pursued reckless pleasure and so often found trouble? Where did the fault lie? Ambrose ignored a twinge of guilt. He couldn't be swayed by emotion right now. He nodded in reassurance. "Go on."

"I heard a loud noise in the room next door. I paid no attention because one hears all kinds of things in a brothel . . ." This time Martin cleared his throat. "But then the same sound came again and a female voice cried out."

"Some blokes like to play a role. They pay extra for that," Madam Violet huffed.

"But it wasn't like that. I mean, these sounds were akin to distress," Martin asserted.

"Some customers find pleasure in pain."

No one commented on the madam's quick rebuttal this time and then after a beat, Martin continued.

"The female voice expressed panic. Still, I tried to ignore it," Martin went on. "I was in the middle of my own enjoyment and it was damned difficult to keep my flag flying with so much distraction."

The otherwise silent enforcer grunted and Madam Violet twittered as if amused.

"Then what happened?" Ambrose needed to hear the details

to determine how to proceed. Of course, none of this would have transpired if his brother hadn't made yet another poor decision, but any desire to console was easily overridden by a stronger urge to throttle Martin into next week.

"I heard that same high-pitched, emotional voice object. The girl refused to do something the man said, repeating *no* over and over again. Then it grew strangely quiet. Afterward there were other noises and what sounded like a dull thud, as if someone fell to the floor."

"Someone or something. You can't know what happened. You've got yourself an active imagination." Madam Violet shook her head vehemently. "You were in another room with the door closed. How would you know what transpired elsewhere? Besides, I told you, some of the paying customers enjoy a bit of rough and tumble, but no one hurts the girls," she insisted, her temper alight. "What kind of place do you think this is? People come here to seek pleasure."

Ambrose clenched his teeth to keep an objection at bay. There were places in London that for the right price, anyone could purchase any kind of experience, so Madam Violet's outrage seemed misplaced and narrow-minded at best. He had no way of knowing if Madam Violet would turn a blind eye to fatten her pocket. Considering her fervent defense, he suspected she would overlook wrongdoing if it increased her wealth.

Martin shifted in his chair, and clasped his hands tightly as he leaned forward. "I might have dismissed it all, but the girl keeping my company looked frightened, as if she knew what had happened. I didn't know her well, as she wasn't my regular girl, but I can recognize fear and dismay. Everything about her demeanor changed when she heard the noises through the wall. There was no way I could continue. I feared someone may have been struck and I couldn't very well do *nothing*." He paused, as if gathering what he would say next. "I put myself to rights and went into the hall. The door to the next room was left ajar so I peered inside, but no one was there."

"See! This is all an elaborate ruse to shirk what you owe and explain away the ruckus you've caused," Madam Violet interjected, her burly enforcer straightening his posture as if anxious to be called into action. "He alarmed the other guests and cast aspersions on my establishment for unfounded reasons. I don't need the *ton* looking down on what happens here when most of my clientele spends their days in Mayfair and then slinks to my back door when the sun goes down. I've a business to run."

"Allow him to finish speaking." Ambrose's tone was stern and the room fell silent again. He found it ironic Madam Violet worried about the brothel's reputation when she'd only just threatened him with slander.

"I thought I'd catch a glimpse of someone if they were settling their account or hailing a hackney, so I hurried downstairs and out the front door, not thinking I'd be accused of stealing. Not thinking of anything other than my concern someone could be hurt and another individual may have inflicted harm and was walking away. It all happened rather quickly and that's when he became involved." Martin eyed the enforcer with malevolent distaste.

"I see." Ambrose sighed. While the result was an inconvenience and easily assuaged with generous compensation to Madam Violet, at least nothing worse had befallen at his feet. Martin was well and showed appropriate concern and action had he truly believed someone was in peril. Ambrose would have reacted in the same fashion except it never would have occurred because he'd never have frequented a brothel in the first place.

Ambrose kept his interactions with women brief and noncommittal, a form of physical release only. He had no desire to entangle himself in a lasting relationship at the moment. There was time enough for that when he'd need to get on with producing an heir. Nevertheless, even with his lack of mistress or entanglement of amorous escapades, he'd never looked favorably on bawdy houses, a quality he decidedly didn't share with his brother.

"How much does my brother owe you?" He steeled himself for

Madam Violet's reply, knowing the sly businesswoman would pad the amount for her inconvenience this evening.

"We'll settle the matter in my office with the understanding your brother doesn't visit this establishment again. I don't need him scaring the girls or spreading lies about what occurs within these walls."

Ambrose settled his gaze on Martin, prepared to vent his spleen if his brother voiced the slightest objection, but with a shred of intelligence his brother remained quiet. Perhaps the night wasn't a total loss if Madam Violet's edict would assist in keeping Martin on the straighter path.

Any gratitude Ambrose may have experienced evaporated by the time he'd settled in the carriage with his brother. "There goes time and money I'll never see again." He summoned the last bit of patience within himself and leaned against the cushions. "You might want to reconsider your generous friendship with Kilbaren. You didn't mention the outstanding debt you'd incurred with him. It practically doubled the obligation you'd already incurred."

"KK comes frequently." Martin stifled a wry chuckle at his poor choice of words but sobered immediately. "I sent him home at the start of trouble. No sense in having him inconvenienced on my behalf."

Ambrose drew a deep breath. "Indeed." His tone turned lethal. "Why cause inconvenience?" He closed his eyes in a long blink meant to calm his irritation. "After our discussion earlier, I wrongly assumed you'd take your future more seriously."

"I intend to do so." Martin met his attention. "But these circumstances are different."

"They always seem to be."

"No, I haven't told you everything. I needed to wait until we were alone."

Martin's expression was a rare mixture of contrition and regret and this, more than his flimsy excuses, gained Ambrose's attention. "What else is there to tell?"

"I couldn't speak plainly in front of Madam Violet. Most especially when I believe something's not right at the brothel and she's likely aware but allows it to continue."

"What are you talking about? Did you tell the truth or not?"

"No, I did." Martin shook his head vigorously. "I just didn't tell *all of it.*"

"Will this additional information provoke me to exonerate your blatant lack of respect?"

"Well, no, but you may view this evening differently when you come to understand the circumstances that prompted my actions."

"Go on." Ambrose encouraged him—against his better judgment.

"Before I dashed from the room, I asked the girl I was with what happened to Daisy."

"Daisy?"

"She's my regular at The Scarlet Rose. We have a standing arrangement."

"How romantic," Ambrose muttered.

"I take exception to that. It's hardly bad form. I'd wager half of Parliament visits one brothel or another. You'd be surprised who frequents The Scarlet Rose habitually."

"I don't want to know."

"Of course you don't." Martin appeared affronted.

"What's that supposed to mean?"

"Nothing." But Martin thought better of his reply and persisted. "How is my affair any different than the mistresses you've kept in the past?"

"We don't have time for that conversation." Ambrose heaved an annoyed sigh.

"As I see it, my way of it is far less taxing. I visit Daisy with the understanding that our relationship lasts an hour or so. There's no emotional drama, no obligatory gift giving." Martin waved his hand through the air, the gesture supporting his suggestions.

"We're not using this time to debate the difference between prostitutes and mistresses. We've more important topics to discuss."

"Of course, you would say that," Martin muttered. "Anyway, no one has seen Daisy. It's like she just up and disappeared without a by-your-leave."

"It's a brothel, Martin, not a tea party. No one needs to tell anyone else about their comings and goings. Beneath that veneer of decorative velvet and polished plaster, it's still a place where women sell their bodies." Ambrose drew a deep breath. "Regardless, it's out of your hands now. You're not to return so there's nothing left to say." It wasn't that he was unsympathetic to the plight of the working girls at the brothel, but he couldn't begin to understand what his brother expected him to do about it.

"I think Madam Violet doesn't want me to return because she knows that I know something's not right there, but I can't just leave it that way." Martin splayed his hands in front of him as if the proposition was unacceptable.

"What is that supposed to mean?" Ambrose wouldn't have his brother return to The Scarlet Rose and cause further trouble. It would be all over the morning edition of the *London Times*.

"I think we should ask a few questions, at the least."

"Have you already forgotten you've been banned from the place? You can't return there." Ambrose pinned Martin with a meaningful glare.

"No, but you can."

He stared at his brother a long minute, the sound of carriage wheels on cobbles the only interruption to his steeping temper.

"Say something," Martin persisted. "Daisy wouldn't just disappear. I visit her often. I pay her well. You know the idea of any female being hurt is unacceptable."

"Agreed," Ambrose answered immediately.

"So then, we should find out what's happening. It's our obligation as nobles."

"Martin"—Ambrose shook his head in the negative—"London is filled with hardship and turmoil. We can't right every wrongdoing. We'd be at it all day long."

"But this is different. Isn't caring for society part of the responsibility of the dukedom?"

"In relative terms. In Parliament. Through decisive governing that takes years of deliberation and implementation."

"That seems a bit obtuse." Martin leaned back against the cushions, his mouth twisted in disgust. "What good does government serve if it keeps old men arguing beneath a fancy roof but takes decades to help the neediest people?"

Ambrose agreed with his brother on this point but saw no easy answer to Martin's request. "I suppose I can make a few discreet inquiries."

How was it he was being pulled into Martin's mess instead of extricating both of them out of it? He sighed and probed further. "What else did you learn? Did you see anything? Did you catch a glimpse of a suspicious blackguard?"

"No, I left the room and nearly collided with a cloaked woman in the corridor. Our near mishap impeded my progress. By the time I advanced to the stairs, no one was in sight."

"A person in a cloak?" His mind recalled the woman from earlier who'd entered behind him. Could she have already come and gone and then returned to the brothel? Her appearance hadn't raised questions by either the burly enforcer or Madam Violet and then she'd all but disappeared once he'd moved on.

Where *had* she gone? Did she work at the brothel? That didn't seem right. A female that attractive and neatly assembled was a stark contrast to the garish display offered by the working girls. Was her intrusion on Martin's pursuit a coincidence or purposeful foil? A black cloak was too commonplace to be considered more than an ordinary sight. It might have been anyone abovestairs.

Were the girls in danger? Did something untoward happen to the one called Daisy? There was no way to know unless he returned to The Scarlet Rose and questioned a few people. More importantly, if he happened upon the same mysterious woman, she might know something. Gut instinct told him she might be connected to the happenings at the brothel. "I suppose no harm can come from ensuring everyone is safe."

Martin smiled. "I knew you would see reason."

"Is there anything else you can share?"

"Daisy had mentioned on occasion that not all the girls were treated properly by gentlemen customers, but they hesitate in telling Madam Violet for fear she'll put them out. That being so, the girls endure the abuse and rationalize the soreness will subside after a week or two. Although others have left and never returned after a customer has become too rough."

Ambrose couldn't ignore the atrocity of anyone being willfully hurt, never mind a man mistreating a woman and perhaps, in this case, multiple women. How would someone in such a situation endure such exploitation or furthermore, escape? Likely, by running away. Which no doubt would ultimately explain what happened to Daisy. It was a sorry result, but would probably prove true.

"Someone must have previously mentioned something to Madam Violet. That woman looks like she knows what I ate for dinner, never mind what happens during arranged brothel business transactions," Ambrose grumbled in frustration.

"That's just it. Daisy said Madam Violet condones everything that happens beneath her roof and doesn't act on the information, that she still admits the same gentlemen despite the few girls brave enough to express concern. And no one pesters Madam Violet because The Scarlet Rose brings in far more than other brothels and no one wants to be told to look elsewhere for work. Girls age in and out, but they all want to earn as much as possible while in good favor and Violet warns them against driving away clientele with deep pockets."

"That's horrible." Ambrose struggled with his immediate reaction to his brother's story. "They're trapped by necessary desperation."

"One can hardly fault a person who works to keep food in their belly." Martin's voice was the core of sincerity. "You will help, won't you?"

"Yes." Ambrose paused, the weight of his commitment an uncomfortable fit.

"Good. I appreciate it. Lest we forget, a man is only as honorable as his word."

"Damn it, Martin." It was just like his brother to remember a singular aspect of their earlier discussion and then use those very words to force Ambrose into action. In need of a brandy, he suddenly wished he carried a flask. "What the hell did you get us involved in now?"

CHAPTER 5

Scarlett obscured herself behind the same shrubbery she'd chosen the previous evening and kept a keen focus on the back door of The Scarlet Rose. The area was nothing more than a glorified pathway, purposely situated between the neighboring buildings to give the illusion one wasn't at the edge of Vauxhall. Still, it served her purpose and kept her hidden from view.

Earlier she'd visited Madame Ivory's Emporium to discover the modiste in high temper over Linie's failure to appear at work for three days' time. The dressmaker complained of unfulfilled orders and unreliability, but Scarlett's fear was for Linie's safety. Why would the young girl all but disappear without a trace?

Now, ensconced between two thick hedgerows with little more than ten strides worth of space, she deliberated how to breach the brothel or, as an alternative, how to approach one of the girls when she left. The latter seemed a wiser choice and she waited, unfamiliar with the hours of business or the habits of the girls who worked there.

Her mother hadn't conducted the sale of her body in any formal manner, but the result was the same regardless. Scarlett was too young to remember details clearly, but she learned quickly enough what her mother endured to keep food on the table and shelter over their heads. It made her heart clench with an odd mixture of anger and sadness whenever she considered the burden her own life had placed on her mother. An unexpected pregnancy, a bastard child, another mouth to feed.

Then the reality of it all. Her mother couldn't work with an infant on her hip, couldn't hire someone to watch the baby when she barely had enough coins to provide food, couldn't seek employment when she had no one to care for her bastard. It wasn't an illogical choice to entertain men in the two rented rooms where they lived. As she grew older, she understood more and more how the regulars came and went, the sounds of their activity, the exchange and bawdy comments. And then, the horrific discovery that still haunted her nightmares.

Reality pierced through the haze of her memories. A hackney rolled across the path and she shook herself. Enough of inner reflection and unresolved disappointment. It was time to focus on the task at hand.

In a scene not unlike her last visit, a man stepped from the cab and within a heartbeat, she realized he was the very same gentleman. Though tonight, when he approached the back door, he paused, seemingly hesitant and not at all as eager as on his previous visit. Scarlett watched and waited. Still, he didn't knock. Instead he glanced in her direction, just as he'd done before. Shaking away the absurd uneasiness caused by his attention, Scarlett held her breath. He turned away from the brothel and began walking toward her. Did he mean to use the narrow alley created by the overgrown hedges? She pulled her cloak more tightly around her body and slid her hand into one of the inner pockets where she kept a small dagger, easily concealed in her palm.

She couldn't retreat without revealing herself, nor would she advance toward him. Curiosity held her captive. Fear had no place in her disposition, but she did wonder what he intended. A man who entered a flash house by the back door rarely went seeking attention otherwise.

His heels crushed the broken shells on the path as he stepped nearer, the waning glow of the last light of dusk glinting off his polished boots. No doubt he was quality, so what did he seek in the hedgerow this evening? Hadn't he found satisfaction in the brothel? Surely he had, as he returned again this evening.

Her heart seized when he stopped not two strides from the hedges where she hid. Had he sensed her presence or did he simply need to relieve himself? Still, she couldn't imagine why a man of such fine breeding or tailoring would seek the trouble awaiting in the shadows of a brothel. She measured each breath with her fingertips arrested on the edge of her blade. One never knew from which direction danger advanced. How many times had things appeared differently than reality? Her joust with Felix a few days prior proved that theory. Scarlett had learned to be ever prepared.

The gentleman was in clear view at close range now, the night not dark enough to eclipse his fine features or intense expression. Shadows prevented her from discerning the exact shade of his eyes and her attention came to rest on his mouth, his sensual lips in contrast to the otherwise rigidity of his bearing. He stood motionless as if tentative with unease. Perhaps he came to the brothel to relieve his anxiety.

Still, why didn't he move on? Her heart thudded a heavy beat. Her pulse thrummed in her ears.

"Show yourself."

The deep timbre of his voice rippled through her and she gripped her knife tighter, sliding her fingertips away from the blade. He spoke with the authority of a man who got what he wanted at all times. *Privilege.* In this case, privilege beyond the usual boundaries of upper society.

Scarlett prided herself on bravery. She wasn't a coward. She also wasn't a fool and saw no need to expose herself of yet. She ignored his command. He might very well have his look and walk away. But he didn't.

He did what she would have done.

He waited.

*   *   *

Ambrose cursed silently, at the ready to label himself a fool. What was he doing talking to a thick hedgerow at the rear of a brothel? Had his brother driven him to the brink of madness? No, that wasn't it. Ambrose sensed someone hid among the dense shrubbery despite he couldn't see anyone there. Something inside him foretold he wasn't in danger, though only a fool would go poking around dark alleyways and secluded alcoves with his fists as a singular means of defense.

With two long strides he backed away and edged along the lined hedgerow to see where he might gain access and view the shrub-lined curb from the opposite side. If someone lay hidden in watch of the brothel, they could very well have information he needed, even if it appeared nothing more than commonplace observation.

By the time he found an area wide enough to permit his passage, he'd convinced himself twice over he was indeed a fool and his investigation would prove nothing except that fact. Pushing through the bushes, twigs raked across his coat and snagged the threads in protest. His valet would not be pleased. Darkness had already fallen, the sky an inky blanket of blue-black velvet with ominous clouds. It was a moonless night.

He moved with as much stealth as he could manage, unaccustomed to the practice. Life as a duke prepared him more for society's speculative eye than for a desire to blend into the background. When he reached the spot adjacent to the brothel's entry, he found nothing. As he returned to the back door, he detected the lingering scent of rosemary and mint. The fragrance was so vivid he was immediately transported to his childhood home where Cook made the most delectable biscuits flavored with the herbs his mother had grown in her garden. He allowed a reminiscent smile before he shaking his head dismissively. Maybe Martin had succeeded and truly broken his brain.

As before, Ambrose was admitted to the brothel and, with a flimsy request to pay for company in a private room, he followed the hulking enforcer he'd met the previous evening. Martin had stated the bedrooms were up the stairs to the right. The drawing room on the first level appeared to be one ongoing party where working girls mingled with gentleman before the customer made his selection. Ambrose tried to don an expression of indifference, but wasn't sure he achieved that goal.

His eyes settled on a timid girl who lingered near a far corner, her eyes filled with trepidation. She stayed within the room's company but appeared as if she wished she was invisible. Without a doubt she would be an ideal person to question. Ambrose had no intention of taking advantage of the girl, nor would he intimidate her, but he needed to pursue the suspicions Martin planted in his mind. A misuse or abuse of any person, never mind these misguided young women, could not be tolerated. Now that the idea had been suggested, integrity prevented him from ignoring the possibility.

"Decided you liked what you saw last night, eh?" Madam Violet sidled up to him and nudged his elbow in what could only be her idea of camaraderie. "No offense meant, Your Grace, but your brother ruined my usual hospitality. I'll need the promised payment first before you venture upstairs."

"No offense taken, madam." Ever prepared, Ambrose discreetly removed funds from his pocket and pressed it into the waiting hand beside him. "As we discussed, the money owed to you by my brother is included."

"Very good." The madam accepted the payment and turned to him, her expression instantly more congenial. "You expect a high standard, Your Grace, and I wouldn't wish to disappoint. I seek fresh girls all the time in an effort to appease the appetites of my customers. I have the perfect companion for you. She's exceptional in her talents and will wait for you abovestairs in the first room on the right. Of course, if I'm wrong about your preferences you have access to any girl to your liking. More than one if you prefer." Violet gave him another wide smile and when he didn't say more, she strode away.

Ambrose was often labelled as charming. He was considered

a prime catch, though he never made a habit of reading the gossip rags or newspaper's social page where eligible bachelors were described as intricately as the latest fashion plate. Still, he was a duke with an immaculate, well-respected lineage. He possessed wealth, all his teeth, no degenerate tendencies and an affable disposition, the latter of a changeable nature contingent on the situation. Still, he had no idea how to interview a young girl who waited tentatively for a man to take her upstairs and exchange sex for coin. Eyeing the stairs, he drew a breath of resolve and forged on.

Scarlett entered the brothel in much the same manner as the night before. Picking the lock on the back-door latch posed no challenge. Easing inside, just so. Yet once she climbed the stairs and proceeded through the hall, she realized she was beyond her element. Unwilling to be caught, she listened intently beside a nearby door and when she'd ascertained it remained empty, cracked it open and slipped inside. The interior was mostly as she'd expected, with a large opulent bed swathed in velvet pillows and a voluminous coverlet. There were two overstuffed chairs and a small table near the far wall where the room took a turn and a dressing screen angled into the corner to provide for privacy. The linens appeared clean and were neatly drawn up to the headboard. A small oval table held a basin, towel and ewer of water. She released a long sigh, relieved the room was empty and she hadn't happened upon anything she didn't wish to see.

But how could she learn of Linie's disappearance if she didn't speak directly to some of the girls? Lurking abovestairs with the risk of being discovered seemed a poor plan but once the inquisitive lord from downstairs entered the brothel, she'd felt compelled to do the same.

How had he known she'd waited beyond the shrubbery?

The door opened before she formed her next thought and as if conjured from her memory the same gentleman from outside the brothel entered the room. Their paths seemed fated to intersect.

They stared at each other a long moment before he turned and closed the door.

"Are you here to see Martin?" She didn't know why she baited him. Perhaps if she did so, he would decide any other room would suffice and then move on.

"Martin is my brother."

His annoyed tone gave her a measure of satisfaction. She watched as a series of emotions played over his handsome features. Why would a man of attractive appearance and obvious wealth seek a woman in a bawdy house? Were aristocrats never satisfied with the lion's share they already possessed? He could only be someone important. His presence exuded power and composure without effort. A commanding yet quiet authority surrounded him the same way air filled the room.

"That *is* peculiar," she said offhandedly; she didn't expect him to answer. They stood several paces apart, neither one of them having moved, yet their words reached across the room, a fission of tension at war between them.

"You misunderstand."

She enjoyed the way his eyes flickered with anger when she provoked him and how a moment later, he marshaled that same emotion and squelched it, his disciplined self-possession restored. "I don't need to."

"What is your name?" He took a step closer and she backed away.

He thought her a whore. A girl here for his use. The assumption offered the ideal subterfuge to her true identity, but the purposeful deception still rankled. "You can call me . . ." She hesitated long enough to portray indecision. "Scarlett."

"How apropos."

"Pardon?"

"That you carry the name of this establishment." He splayed one hand wide to indicate the modest room. "Madam Violet mentioned she had someone special in mind for my visit."

Scarlett didn't reply. She was thankful she'd worn a skirt over her trousers and for the dagger easily accessible in the pocket because if the gentleman before her expected she'd offer him any kind of pleasure she'd need to make a swift escape. Still, a spike of curious intrigue chased that decision. Had he hoped for special treatment from one of the females downstairs?

"Do you visit here often then?" Perhaps she could discover a useful clue if she was able to keep him talking. Could he know of Linie by having paid for her company?

"No."

He decreased the space between them with another long stride. His hair was a mixture of brown and black, darker than the strong coffee she drank each morning, his eyes the same, though for all their darkness they held layers upon layers of intense boldness. He assessed her with interest and she held his gaze with equaled strength. She would not cower. When he took in her clothing from head to toe, she straightened her shoulders. Was he imagining her undressed? He believed her one of the working girls, didn't he? Or was he measuring her worth?

"Your cloak is fine wool and your skirt neatly tailored. You don't look like you belong here."

"Nor do you."

"Because I don't. But there are circumstances . . ." He shook his head slightly. "I'm seeking information with this visit, not pleasure. Were you here yesterday?"

"Yes." She narrowed her eyes as she answered. "You know that because you saw me here."

"Were you here earlier in the day?"

"No." Why she granted him answers to his questions posed a question in itself. She needed to move beyond this room and discover the information she sought. "I'm leaving now and I've no desire to be discovered, so I must insist upon your discretion." She began to move toward the door, but he raised his gloved palm as if to stop her.

"My discretion?" His features created an expression of indignant befuddlement. "Do you have any idea—"

Scarlett would have continued their verbal jousting if the latch hadn't jiggled, the sound quickly followed by two hushed female tones just outside the panel. The door opened partially and paused as if whoever meant to enter remained undecided. Scarlett diverted her attention to the gentleman in the room. He looked ready to object, his brows lowered and lips parted but she couldn't afford to lose the opportunity to eavesdrop if the girls decided to enter the room and discuss brothel business.

Waving her arm to snare his attention, she pressed a bare finger to her lips while she moved behind the dressing screen, unwilling to be caught where she didn't belong. Any gentleman found in a random room would be thought just another customer, his presence easily explained away, but the girls who worked at the brothel would immediately know Scarlett didn't belong on the premises and she couldn't take that risk, especially if she was recognized from yesterday. Thankfully the thick scattered rugs dulled the thud of her hurried boot heels.

"Come here. This room is empty." The careful tones continued in the hall.

What Scarlett hadn't expected was the lofty gent seeking refuge behind the screen as well. There was hardly any room for herself in the cramped confines and the only portion high enough to conceal his height was along the abutment where the screen attached to the wall—the same area Scarlett occupied, hoping she'd be lost to shadow and left undetected. If the girls didn't venture farther into the room all would be well. But a familiar feeling, one of annoyance and impatience, signaled to her things weren't all as they seemed.

Her heart seized midbeat as he moved farther in to crowd her. He shifted until he stood directly behind her, not touching her person, but invading the narrow space. Meanwhile the door closed and a low-toned conversation ensued. She had no time to object. She needed to glean every shred of information from the conversation unfolding beyond the screen and yet her mind began to catalog each detail of the man who shared the space behind her.

He possessed a broad build. She knew that before he'd moved as close as her shadow. But now his heat suffused her body, permeated the air and provoked a sensual awareness as sharp as if an arrow pierced her skin. She instructed herself to breathe. The simple involuntary act of drawing oxygen and exhaling afterward demanded her complete attention. Yet how would she gain the knowledge of the whispered discussion within the room if she couldn't hear a word over the thrum of her pulse in her ears?

And why would she have this odd reaction anyway? She'd pressed against a male body before. On the street, in the crowded squares, or at times in a maneuver of self-defense that required fast action and unyielding strength, but never had she danced or dallied in a way to become accustomed to a well-muscled physique at close proximity such as the gentleman nary a hair's breadth behind her.

How dare he unsettle her.

Anger was quick to replace curiosity.

Enough of these thoughts. She strove to listen to the goings-on beyond the screen, yet she was still too distracted, too aware of his masculine body. It was as though his solidness surrounded her.

He would keep you safe.

She clenched her jaw tighter. She required no one to ensure her safety. She kept herself from danger without a man's interference or assistance. Dependence on another posed a danger, a weakness, and thoughts like that broke one's heart. Pulling her shoulders straighter, she fought to dismiss his presence no matter his heat resonated through her.

Then blinking hard, twice, she strained her ears to the conversation.

CHAPTER 6

"Hurry. I've only a few minutes to spare. What did Clive say?" one of the girls spoke, a mixture of eagerness and skepticism in her voice.

"He promised to set me up in a fine cottage, with servants no less. He said I'd have a dozen new gowns and a box of pretty jewels to match."

"Truly?"

"And use of his carriage, a lovely brougham with a fine pair of chestnuts. He told me so."

"I can hardly believe it." A slight pause ensued before curiosity won out. "And when will this happen?"

"I've only to tell him when I'm ready and he'll take me away from here."

"Are you sure? I don't know about this. His promises seem too good to be true."

"You wouldn't be jealous now would you, Missy? That he passed you over and chose me instead?"

"No." Anger colored the single word. "I worry about you, that's all. Some say Annie was found in the Thames after she left."

"That was months ago and Annie was foolish. She never had a care for her own safety. If something untoward happened to her, she likely brought it upon herself. Besides, no one knows if that's true or not. It could be she ran away and that's why we've never seen her again. As far as I'm concerned, it doesn't matter now. This is my chance to better myself. Off my back and on my feet for a change. My brother won't have to work mudlarking for Tommy Crow any longer and if everything goes as planned, I'll be able to send Willie funds. We'll have full bellies, new shoes and clothes that fit. No more cold mornings and nights without firewood."

"But how do you know if Clive is telling you the truth? It could all be lies. He might not have a farthing. If he's all that he claims to be, why is he sniffing around a brothel? Why wouldn't he be out in society with the fancy ladies in their velvet gowns?"

"You see all the nobs that come in and out. He wants to help, that's all. He wants to help *me* because he fancies me. And you wouldn't doubt he's deep in the pockets if you saw his clothes and the ring on his finger. It's a ruby fatter than my pinky nail, red as blood, and that's not all. Six round diamonds dance around it as pretty as the stars we wish on at night. I could lie on my back forever and I'd never have enough to own a ring like that. But once I leave here, everything will change."

"All this talk of leaving makes me scared for you, that's all. Remember Jess. She was propositioned just the same and we never heard from her after she left. If it's such a good life, why didn't she come back to tell us about it? And what of Linie? Where has she gone?"

"Linie always had bigger dreams to chase and as for Jess, I suppose once set free she doesn't want to look back," the first girl answered quickly. "Besides, if she's passing for a proper lady now, why would she ever dirty her new silk slippers by returning to this place?"

"That could be true."

Indecision hung in the air until the girl with Missy spoke again.

"I'm going to tell him I'm ready the next time he visits."

"Are you sure you can trust him?"

Silence held the room hostage and Scarlett waited, silently begging the girls to reveal more.

"I've got nothing to lose. Clive wouldn't do me wrong."

"Then I'm right happy for you. I truly am."

The shuffle of shoes and dull thud of the door marked their exit.

Scarlett exhaled fully, both relieved she hadn't been discovered and invigorated the girls had offered her substantial clues. And while nothing connected Linie specifically, if someone was propositioning the girls at the brothel and promising a better way of life, Linie might have decided it was worth the risk although Scarlett doubted that would prove true. The seamstress wouldn't turn her back on her dream and become a kept woman. The pieces to this problem still didn't fit together.

Swiftly moving from behind the screen and all too aware that the other body in the room did the same she pasted a congenial expression on her face and turned toward the gentleman behind her.

"Thank you, Aylesford." His brows rose with surprise at the use of his name and yet he must have realized she'd heard Madam Violet address him the night before. Scarlett kept an inventory of facts. One never knew when a bit of information would prove itself important.

Aylesford appeared momentarily out of sorts and remained silent a moment. When he spoke, his voice was low and careful. "That was an earful."

"Information we'd never have gained were one of us to ask the girls directly. I suspect they protect their own fiercely." In fact, Scarlett knew it with certainty as she lived by the same code. She'd never expose another Maiden of Mayhem, confident in their mutual loyalty. "Perhaps something you heard will aid you in your search." She began for the door.

"That seems doubtful." Aylesford shook his head, his expression confounded. "Aside from the mention of an expensive ring, which I can attempt to investigate through Bond Street's better jewelers, I've little to pursue. I'm not familiar with the population in this area of London."

In other words, you're a prig.

He pressed his lips tight, seemingly uncomfortable and growing more agitated with his frustration.

"Surely a man such as yourself has an endless list of resources to command." Scarlett did, and she wasn't some toff who kept London on the end of a silken string.

"I may be a nobleman, but I've a lot to learn about this type of pursuit." He shook his head slowly. "What has my brother drawn me into this time?"

"I honestly cannot say." She knew the question begged for no answer and that's exactly why she replied, "And so then, I'll take my leave."

She almost smiled at his awkwardness but she didn't dare offer him an opportunity to further their conversation or prolong their association. Besides, she now had a name and a name was a lead. Finding a man named Clive in the city's populace would prove daunting but she'd gathered a number of additional facts and at least she knew her next step. There was mention of Willie, the girl's younger brother who worked mudlarking for Tommy Crow. Anyone with that ominous moniker shouldn't be too hard to discover if one knew which rocks to look beneath. Luckily for Scarlett, she was very familiar with men such as he.

As Ambrose settled into a corner at the club, he took time to deliberate all that had transpired that evening. He hadn't bothered going home. Aside from the threat he might throttle Martin for ensnaring him in a questionable circumstance, no peace would be found there. Not with so many questions crowding his brain. And it wasn't just the working girls and their conspiratorial conversation that weighed heavily. Overhearing the insecurities and worrisome challenges of the girls firsthand pricked his conscience with the notion he should be doing more and somehow engaging in purposeful standards of improvement. Not charity, but more in a cause that initiated a difference.

Who was Scarlett and why was she so interested in the brothel?

At first he'd mistakenly assumed she was a woman for hire, yet their brief exchange made it clear that was not so. And while he sensed she was strong, perhaps *too* independent for her own well-being, he also knew she had intelligence to match.

She wasn't gentry, although she held her shoulders with a proud bearing and her chin at an indignant angle that somehow pleased more than irritated him. Not that it mattered. He'd likely never see her again. Still, something in him, some innate and at times misplaced sense of duty and honor, urged him to protect her. Which was ludicrous. Or so he told himself repeatedly.

The image of Scarlett wouldn't be so easily dismissed. Instead, as he ruminated with a brandy in hand, he recalled the scent of rosemary and mint, light and fragrant as it drifted around him, enhanced by the heat of their bodies in close proximity hidden behind the dressing screen. It *had* been she behind the hedgerow. Had she passed through on her way to the brothel? He wondered if she'd given him a fleeting consideration since they'd parted and what she might be doing at this hour, half ten. Was she asleep? Or did she prowl the streets after the answers she sought so vigilantly?

"What has you at sixes and sevens, my friend?"

Galway approached, his affable smile and easy attitude a balm to smooth away troubling thoughts. At least, that was the usual way of their friendship.

"Martin. Martin and more Martin, I'm despaired to say."

The viscount signaled for a brandy and settled in the chair beside Ambrose.

"I take it no good news came from your sudden summons last time we were here."

"In a word, no."

A footman arrived with Galway's glass and a stretch of silence ensued.

"Do you know anyone who wears a ruby ring surrounded by round diamonds?"

Galway was out in society and privy to the most current news and happenings, unlike Ambrose who shunned the gossip rags and hardly left his study. And too, the viscount was befriended by everyone, whether titled gentleman or flirtatious debutante.

"No one comes to mind. Has a certain lady caught your eye?"

"No." Ambrose took another sip of brandy. "I'm interested in locating a gentleman who wears a ring in that design, not a woman."

"Has Martin found trouble again? Does he owe money to a sharper? Or has he won the ring and you seek to return it to its rightful owner?"

"If only resolving the problem Martin dragged me into was as easy as paying his vowels." Ambrose set his glass down on the table, hesitant to discuss the situation in entirety. The more people pulled into the mess, the more complicated it would become. "Do you know a reputable jeweler who designs and creates gemstone pieces and also practices discretion?"

"I know the same retailers on Bond Street as you do, so I'm afraid I'm no help."

Ambrose paused for a moment. "That said, do you know a less reputable one?"

Galway looked tentative, but answered quickly enough thereafter. "If you'd truly like to speak to a merchant who deals with unsavory characters and not so legal transactions, an individual does come to mind."

Ambrose quirked a brow and waited. As he'd predicted, Galway possessed all the right contacts.

"He runs a quiet business out of a storefront on Shadwell Street near Wapping Dock. Works on commission mostly for customers who'd like something specially made or pawned without a trace. I suspect keeping that location enables him to smuggle the best contraband coming in from the ghost ships but one can never be sure about such things. What's this all about if you don't mind me asking?"

"You possess a notable inventory of information, Galway." Ambrose was impressed. By his own account, his friend led an unrestrained lifestyle. Ambrose needed to get out more. Still, the thought of venturing down to the waterfront caused his shoulders to tighten. One could only imagine the unsavory types who dwelled in that area. He hadn't married or produced an heir and were he to meet his demise in a dark alley of Wapping, he'd be stripped clean with his clothes pawned and body dropped in the Thames before the sun rose over London. The thought of Martin assuming the title caused Ambrose to swallow the remainder of his brandy in one gulp.

"This jeweler you mentioned, can you give me his direction? I'll visit the legitimate establishments tomorrow during shopping hours, but if my inquiries fail, I'd like to talk to this gentleman on Shadwell Street."

Galway chuckled before he thought better of it. "He's no gentleman and you probably shouldn't go down to Wapping alone. He's a fencer. If Martin was the one who threw you into this mess, you should take your brother with you. It isn't safe for you to venture into that area by yourself. Never mind no one would know of your whereabouts."

"Perhaps." Ambrose knew he wouldn't bring Martin along. His brother invited trouble wherever he went.

Scarlett adjusted the hood of her cloak and trailed her gloved fingertips over the craggy stone wall running alongside the roadway. Ratcliff Highway was hardly a safe environ, never mind in a few hours the sun would set and blanket the area in blackness so thick one wouldn't see their own boot tips. There were no lamps along Ratcliff and if the stars were obscured and the moon behind clouds, the invidious dark would surround her.

This caused her no ill-ease. She didn't blink an eye at the threat of danger as she walked along the edge of the steep embankment, the red sandstone drop-off a peril to anyone who didn't navigate the area well. She knew of the smuggler trade here, tea, nutmeg, flax and lace, all easily portable and yet highly valuable in the hands of the right buyer. And then of course, there were Wapping's opium dens along Dellow Street, where men lost their minds and forgot their troubles for no small price.

But Scarlett sought Tommy Crow, not a head full of smoke and euphoric delirium, and she'd learned easily enough through well-aimed inquiries that the man in question was a leech collector who turned a pretty coin at his trade.

Tommy Crow was exactly where she'd been told to look and this discovery *did* surprise her. Crime kept no schedule but perhaps today, luck favored her. The man's bent form was knee-deep in the murky waters along the low-lying tidal marshes beyond the embankment where she'd walked. A large lantern burned atop a dented pewter pail with a scrap of cloth draped over the top near where Tommy Crow lowered a glass jar on a length of string into the inky black dredges below the dockside pilings. He worked several containers at once, draining the water with alacrity and depositing leeches into the glass bowl in the same way one might collect pretty shells from Brighton's crystal shoreline. He mumbled to himself and as she neared Scarlett realized he sang a ditty.

"Might I have a word with you, Tommy Crow?" She had no reason to fear the old man, having already decided an honest confrontation would do well to cut through wasted time and energy.

"It depends who's asking." The old man turned and squinted in her direction; his fingers still occupied with a multiple of strings. "It must be something important to bring you down here where the edge of your skirt will grow damp and muddy."

"I'm looking for a friend and the search has led me to you."

"I doubt I can help you. I'm nothing more than a leech fisher. I supply most every physician in this area who needs to breathe a vein."

Tommy Crow turned back to the jar he held and it wasn't until he stood in profile that Scarlett recognized the disturbing task at hand. She watched as he waded along the shoreline, lethargically pushing through the bulrushes and weeds, his legs bared from the knee down. Every few steps he'd stop, reach below the water and remove a leech that had attached to his leg. Then he'd swiftly deposit it among the cluster he'd already collected in his jar, the everted lips of the container preventing the hapless creatures from escaping.

"I'm ready to compensate your time. I've a pocketful of coins that will save you from the chill of water this evening."

"I'll take your coin but I won't abandon the task at hand or the doctors and piss-prophets will have no leeches upon the morrow." He drew himself up a little straighter. "They depend on me."

"True enough." Scarlett stepped as close as possible without entering the water. "Then I won't take up much of your time and you'll still have a pocketful of coins when I'm through."

This seemed to mollify the old man and he stepped away from his purpose, allowing the lengths of strings tangled in his fingers to fall free. "What is it you wish to know?"

"I'm told you know every secret here in Wapping, that you possess an inventory of knowledge curated from mudlarks, smugglers and otherwise unlawful scoundrels, to daring free-traders and pirates."

"Aren't you one to turn my head with flattery." Tommy Crow moved closer and in the waning flicker of the lantern she saw beyond the grime and weathered wrinkled skin the eyes of a man who possessed an inner strength that marked him a survivor no matter the challenge. "I do keep myself informed."

"Exactly." Scarlett glanced toward the water. "I'm interested in a body that washed ashore not long ago. Do you know of a young woman who may have found her death in the Thames recently?"

"Bah." Tommy Crow stifled a misplaced scoff. "It's not a far tumble from a rowboat to a watery grave and many a bloke, whether toff or no-gooder, uses the Thames for their disposal."

"And?"

"I see too many things, too many bodies." Tommy Crow shook his head and made a motion toward the water. "A pretty gel, with long yellow hair washed up not long ago. Just beyond the dock there. The current spits out naught but debris where the bank hems in and the river narrows, and that's where the corpse was caught. She was young, her skin bruised blue-black, but there's no way to know whether she found that condition before she died or after."

Scarlett swallowed a bitter retort. The abuse of women took so many forms a fresh lick of anger ignited in her soul. Yet just as quickly, a rush of relief assuaged her worry. Linie had short dark hair. She prodded for more. "And?"

"There hasn't been so much as a whisper as to who she was or where she came from." Tom nodded. "That proves she was part of something important and not the opposite as one might think."

"Because someone went through great trouble to keep her death a secret."

"That's right." Tommy Crow extended his hand, the scarred skin of his palm a map of his life's hardship. "I haven't seen any of the coin you spoke of yet."

With a slight smile Scarlett removed a pouch from the pocket of her cloak. "You need not worry about me keeping my word." She dropped the entire thing into Tommy Crow's hand and the old man reacted with a start. "I'd like to think we're forging a profitable relationship. I'm looking for a friend. Her name is Linie."

"I can't say I know her. The whores by the docks don't pay me any mind."

"Linie is a friend of Darla's and you employ Darla's young brother as a mudlark. His name is Willie. Do you know of whom I speak?"

Tommy Crow glanced to her, his eyes narrowed as if he examined her worth and how much truth to share. "I do. The lad may have the information you need. You can find him near the South-end culverts at sunrise. He's a headful of red hair that sets him apart from the others."

"Thank you. I'll leave you to your work."

CHAPTER 7

Ambrose paid the hackney driver before he pulled the collar of his greatcoat higher and brim of his beaver hat lower. Then he headed down the alleyway with unbreachable confidence.

He was a duke. He did not cower when confronted with danger. Centuries of history and decades of heritage bolstered his bravery.

He found the jeweler's storefront easily enough. Galway's directions proved accurate. The shop was nothing more than a narrow facade sandwiched between a two-story tenement and an abundance of sailors' victuallers in succession. He'd decided to venture to the dockside community during the evening hours to protect his own identity but realized the fault in his thinking as his plan also invited the most unpleasant characters who lurked about corners in search of easy prey to mark him as their next conquest.

Refusing to be mistaken as such, he approached the shop with righteous confidence. He was nearly at the door when a fellow exited, causing him pause. He eyed the stranger warily, and yet the presence of another innocuous visitor did much to chase away any trace of apprehension.

"Excuse me." The fellow looked at him directly and Ambrose glanced away as he stepped to the side. The other patron hesitated, raising his hand in what Ambrose thought would be a gesture of greeting but became a motion to swipe at his nose.

"Good evening." The other man nodded and continued on his way.

Unwilling to lose momentum, Ambrose entered the shop and walked straight to the counter. "I need to speak to the owner of this establishment."

"Ain't here," the scraggy man behind the counter answered quickly.

Ambrose blew out a breath and repositioned his shoulders. He wasn't accustomed to conversation of this nature, short on information and impolite. Yet he couldn't employ his ducal authority in an effort to preserve his reputation. "I only need a moment of his time. I have a few questions I need answered."

This caused the man behind the counter to grin. Perhaps Ambrose was making progress.

"Ain't here. Definitely ain't here for some nob who keeps the world in his pocket."

Or perhaps not.

"I'm interested in a very specific piece of jewelry. A ruby ring with diamonds encircling it. Have you seen anything that resembles that design in this shop? I'm willing to pay for your assistance." Consternation caused Ambrose to offer compensation quickly, though he realized the error of his statement just as swiftly.

"No doubt you are." This caused the man's grin to widen. He glanced toward the door and Ambrose did the same. "You should take your coins and enjoy a three-penny upright in the alley out back. Jenny will do you one good. She'll give you a taste of the slums and a story to tell at your club. Otherwise, there's no business for you here. Make your way round the corner or down the road, but I'd beware of cloak-twitchers and pickpockets. That's a bit more of free advice for you. Upstanding chap like yourself wouldn't want to tempt fate and find yourself inside an eternity box."

The mention of a coffin smacked Ambrose into action. He turned and left the shop, annoyed and frustrated to be so far out of his element he'd hardly understood the shopkeeper's warning.

Worse, Ambrose had released the hackney without thought to his return and was now faced with walking north to High Street where he might find another for hire. He bundled his coat tighter around his person and with his head down, began to move. He was strong and fit, his body honed to healthy muscle by a rigorous schedule of boxing and horsemanship. But he wasn't familiar with street fighting and he didn't wish to become acquainted either. Aristocracy had buffered certain aspects of his life. While he held no doubt he could defend himself, he cursed silently for allowing his world to have become so microcosmic. He needed to do better. Get out more. Experience life more fully and understand London beyond the confines of the duchy.

He raised his eyes and kept a vigilant watch on his surroundings as he walked. He was a member of Parliament and one of the highest-ranking officials of England and yet this section of London might have existed on another planet for all he knew of the environs and its inhabitants.

He would learn more of the plight of the poverty-stricken. Thoughts such as this had crowded his brain since his conversation with Martin and his visit to The Scarlet Rose. The image of that young girl, lingering on the side of the room with abject fear in her eyes, remained a vigilant reminder that he as a duke had become negligent in his regard of lower London. While he was ensconced in the House of Lords elbow to elbow with men in somber suits who sought political alliance and debated supercilious ideas, so many others struggled for the most fundamental necessities every single day. An unsettling stroke of disappointment accompanied the realization. He would do better.

Perhaps he could motivate others to join and assist in efforts to offer relief to areas such as these. He had influential comrades and equal means at his disposal. To begin, he could establish foundations and charities to assist young women so their own choice didn't have to be such a despairing sacrifice. He would enlist other members of the House of Lords to work with him. By nature of lineage, the aristocracy considered themselves ameliorated, elevated, but in truth no one's life was more valuable than another's simply because of the advantage of birth. Martin, for all his buffoonish pleasure-seeking and misguided intentions had taught Ambrose a valuable lesson in a handful of days.

Deeply enmeshed in these thoughts, he crossed the street and rounded the corner only to find his path intersected by two large men, their ominous expressions echoed by the cudgel each held in their bare hands.

"Look who's out slumming this evening."

"He's a pretty one, isn't he?" The stocky man chuckled. "But we can fix that."

Ambrose matched eyes with the thugs and straightened his shoulders, his gloved fingers curled into fists at his sides. "Back away. You don't want to harm me. I'm the Duke of—"

"A lofty title won't protect you. You're made of skin and bones and bleed the same way we do. Everybody's equal in Wapping."

Ambrose tensed. He was good with his fists while at a practice session pounding a stuffed bag, but he hadn't engaged in fisticuffs since his youth. Still, had the men produced a knife or pistol, things would be more difficult. A few strikes with a wooden club wouldn't bring him down tonight. First though, he'd attempt a civil exchange.

"If it's money you're after, I'm willing to assist your plight without the inconvenience of violence."

One of the men snorted as he turned to the other. "Oh, we've got a dimber cove here. Listen to all them fancy words. He's going to assist our plight. He doesn't want to inconvenience us with violence."

"But we like hurting people. That's the best part. It's how we have fun since we're not invited to all those jolly rows in your ballroom," the other looming thug answered.

This gave Ambrose considerable pause and he didn't attempt further reason. Drawing up his shoulder, he leaned forward and burled into the first chap, knocking him to the dirt road with enough force to jar the weapon from his grasp. He landed a punch to his assailant's jaw, the crack and thud of the miscreant's head striking the roadway effective in subduing further violence. Still, all the while the other man rained blows on Ambrose's back. One crack to the head would leave him unconscious. Seeking to avoid that fate, he rolled off the first thug and hurried to his feet only to be struck again above his ear, this time the blow more accurate. Ambrose felt the jarring impact as it radiated through his bones, straight to his heart.

"Son of a bitch, nob."

The second blow struck him from behind and much like the dead night of their surround, blackness swamped Ambrose's vision. He shook his head and raised his arms to ward off another hit as he struggled to gain his footing and move out of harm's way. The thug on the roadway had rallied himself and as Ambrose stepped backward, he felt the grip of the first assailant wrap around his leg in an attempt to force him to the ground.

Then circumstances changed.

Quickly.

The upright ruffian cried out in pain, gripping his shoulder where the hilt of a knife suddenly protruded at a troubling angle, the blade buried beneath his flesh. An eerie calm blanketed the three of them and Ambrose cautiously glanced left and right, uncertain where the dagger had come from and how it had found its mark so efficiently in the darkness. But whoever sought to offer him assistance apparently wasn't finished. Another swift whisper cut through the air and a second blade found its mark in the leg of the thug on the ground. The man's sharp yelp resounded off the empty stones in an unnerving cadence of agony.

Ambrose backed away with caution, unsure if a third knife was meant to find his person, but as he turned to gain speed and leave, he caught a flutter of movement on the roof of a building across the roadway. All he could recognize with certainty as the figure departed was the flapping cloth of a billowing cloak. Could it possibly be the same mysterious woman as earlier? *Scarlett.*

The silhouetted figure fled so quickly he almost convinced

himself he imagined the entire scene, until he forced his feet into motion and gave chase into the dense alleyways of Wapping.

Scarlett untied her cape and left it in her wake, a flapping shadow as it drifted across the eaves and down to the cobbles below. Next she unfastened her overskirt and dropped it over the rooftop. She couldn't move freely with all the cumbersome fabric until she shed their weight and wore only her tight-fit trousers. Now with the layers discarded, she sat on her bottom, slid down the shingles to the guttered edge of the tenement building and shimmied her way to the ground by use of an ironwork railing.

After leaving Tommy Crow she'd made her way toward High Street until she'd stumbled upon some trouble. Her heart beat double time when she recognized Aylesford's prone form and the two ruffians who thought to relieve him of his boots, his purse and most likely his life. Why would the gentleman come into Wapping alone? Was he unarmed? Nobles and their misguided perceptions, which too often overrode common sense and intelligence. The thought would have provided amusement if the situation hadn't proven so dire.

She'd climbed to the roof of an adjacent building to ensure she'd have clear aim and then set to work freeing the troublesome toff who somehow seemed to have become her unlikely nemesis. With the miscreants felled, she paused only another breath to ensure Aylesford was able to carry on, then turned to leave in hope he would rid himself of the area as soon as possible.

He had no reason to pursue her now. She wished he wouldn't. And yet she heard him gaining ground no matter she ran as hard as she was able. Apparently, he hadn't allowed himself to go wobbly in the middle like most rich dandies. Whatever kept him in prime condition aided his focus in equal measure because he wasn't lost to the alleyways as easily as she'd intended and with an agile glance backward, she saw him, a flash of pale shadow and motion in the darkness.

Confident her stamina would outlast his, she maneuvered

through a series of filthy dank passages in hope she would disorient him and deter his pursuit further. She hated to lead him into confusion as he'd likely not recovered yet from the attack, but it was he who gave chase when he was better off hailing a hackney to return to the comforts of Mayfair. Having mollified her conscience for the moment, she exited the strait of narrow cross lanes and flattened her back against the nearest brick wall to catch her breath.

"Scarlett?"

Bloody hell, did he mean to wake the dead with his call? Had the man no sense in his head?

He strode forward through the darkness and stopped not two paces from her. She had to give him credit. While they were both winded, he didn't seem that much worse the wear for it.

"Why did you follow me?"

"What are you doing here?"

"Saving you, apparently." She drew a deep breath and released it slowly, pushing from the wall so she could engage in the conversation while also preparing to take her leave. "You're welcome, by the way."

"It's dangerous. You shouldn't be here."

For the slightest moment, her chest squeezed. How long had it been since anyone cared about her welfare? Thought of her safety and security? She'd survived on her own for so long, she almost didn't recognize the feelings pricking at her heart now. She couldn't let them in. To care for someone was the one mistake she couldn't make. Besides, she didn't need someone to worry on her behalf. The very idea rankled.

"Nor should you." She took a step, knowing her only way to freedom was beyond his reach and out of these intersecting alleyways. They stood at a dead end where only a few dark alcoves snaked between tenements and offered shelter. "You took too great a chance—"

"You're wearing trousers."

The awe in his voice caused a ripple of amusement to wash

through her and it served well to release the tension of the evening. She almost allowed herself to laugh.

"I am."

"I saw a gown, some heap of clothing as I pursued you. I didn't know." He sounded thoroughly confused.

"I can't run, jump or scale things with all those bothersome layers males insist women wear. Men are forever casting aspersions on females when at the same time enforcing limitations of every kind. Is it any wonder women resort to using their bodies, when men won't allow them to use their minds, their intelligence and ingenuity?" Aware she'd gone on too long and likely sounded the bitter shrew, she drew another breath and shook her head, reclaiming her singular determination to be rid of the man and return home. "It doesn't matter. I—"

"No. I understand."

She doubted he did, but this was no time to initiate a debate. A change of subject was in order. "What are you doing here?"

"I'm seeking answers to a problem. It was suggested I speak to a jeweler near the docks, but he wasn't available to meet with me."

She laughed this time. She couldn't help it. "He wouldn't speak to you? You likely addressed the man you sought to locate. The same man who turned you away. Did you expect several workers on staff?"

He remained silent and the moon cut a shaft of light between the clouds to at last allow them a modicum of visibility. It was then she noticed how disheveled he appeared. His clothing was worse for the attack he'd experienced and his hair was no longer combed into order. Still, somehow these elements caused him to become more attractive than when she'd seen him at the brothel. A rugged handsomeness had replaced the polished aristocrat whose haughty demeanor repelled those who didn't belong in his hemisphere. The man before her had the opposite effect. Attraction took hold, strong and fast, and she looked away from his unwavering gaze, afraid if she stared too long at him, she might yield to their powerful chemistry.

The sound of unexpected footfall broke through her thoughts with the steady beat of someone headed their way. There was no time for prevarication. She scanned the area and motioned in his direction. When he didn't immediately move, she reached out and tugged on his arm, sliding her bare hand into his and urging him forward.

"This way. Now." She only had two small daggers left on her person and neither would be effective against a true threat at the moment.

He followed without question. When they reached the corner, she shimmied into the farthest alcove, nothing more than a widened crevice between two tenement buildings, and indicated he do the same. There wouldn't be ample room to allow them separate positions, but at the moment it was their only choice and the area was completely dark without so much as a hairbreadth of light.

She flattened her body against the boards as he stepped farther into the alcove, her back against his chest, their forms enveloped by the blackness and sealed as closely as possible. There was no way they were visible from the alley, not unless someone decided to enter and search each alcove individually. It was a distinct disadvantage to not have a visible line of sight. She'd have liked to have known who pursued them. Was it a common thug, a deranged vagrant or someone who had more than thievery on their mind? The situation did not allow her this luxury though.

Another breath and her body no longer responded in the manner she'd expect. Her muscles tightened, but not from the danger of their pursuer. Aylesford blanketed her completely. Nary an inch of her person wasn't pressed against his. He was as close to her as a lover's embrace. She stiffened with this realization. His chest buffeted her shoulders, his hard thighs bracketed her hips and pressed against the softness of her backside. A lick of desire heated her skin as the air around them took on a palpable sensuality.

She didn't like being touched without giving someone permission, unless of course she fought for her life. But by degree, she relaxed. His breath fanned against her temple and she cursed her hair, wrapped securely into a bun and pinned tight when it might have provided another barrier to his heat. Every exhale, despite they were shallow and predictable, encouraged the spark of desire and fanned that flame to ignite. She fought against it.

Still, clear thinking became elusive as awareness of every point of contact took control, each one sensitized and consuming. Emotion and feeling held her tight in its grasp. She wouldn't allow herself to notice this powerful attraction or yield to its carnal command. She strained her ears and forced her focus to the sounds of the night. Not his breathing. Not the slightest scruff of his coat against the fabric of her blouse. Not his boot pressed aside hers. Not his heat or his strength.

The footsteps that had chased them materialized into another's presence. She couldn't see, but she knew and too, this person who gave hunt sounded bold in his pursuit. She could hear the dull clack of his bootheels on stone as he entered the same dead-end alley where they hid. He made no attempt to conceal himself, which meant he was armed and unafraid of danger.

CHAPTER 8

Ambrose tried holding his breath, but there was nothing for it. He inhaled deeply, Scarlett's scent of rosemary and mint a drug more potent than laudanum. He didn't move, his body unable to bear the agony of their position without the possibility he'd dishonor himself. He'd never seen a woman in trousers. He'd not even imagined it. The slope of her hips and gentle curves of her figure would forever be burned into his memory now. How she moved with efficient grace and strong agility was a marvel. She was fierce and brave and yet so soft and delectable against him. She'd saved him from certain death. His mind and emotions were a morass of confusion.

He shifted the smallest degree and his palm brushed her thigh, his fingers trailing over the fabric pulled taut across her smooth skin. He swallowed, his heart in a rapid beat.

Nothing prevented his body from making contact with hers except a few layers of cloth, barely a barrier considering the heat exchanged between them. Each of his senses heightened, attuned to every nuance of her body and he could hardly withstand it. It must be the attack he'd experienced tonight that brought all these reckless emotions to the surface.

Some ridiculous streak of masculine pride suggested Scarlett was different from any woman of his past and liked him for who he was as a person and not the title that claimed his existence. She'd have no expectations. But did she find him attractive? He flexed his muscles in an unexpected moment of vanity and then stopped himself from further embarrassment. A hard throb of lust pumped through him. How long would he have to endure this torture? He struggled to listen for the same noise that drove them into hiding and was rewarded with the sound of approaching bootheels. They still weren't safe.

She wasn't safe. An intense urge to protect her rose up inside him proving him more the fool. She'd saved him tonight and not the other way around.

Once they were freed from the alcove and separated, when he could breathe openly and think clearly, he would see this for what it was, nothing more than a reaction of misplaced desire brought about by his brush with violence. But at the moment, his need was real, a potent demand that begged to be obeyed.

Without warning, moonlight flooded the alley. The clouds had moved on. From the shrouded darkness of their shared alcove he spied the man who'd followed them. He didn't appear a typical criminal, though dishonest people took many forms. When the stranger edged closer, Ambrose recognized him as the same fellow who'd exited the jewelry store when Ambrose had entered. So, he'd been followed? For what reason? Was it the mention of the ring or was his imagination seeking any easy connection to solve Martin's problem and get on with normal life? He didn't know. With Scarlett facing inward there was no way for her to perceive the encroacher, but perhaps that was for the best. This night needed to end so he could see her home safely.

Their silent, motionless patience paid off and after another interminable minute, the stranger turned and left. Ambrose willed his body to relax and stepped from the alcove, offering his hand to assist as Scarlett wriggled free from the crevice and quietly brushed off her pants. This action brought his focus to her legs, encased in form-fitted buckskin, slender and endlessly long. If she turned and he viewed her bottom, he didn't think he'd be able to discourage his erection for the rest of the evening.

"That was too close." She shook her head and eyed him directly. Did she speak of their near discovery or the way they'd melted against each other within the alcove?

"Well, it's over now." He breathed deeply. "And I owe you my thanks. You saved my life back there."

"You'll be sore come morning." Her eyes ran over him and settled on his chest. "Did the thieves land many blows before I arrived?"

He straightened and rolled his shoulders to test for soreness. Then they began to walk slowly. "I'm fine. I'm actually more troubled for your welfare. How will you return home from here?"

"Peculiar how we've opposite concerns. I wondered the same about you."

They walked on in silence for a short stretch but Ambrose had too many unanswered questions to keep quiet for long.

"How did you learn to throw a knife like that? It's hardly a conventional practice for a lady."

"I'm rather unconventional, then, and . . ." She kept her eyes on the roadway ahead. "I'm not a lady, at least not the kind to whom you refer."

"Prickly, aren't you? Such sharp edges." *Such lovely curves.*

"Your edges have been polished smooth by years of wealth and advantage, a result evidenced by the life you lead. Our differences are far greater than our similarities."

He couldn't help but think she was drawing a line between them. Erecting a wall and stating the rules. But for whose benefit?

She picked up the thread of conversation she'd abandoned, seemingly anxious to divert attention to a subject worthy of her time.

"We helped each other tonight. I thank you for that, but now our association comes to an end."

"It is I who owe you my gratitude. Let me repay you. I can help in your search. As you once mentioned I have many resources at my disposal. I am the Duke of Aylesford."

"Aylesford," she repeated. "And a duke no less. That compounds the point I made earlier, Your Grace." She offered him a mock curtsy though she gifted him a genuine smile. "It would be the veritable scandal were you to associate with the likes of me."

"I am Aylesford. I'm a duke. I'll do as I please."

"I'm my own woman and I do as I please," she countered.

"Is it that simple?"

"Of course." She spared him a fleeting glance as they continued to progress toward High Street. "At least my decisions belong to me. You belong to the people."

"Perhaps. Although my title allows me complete freedom."

"Freedom to choose from prescribed choices, Your Grace. Freedom to conduct a future that has already been planned for you. Is that a choice at all?"

"In return I have the attention of greater society."

"You say that as if it's a desirable condition." Exasperation and amusement laced her reply.

"It is."

"To have everyone listening and measuring every word you speak?"

"Not every word." He stopped and she did as well. They'd almost advanced to High Street.

"What brought you to Wapping tonight?" She assessed him knowingly, as if she knew the answer but asked the question anyway.

"As I stated, I was seeking information."

"The same matter that brought you to The Scarlet Rose." She nodded in the affirmative. "Did you find it here?"

"No." He paused, unsure of what she sought with her questioning. Unsure of what he felt about anything at the moment. One thing pierced through his haze of confusion though. He needed to do better. Routine donations to causes and charities hardly scratched the surface of what must be done. "And were you successful in your hunt?"

"I was." She smiled and he felt an unexpected pressure in his chest. "But the terms for me are different. Your ducal tone and assumed authority won't earn you any cooperation here, Your Grace. This isn't Mayfair."

"No, even a blind man can see that." He stared into her gaze and wondered at her secrets. It was the first time he gave her face unabashed attention at close proximity and he took in every detail noting a slender white scar near the corner of her left eye, the exact path a teardrop would travel. Realizing he'd stopped speaking abruptly he forced more words from his mouth. "You know a lot about the riffraff here and their way of life."

"Not everyone here is unlawful, but they are all poor." She began to move again and he was inclined to follow. "Criminals live by a code just as you do, and loyalty and unity play a large part."

He hesitated before he continued. "We could help each other. You know this area and could assist me—"

"I work alone."

"But together we might—"

"I'd rather not." Her expression compounded her blunt determination.

He had no explanation for his rash need to continue their association whether fueled by the desire to protect or connect. He only knew he was intrigued and as so little caught his interest beyond the mundane duties of the duchy, he refused to allow the opportunity to escape.

They paused below a lamppost on High Street, their walk seemingly at an end under the pale glow of candlelight and moonbeams. There was nothing romantic about their environs and yet he fought hard to quell the need to touch her. Perhaps his brush with death indeed brought on the incessant desire.

"Who did this?" With a boldness he'd never asserted with a lady of the *ton* he ran the pad of his thumb over the scar near her cheekbone. He traced it again as if he could somehow erase the pain that caused it, along with the lasting memory. Still, experience had taught him the worst scars weren't visible. Especially those carved into one's heart.

Her skin was warm beneath his touch, soft and smooth, and the notion her entire body was a decadent paradise to be explored caused a rush of blood to tighten his groin. He leaned in closer, telling himself it was just so he could view her more easily, the lighting insufficient, but his breathing slowed and he noticed her own seemed to hitch as he advanced.

She licked her lips before she finally replied, "That was the work of a fool long ago."

"You have only to tell me his name and I'll find him and make him pay for hurting you."

"How chivalrous, Your Grace." Her lips turned softly as if he'd amused her, as if she'd kept her true thoughts to herself. "But you assume too much."

"In what way?"

"You can't find him because *she* stands before you. That wound was caused by my own hand in an act of foolishness. No matter, I learned a valuable lesson that day."

"I believe you."

"Why? We've only just met. You wouldn't know if I was telling the truth, would you?"

"Look at me."

She did.

"Eyes never lie."

They stood that way a moment longer but the profound chemistry that had held them tense within the alcove had now dissipated. He hailed a hack and watched her climb inside, his last glimpse of her slim figure clad in trousers enough to revive his erection. Then he summoned another driver for hire and left Wapping behind him.

CHAPTER 9

Scarlett leaned against the cracked seat cushions and closed her eyes, Aylesford's intense gaze still vivid in her memory. Did she imagine it? He no longer touched her and yet his heat lingered against her skin. When he'd called her name, his deep voice caused a tremor to skitter through her, swirling like a whirlwind into her stomach, unable to settle and find an end. She could only explain it away as unexpected trauma from their experience together. Each moment held a specific distinction she'd never forget. The heated masculine scent of his body pressed so closely to hers. The brush of his fingertips across her hip. The sensual warmth of his exhales against the back of her neck. It was as though every pinnacle of contact was now imprinted with his touch. A rush of heat swept through her and she breathed deep to expel the nonsense.

Yet later that night when the hour had grown quiet, she still wondered over the experience. Surrendering to her restlessness, she climbed between the sheets doubtful she'd find respite. Come morning she'd been proven right, her dreams persistent and unforgiving.

The first was of her mother, but not in happiness as she'd choose to preserve her recollections. Instead the horrific image of her mother, beaten and broken, left to die in a pool of blood on the bedchamber floor had forced Scarlett to consciousness, her heart objecting and her palms sweaty.

When she'd managed to find sleep again, a different but equally disturbing visage took hold. She stood in Southwark, visibly distressed, where she paced near the docks at the water's edge. For what she waited she couldn't see, the air too heavy with looming mist. Nevertheless, she searched as the murky waters blackened the hem of her cloak and her emotions grew more agitated with each step. The sluggish tide begged her closer, drew her forward until inky-black leeches clung to her boots and inched upward toward her ankles and calves. Still, none of this forced her away from the lapping waves. She remained in place, transfixed to the ebb and flow.

At last she saw the body, facedown and out of reach. With anxious trepidation, she watched as it floated nearer. A single blade protruded from the poor soul's back.

Was that her knife? Had she done this? She needed to know.

Rushing forward, heedless of her skirts and the filth that soaked through to her skin, she waded closer and heaved a breath of relief. The handle of the knife was studded with rubies and encircled with small round diamonds, the gemstones agleam in the fractured moonlight. This weapon was far more valuable than any of her belongings. Still, the blade had found its mark and killed the unfortunate stranger. With her heartbeat in her ears, she reached beneath the corpse and heaved it over in the lethargic tide. Aylesford's handsome face stared back at her, his skin ashen and his lips tinged blue.

She awoke with a wild scream, though soon after tears clogged her throat and muted the sound. She clenched her eyes closed again as if by doing so she would erase the image, but Aylesford's death-pale features wouldn't disappear. Why? Why would she dream such ghastly morbid images? She'd saved Aylesford from danger, or so she believed. Did she somehow inadvertently place him in harm's way? What was this strange thread that bound them together even in her dreams?

Most of the morning had passed before she regained a sense of calm. She dressed quickly, able to do so with astounding alacrity, her front-fastening undergarments a unique advantage created by Linie's ingenuity.

What had happened to the girl? Had Linie returned to work at Madame Ivory's Emporium? Scarlett hadn't received word from the modiste. Too many questions bombarded her and demanded answers. Scarlett would seek advice from the other Maidens of Mayhem and collectively they'd work to discover the truth. She just hoped she wasn't too late. For Linie's sake. Mayhap Aylesford's as well.

Ambrose settled into a corner at White's. The view from where he stood was unobstructed.

Here at the club comfortability would return. This was where he'd regain his footing, in this domain, a collection of rooms devoted to titled gentleman and their masculine pursuits. Or so he hoped. He knew no other way of life. White's represented tradition and its staid ancestral honor. When entering the club, one was secure, safe and among others who valued the same qualities. Men who would protect their own at any cost.

But what of those who dwelled on the outskirts of London central? Those in Southwark, Seven Dials and Wapping? How did they secure their footing, keep their loved ones safe? He was ashamed to admit he'd never given their fate thoughtful consideration.

That was, until last night. And now he could no longer ignore what existed not so much as a stone's throw from many of the roadways he'd traversed while going about his daily business.

Scarlett seemed at home among the narrow alleyways and darkened streets. She'd saved his life without hesitation and refused compensation or remuneration by any measure. And in his gratitude and admiration, he found his thoughts returning to her again and again. He should reconcile a way to repay her. To learn more about her and improve her life. Although he could be assuming too much. There was nothing about Scarlett that bespoke her wanting a thing, whether it be material or otherwise.

Considering all that had occurred last evening, he hadn't expressed his appreciation properly and he still grappled with making sense of the muddle of events and emotions. He didn't know her, nor her history. He scarce knew anything about her at all and yet he yearned to know her with an insistent desire no genteel lady or delicate debutante had evoked ever.

It could only be she was so unlike any lady of his acquaintance within the *ton*. What would she think of a social event during the height of the season? Would her lovely gray eyes grow wide with enchantment? She'd transform into a diamond of the first water encased in velvet or silk, her golden brown hair arranged in an elaborate style, ashimmer beneath the candlelight. Would participation in a grand ball soften her view of the aristocracy? Pity, the gossipmongers and tongue-wags would destroy any joy found if they were to appear in society together. Still, he was intelligent enough to recognize he needed to meet her at least once more if only to assure her safety, satisfy his curiosity and in some way offer his gratitude. The only way to cure the questions she stirred in his soul was to speak to her again and placate his misplaced wonderment.

She'd thrown her knives with perfected accuracy. How does one come by such an avocation? He noted how easily she'd evaded questions so one didn't notice until later that her answers were never supplied. She'd shown no fear during their pursuit, no histrionics at the outcome of the evening. She was stronger than most men who capered around White's, their boasting and preening a sorry exchange for the brave courage he'd witnessed in a young slip of a woman who had likely experienced more hardship than pleasure in her life.

And those trousers . . .

He hadn't recovered yet, although he attempted to drive the frequent image from his memory or he'd suffer an everlasting erection. Why would a woman eschew fashion for a man's tailoring? So many questions needed answers and yet he had no idea how to find her again.

Uncanny, how their paths had crossed three times in a handful of days. Was she following him? Investigating her own interests? Clearly, their queries intersected. She'd refused his offer of help and resources with definitive immediacy. Ambrose wasn't accustomed to being refused anything. Such was the way of the dukedom.

"Something has your brain tied in knots."

Blinking hard, Ambrose shifted his stance and turned toward the voice. "Townshend, good to see you. Sorry to hear of your difficult predicament."

Will Reid, Viscount Townshend, was a likable fellow who often landed on the wrong side of things by no fault of his own. His recent engagement to one of society's darlings had ended abruptly in a damaging public jilt. Ambrose could only imagine Townshend's bruised ego, most especially as society continued to speculate feverishly as to the reason for the lady's sudden change of heart.

It was good to see Townshend out and about though.

"I've been making the rounds," Townshend said. "Won't do for me to retreat inside and lick my wounds indefinitely."

His friend didn't continue although Ambrose suspected there was more to the story. He signaled a footman for brandy. "True enough. There's nothing like a bit of distraction when life is uncooperative." The words gave him pause. Not just because they sounded disturbingly similar to something Martin might say, but too, because they mirrored the exact reason Ambrose had come to White's in the first place.

"That's a word for it, I suppose."

The brandy arrived and a few minutes were spent in appreciation of their liquor.

"I haven't seen your brother at the usual locales. Dare I believe Martin has adopted a more responsible agenda for his evening hours?"

"And there you have it, the main reason my brain is tied in knots." His brother was an unsettling subject at best and Ambrose hadn't spoken to him in days. Was Townshend's observation an indication that Martin sought to mend his habits or a death knell warning another impending disaster was imminent?

"How two brothers could be more opposite in nature, I do not know."

"His tomfoolery reminds me daily of my duty," Ambrose replied.

"I suppose, although your differences offer your relationship balance, no doubt." Townshend nodded.

"How so?" The turn in conversation aligned with Ambrose's earlier thoughts about how dissimilar he was from Scarlett, yet an unspoken affinity had formed between them. At least on his part.

Townshend hesitated and took another swallow of his brandy, but then his face became somber and he continued in a low tone. "The end of my engagement came as no surprise to me. The lady and I were quite compatible. Brilliantly so, actually. Why, she could finish my sentences and I, hers. More often than not we chose the same topic of conversation, identical activity or event to attend. Our similarities overlapped to the point of coagulation."

Ambrose struggled to follow Townshend's thinking. "But isn't that good? To be so much alike demands very little effort and I'd believe scarce disharmony."

"What we once found charming soon became . . . ordinary. We grew bored quickly. Our relationship was routine instead of special and we are both intelligent enough to realize we didn't wish to spend the remainder of our days as brother and sister rather than husband and wife. And so, the jilt was engineered to salvage the lady's reputation."

"A chivalrous act." Ambrose nodded in admiration.

"It saved me as much as it saved her." Townshend glanced about the room and the topic died away. "So you see, to my point, a good degree of attraction is surprise and discovery. That way the spontaneity and unpredictable nature of being in a person's company never grows stale."

Ambrose allowed Townshend's conclusion to settle, his mind acutely focused on how he'd only just considered the difference between Scarlett and ladies of the *ton*, her lifestyle and his title. Unwilling to delve into his misplaced distraction, he returned his mind to talk of his brother.

"I wouldn't complain if Martin decided to live a more mundane life."

"I've no doubt." Townshend grinned in agreement. "He thrives on adventure undeterred by past outcome. I'll never forget the look on his face when he lost that hand of faro to some ostentatious old gent at Boodle's last Thursday. Martin never should have played in the first place. One look at the fellow with his embroidered waistcoat and gleaming ruby ring was enough to warn off a wiser man, most especially your brother with his shallow pockets. Two thousand pounds is not a small sum by any standard."

Ambrose jerked to attention, reacting as if Townshend had punched him in the jaw. "What did you say?"

"I mean no insult, Aylesford. I assumed your brother told you about the debt. You know me well enough, but your brother should—"

"No, before that. What did you say about a ring?" Could it be he'd found the man the girls mentioned in the brothel?

"Only that the faro player, the swell Martin lost to, was bedizened head to toe with fine tailoring." Townshend gestured with a sweep of his free hand. "Polished Hessians and valuable gemstones, the man was entirely in twig. He wore a ruby and diamond ring on his finger and matching encrusted stickpin at his throat that bespoke of old money and a lot of it."

"Who was he?" Ambrose rushed on.

"I haven't the foggiest, but surely your brother knows. He owes the man two thousand pounds." This was said in a low, commiserate tone.

"Thank you." Ambrose set down his glass and signaled a footman for his coat and carriage, eschewing the warranted apology for interrupting. He hastened to make an abrupt departure. "I need to speak to my brother. Good to see you, Townshend. Best of luck." And then before his friend could reply, he headed for the door.

CHAPTER 10

Anxious to shake off the niggling ill-ease of her nightmares, Scarlett ventured to Mortimer Street. She sought out her friends in hope of becoming distracted and while she still intended to discuss Linie's situation with the other Maidens of Mayhem, she wished to find a little peace before she plummeted into the subject. These women were her closest friends and makeshift family. Their bond of trust and friendship made confiding in them easy, although her interaction with Aylesford was different somehow and she hadn't decided whether or not to mention His Grace as of yet.

"Scarlett, you look troubled. Come into the kitchen. We've just put a fresh pot on for tea."

Julia's welcome was comforting and Scarlett began to relax simply by the knowledge her friends were always there for her. It was a good decision to come to Wycombe and Company. She followed Julia into the kitchen and settled on a chair at the table beside Phoebe. She couldn't remember the last time the four of them were together and she was anxious to hear current news and events. Yet no sooner had she claimed a seat than their chatter stopped and the room fell silent.

"What is it?" Scarlett glanced to each of her friends, unnerved by the sudden change.

"Have you slept?" Phoebe's voice sounded as if she already knew the answer.

"Not as much as I needed. I was in Wapping digging up some answers and happened upon an opportunity to assist a friend . . ." She paused at her use of the descriptor, not sure how to categorize Aylesford. She didn't wish to lie, yet one didn't wonder how it felt to kiss a friend, did one? "An acquaintance, actually," she amended. "And then found little rest afterward."

"Is there any way we can assist?" Diana slid her eyes to Julia and Phoebe, acknowledging their nods of agreement.

"I'm not sure."

"I told Phoebe and Diana about your concern for Linie's safety." Julia poured their tea and passed each cup around the table.

"I sent a message to Madame Ivory, and Linie hasn't returned to the shop. Her unexplained disappearance has me chasing shadows. Last night I went in search of Tommy Crow."

"The leech collector?" Diana piped up. "I'm not surprised he's still down at the water's edge keeping a watch on things. That man knows everything that happens on the Thames."

"In the Thames, as well. He had information of a young girl's body that washed up a few nights ago." Scarlett frowned as she relayed the grim news. "From his description, it wasn't Linie, but it was someone. Someone who deserved better than to be drowned in the river and forgotten."

"How true."

The ladies fell silent for a second time and their shared mutual respect kept questions to a minimum, perhaps each lost in their own memories as none of them were a stranger to some kind of pain.

"So, what will you do now?" Diana broke the silence and Scarlett exhaled deeply as she returned her attention to the conversation.

"All I have is a handful of odd clues, but I thought if I shared what I've learned, we could think on it collectively." It didn't take long for Scarlett to relay the information and a spirited conversation immediately ensued.

"People don't just disappear without a trace, unless they intend to do so."

"Otherwise when it happens nothing good comes of it."

"I have a bad feeling about this one and I may need your help, ladies," Scarlett added.

"Your intuition is not something to be ignored." Diana set her tea down. "Where should we begin?"

"In just one conversation, three different girls were named as having left the brothel. Isn't that unusual?"

"I think so." Julia's expression became troubled. "I wonder if the girls are being lured away with the promise of a better future but then something dreadful happens. But what? And why?"

"It's transient employment mostly," Scarlett stated. Her matter-of-fact tone held telling authority. "Young women age out because many men want the youngest girl available and madams want to supply what the customer demands. Others come and go in hope of making a better income at another location. Sometimes the girls grow too weary to continue. It's a hard life especially if another job is held during the daylight hours. Of course, there's always pregnancy as a reason to disappear, or a botched attempt to rid oneself of pregnancy. Or incapacitating illness. Girls are harmed, injured, misused and bruised by their customers, so they disappear or at least stay away until healed. The profession is grim. It's a pleasure house for men and a prison for women." So many trials in life offered gratification for men and pain for women. Sex and childbirth were two more examples.

Quiet enveloped the room for an overlong beat and Scarlett realized her friends waited on her to continue. "As you already know, my mother was a kept woman."

"A mistress is not the same thing." Julia was quick to object.

"Is it, though?" Scarlett shrugged her dismissal. "There's hardly a difference. I suppose on some levels one could consider a pampered mistress more of a pet than a prostitute, but there's no denying that sex is the basis of either relationship."

No one replied to that.

"What about your runner friend? Bow Street must be aware of all the women who go missing in London." Diana tried to steer the conversation in a more purposeful direction.

"Oh, no doubt they are." Again Scarlett shrugged. "And I suppose asking him about it isn't a bad idea, but I'd guess the runners are too busy with what they consider important crime, rather than what transpires in the bedchambers of a brothel. I'm sure they've given up trying to bring justice to Seven Dials or any other slum in London."

"There's a jewelry fence in Wapping who handles gemstones without asking questions. I wonder if talking to him about the ruby ring is worth the effort," Phoebe suggested.

Scarlett brightened and nodded enthusiastically. "I suspect the fence you've mentioned is the same fellow Aylesford attempted to—"

"Aylesford?" Julia interrupted. "Are you referring to His Grace, the Duke of Aylesford?"

All three ladies turned in her direction and for a moment it was so quiet Scarlett swore she heard the blood moving in her veins. "Yes. We met at the brothel."

Phoebe arched one slender brow. Scarlett recognized her friend's unspoken cue and briefly ran through the details, although she kept the information vague, unwilling to reveal the connection with Ambrose that she didn't quite understand herself. She shouldn't have noticed Aylesford's commanding presence, the strength of his legs tangled against hers or the rhythm of his breathing. But she had and now she couldn't rid herself of the memory.

"Skulking about in the shadows with a duke." A bemused smile played at Diana's mouth.

"I'd imagine he's a stuffy, doddery old prig who believes he's smarter than most. But is he really? Does he fight for matters in Parliament that support progressive politics or is he a slow thinker?" Phoebe asked, her wide-eyed attention fixed on Scarlett.

"We're supposed to be discussing how to find Linie. None of these questions matter right now." Aylesford. Stuffy? Maybe. Doddery and old? Not at all. One thing she knew without a doubt though, he was no dullard. Aylesford was clever and quick to reason, and in regard to her wardrobe he possessed a more open mind than many men of his station.

"You may have more information than you think you do, Scarlett." Diana's expression grew serious, her fingers splayed as she counted off possible leads to investigate. "There are the girls at the brothel who are a wealth of information if you can gain their trust. Sally at the apartment may know more about Linie's history or be able to relay a recent conversation they shared. Sally said she'd had a fitting the day before Linie went missing. And there's the jeweler, a brute named Clive, Howell on Bow Street and Tommy Crow." Finger after finger popped up to tally possibilities for information gathering.

"And don't forget the little mudlark. Most children are more observant than adults. I'd start with the lad if you can locate him," Phoebe added.

"I knew coming here would be a smart decision." Scarlett smiled at her friends. "Thank you, ladies. I don't know what I'd do without you." She stood and pushed her chair into the table.

"I'll walk with you to the door." Julia put down her teacup and also rose.

Together they left the kitchen and when they neared the door, Scarlett paused, awaiting whatever Julia wished to say apart from Diana and Phoebe.

"So, you've spent time with His Grace," Julia began, a gleam in her eye that looked too much like wishful thinking.

"Only because our paths crossed unexpectedly," Scarlett clarified with emphasis. "Don't begin reading anything into it beyond that."

"Oh, I wasn't." Julia canted her head slightly as she stared at Scarlett. "I just worry about you."

"Thank you." Scarlett squeezed her friend's hand. "But you shouldn't. I have everything I need."

"Do you? Don't you wish to find love? Maybe have a family someday?"

Scarlett couldn't keep the surprise from her face. "And you're suggesting I look to Aylesford for a future?"

"No. Not at all." Julia's delicate brows lowered. "I understand the difficult dynamic at play there. But it doesn't mean you can't find a gentleman to keep you company. This little group we've formed can't be all that fills your time."

"I've never had a loving family before. I don't know what I'm missing and therefore it makes little difference now." Scarlett shook her head in the negative. "And couldn't I say the same of you? Or Diana and Phoebe?"

"I've had my chance at love." Julia smiled softly. "I just want you to be happy. You deserve that much. Diana and Phoebe have their own stories too."

"I do all right." Scarlett stepped to the door and put her hand on the latch. "But thank you for your concern. You are a true friend. I'll see you soon." Then she left before Julia could read any more emotion in her eyes.

Ambrose settled in the leather chair behind the desk in his study and exhaled long and thoroughly. This was the room in Aylesford House he sought when he needed absolute quiet. He'd summoned Martin from his apartment at the Albany, but before his brother arrived, Ambrose had much to consider. He raised his eyes to his father's portrait over the mantelpiece. How could one man sire two sons completely opposite in nature? Martin behaved like their deceased father in that he indulged himself and enjoyed life, but while their sire had never shirked responsibility even in his favored pastimes, Martin lived as if the world was his play yard, confident someone else would clean up the mess he always left behind.

Ambrose was the heir, now the duke. Every word and act embodied diplomacy, dignity and apparently all things that began with the letter D. Discretion. Dedication. Duty. It was at the core of every decision Ambrose made and the utmost responsibility of any nobleman worthy of honor. Still, somehow, none of the fine qualities instilled in Ambrose from birth permeated Martin's character. His brother lived in the moment. Ambrose not only carried the esteemed heritage of his past, but was responsible for the duchy's future.

Yet there was another word demanding his attention.

Desire. He closed his eyes and a ready image of Scarlett formed. For the first time in a long time he dreamed of more. No more denial for the sake of the duchy. Lest anyone forget beneath the fine clothes he was only a man.

He shook his head to solidify his resolve. He needed to see her again. Just one more time. He'd find Scarlett and act on his impulses. It was a sacrifice to abet his curiosity. Nothing more. One kiss would satisfy this misplaced longing and unexplainable intrigue. One kiss and then he'd be done. It could only be his recent brush with death that had him considering such an improper idea as a way to rid the woman from his system. It would put an end to his edgy disquiet and then he could return his world to normal. He stood and moved toward the hearth to exercise his restlessness.

With ironic timing, Martin's voice carried from the hall as a reminder of all the trouble left unresolved and Ambrose shut away his earlier thoughts to steel his patience for the conversation. If his brother could identify the man who held his vowels, Ambrose would know whom to speak with concerning the girls at the brothel and at last, one issue could be laid to rest. Life would return to routine. He'd gain peace once again.

After just one kiss.

"You're scowling already." Martin approached though his steps slowed as he entered the room. "We haven't even begun to talk."

Amused by his brother's wariness, Ambrose composed a more welcoming expression and nodded toward the brandy. "Pour us both a glass and let's discuss this predicament."

Martin set to work at the sideboard but as he neared the desk with their liquor his expression transformed from carefree amusement to serious concern. "What happened to you? Your temple is bruised and—"

"A bit of a scuffle in Wapping." Ambrose motioned toward the chair yet his brother stared at him, unmoving. "You almost became the fifth Duke of Aylesford, God help us all."

"Are you all right then?" Seemingly mollified Martin sank into the chair but his gaze remained vigilant. He downed a glass of brandy and failed to relinquish the other.

"I might not have been. The men who attacked me intended brutality, but assistance came from an unexpected place." *She was magnificent.*

"You don't say. They weren't seeking retribution for anything I did, were they?" Martin spoke slowly, warily.

"Common thugs, nothing more," Ambrose assured.

"Deuced thugs, up to no good." Martin breathed deeply, digesting the news and then continued, his disposition somewhat restored. "KK sends his best. He thanks you for clearing his debt at The Scarlet Rose."

"Be sure Kilbaren knows it was a singular act. I won't become responsible for a man who has little more than lint in his pocket and the same between his ears." Ambrose rose and poked at the fire. He glanced again at his father's portrait and strode back toward the desk to pluck the full brandy glass from his brother's hand. "The two of you need to take more responsibility for your actions."

"Agreed."

Martin's expression eased, as did Ambrose's, and for a time just the crackle of the fire lent the room noise.

"I'm heartened to hear your fresh commitment. That said, I've reconsidered the sum you requested for the gambling loss you've incurred. I'd like to visit the gentleman who holds your vowels and issue him payment. If you're to reform your spending, I'd like to solidify your resolve by clearing your debt."

"Thank you." Martin tilted his glass in an attempt to drink the dregs, his mouth in a frown instead of a smile. "But I can't tell you his name."

"What?" Ambrose's temper rose up. "Why the hell not?"

"Because I don't know who he is. He said it was better that way and he would find me and collect when he was ready."

"Unusual circumstance, that. And you just accepted those terms? Gambling large sums with a stranger?" Ambrose speared his brother with a glare of annoyance. Martin was a puzzle with a few pieces missing.

Martin shrugged in answer.

"Where did you meet this man?" Ambrose prodded for more information since Martin wasn't forthcoming.

"At a hall in St. James. The hell comes and goes like a traveling circus. High stakes and high rollers only." Martin gestured a flourish with his free hand. "It moves about London to meet the needs of its clientele. The unpredictability of the gaming hall adds to the allure. Tonight it returns, but then tomorrow evening it will be gone again. That's all part of the experience."

First the brothel, now some dubious underworld gaming den. His brother would singlehandedly see to the death of their pristine reputation.

Warming to the subject, Martin continued. "It operates on reputation only and familiarity by the blokes who run the place. If you're set on clearing my debt, I can take you there."

"No. Just tell me the location. It would be better if I entered as a stranger." Who knew what other trouble Martin might have caused that would evoke retribution? It was better no one realized Ambrose was Martin's brother until it was necessary, *if it was necessary*. And by no means should any of the players discover he was a nobleman. Hopefully, it would simply be a matter of paying Martin's debt and identifying the man with the ruby ring. Yet whatever it was, he needed to see to it done. The sooner the matter was resolved, the sooner routine could be restored.

Although the latter thought didn't excite him as much as it should.

CHAPTER 11

Scarlett made quick work of visiting the brothel after she'd left her friends at Wycombe and Company yesterday afternoon. She didn't gain entry nor was she able to speak to any of the working girls but she did spy Felix as he left through the back door, a curious circumstance indeed.

Did Bow Street have similar concerns about missing women? While part of her thought discussing her concerns with Felix made sense, another stronger compulsion urged she wait until she'd gathered more facts.

His being at The Scarlet Rose could mean nothing at all. Men and their primitive urges were the main reason brothels were necessary. She wanted to believe in love and deep emotion, but aside from a few rare instances, she hadn't seen convincing proof of either. Her mother's exchanges were more business than emotional attachment. Perhaps Felix simply sought uncomplicated companionship.

Unlike the duke. Aylesford was all complication. Not that she was thinking of keeping his company. Not that he would ever entertain keeping hers. Still she wouldn't lie to herself. He intrigued her far more than he should.

Now in the light of a new dawn, she made herself one with the city and eased beneath the culverts on the edge of the Thames. This was a popular place for mudlarks and grubbers to congregate before they began their morning treasure hunts. Finding brass buttons, a silver spoon or a carved wooden pipe would feed a mud-lark for weeks.

Mudlarking was at its best before the Thames came to life, turbulent with the passage of boats and skiffs. Scavengers were early risers who searched the banks for the treasures deposited overnight. Luckily, Scarlett kept similar hours and a jaunt to the water's edge presented no inconvenience, especially if it provided much needed information.

She glanced from child to child, most covered in raggedy cloth-ing in various sizes and stages of disrepair, their small hands and feet stained a dingy shade by river mud, their fingernails ruined. The dank area teamed with activity and swindle, too many or-phans and beggars for Scarlett to comprehend. It was by chance and good luck the lad had a head of flaming copper hair. It made locating Willie more probable and with a few minutes of observa-tion, Scarlett found her quarry. Mudlarks didn't prescribe to the same code as older thieves and pickpockets, especially if it meant the difference between an empty belly or a full one come eve-ningtide. She was confident her coins would work magic.

She followed the lad as he left the protection of the culvert, away from the bridge drains and farther along the embankment until he was separated by a distance from the others and up to his knees in muddy water. Had he the desire to run on her approach he would not be so easily lost.

"Willie, is that you?"

The lad turned as soon as he heard his name though his eyes watched her suspiciously despite Scarlett's keeping her hands folded in front of her, a smile on her face.

"Your sister mentioned you just the other day and how hard you work for Tommy Crow. Have you found any treasures recently?"

His brows eased, though his expression remained guarded. "What's it to you?"

So, he would play it tough then. "I have a pocketful of coins I intend to share with you if you're willing to have a short conversation." She jingled the folds in her skirt to entice his interest. "I've only a few questions. I hope you can help me."

"I'll see the coins first."

Scarlett knew better than to be swindled so easily. If she did as he asked, he'd abscond with the money and she'd never gain the information she needed. "I'll start with a shilling before you tell me one word and then give you another for every question you answer thereafter."

His pale brows shot up so high they were lost in the smears on his forehead, but he no longer hesitated and made his way to the embankment where she waited.

"Well."

He extended his flattened palm and she placed a coin within his filth-covered hand. His fingers curled around it so quickly, their skin brushed as she moved her hand away.

"You know my sister?"

"She was eager to share news about Clive and how he's promised to take her away from the brothel." Manipulating the truth to suit her purpose caused no harm, especially if it resulted in protection of the girl, which by extension would provide for Willie's well-being. If his sister went missing, who would continue to care for the child? "Are you as excited as she?"

He held his palm up and waited. Scarlett dutifully deposited another shilling.

"Course I am. I don't right enjoy mucking through the Thames, but Tommy Crow is a decent sort."

That wasn't the information she needed and Scarlett tried another tactic. "Do you know Clive, the man who plans to help your sister? Do you know where I can find him?"

"That's two questions," Willie said. He shoved his hand deep in his trouser pocket to ensure the other coins were safely kept.

"Do you know Clive?" Scarlett clarified, and waited.

"Is he the toff with the fancy ring?"

"A red stone with diamonds." She nodded, eager to gain more information.

"I know what a ruby looks like. I find all kinds of things in this bloody river. Someday I'll find a piece of jewelry so fine we won't need no one's help no more."

Arching a brow at his word choice, Scarlett prodded further. "Well, your sister may have found a way out of this life for both of you." She smiled at him, genuinely charmed. "Do you know what Clive looks like?"

"He's tall."

Scarlett chewed her lower lip in consternation. Everyone was tall to a young child. "Can you tell me anything else about his appearance? Does he have light hair or dark?"

"Dark, and you're asking a lot of questions." He jerked his head around to look at the water and then back again. "The longer I talk to you, the more chance someone else will find what I should have."

Worried the child might scamper off before she gained as much information as possible, Scarlett compensated Willie and asked another question as she deposited the coins. "Do you know where I can find Clive?"

"Nope."

He thrust his dirty palm toward her again. Scarlett hesitated and then laid another coin into his hand. He pocketed it and turned as if their business exchange was completed. She waited, purposely moving the coins in her pocket to remind him she had more to spend. The tactic worked and he reconsidered.

"What else did you need to know?"

"What else do you have to tell?"

"He's good at cards. Once my sister had me watch for his fancy carriage outside The Pigeon Hole on Garnett Street. You might find him there."

She smiled at him and placed the remaining coins in his palm. "Thank you, Willie. Spend your newfound wealth carefully."

His fingers tightened around the shillings but he didn't say more. Then he scampered away faster than a mouse on the run from a tabby.

* * *

Carriage after carriage, hack after hack, slowed and released patrons at the door of the gaming hell on Garnett Street later that day. The building was nondescript with no marker or distinguishing feature. Each visitor knocked twice and was admitted without question, the business of knowing the location enough to identify the participant as worthy. Unfortunately, each and every one of them wore gloves.

Scarlett cursed softly as she stood in the shadows. "I need to get into that club." She took out a small silver flask and drank a swallow of brandy to ward off the cold.

"You'll never get into that club."

Aylesford's voice startled her and she cursed a second time. When had her intuition failed her in such a way she didn't sense someone's approach? She was losing her edge.

"Again I find you in trousers?"

His voice held a delightfully wicked tone. He *did* like her in trousers.

"Again I find you skulking about in my shadow? Peculiar, how our paths cross continually. I can only assume you've acquired the same information as I." *Or mayhap you're following me.*

Aylesford moved from the corner where he'd hidden and his tall, broad shadow enveloped her. He was no less handsome in the gloaming's dusky light. She forced herself to return her attention to the entrance in question and stop considering the width of his shoulders or the remembrance of his heat pressed against her back. There was plenty of space in the area where they waited now with no opportunity to relive their last encounter or its subsequent inconvenience. Not that she considered the possibility.

"Is that liquor?" His question expressed surprise more than censure.

"Brandy to chase away the damp." She took another sip and waved the flask toward him.

He shook his head in the negative. "While you await the man with the ruby ring?"

"Clive."

"Perhaps."

His doubt snared her curiosity.

"If he's lost the ring in a hand of cards or decided not to wear it, we have no way to identify him. Consider too, Clive may be a fictitious name he used at the brothel. We can't allow assumption to lead us down another dead end."

She noticed his use of the word *us* and fought hard against a pulse of pleasure. She couldn't let her guard down. Not now. Too much depended on her staying focused and besides, her affection was off limits. Most especially for a duke. She wasn't that foolish. Another exhale and she fully rejected the rubbish her imagination conjured. Since when did she visualize personal relationships? Julia's unexpected inquiries were stirring up trouble.

Scarlett gave herself a stern mental shake and replied to Aylesford, "There's only one way to know for sure, and so I'm left to this dingy alleyway." The bitterness of that reality made her words sound harsh.

"But I can gain entry."

This didn't sit well with her either. Men always had the advantage. She was bloody well sick of it. London needed to change. As did the rest of the world. Women should be valued, not minimized. But that wouldn't be accomplished this evening.

"And will you?" She swallowed what remained of her anger and turned to him, resting her back on the bricks of the building where she'd waited. He searched her face for a moment and then his gaze followed the curve of her neck and shoulders, then her hips until his eyes lowered to the high boots she'd worn. Uncomfortable with his assessment, she pulled her cloak inward.

"You are a development I've never considered."

"You say that like it's a compliment."

"It is."

He smiled and for a moment her heart refused to beat.

"It's as though no one knows you exist." His voice held a curious wistful tone though his stance exuded self-assurance.

"While everyone knows of your existence. Yet another way we are of opposite nature. I prefer the shadows while your entire life is on display."

"At times," he conceded.

She smirked as he qualified her answer.

"I believe we need each other."

"Pardon?" His statement was so unexpected she was jarred from her usual defense. "I answer to no one. I live independently."

He eyed her keenly. "And how is that possible? To function in society, one needs funds for food, clothing, everyday living. Are you secretly a duchess?"

She wondered if wishful thinking prompted his ridiculous question. "Hardly." She hesitated. She wasn't in the habit of explaining herself or her situation, but they were confined to a dark corner with nothing but time to pass. Besides, if she didn't answer in some respect, he would continue to pester her and she didn't care to spend the evening answering question upon question about her past.

"Several years ago, I saved a child who was stolen from the streets. Her parents were high-born and affluent. They were also extremely grateful for their daughter's return. I would not accept payment despite their insistent attempts to compensate me and express their gratitude. They left the city and I never heard from them again. But then one day a package arrived by messenger. I opened the box and discovered it packed tight with pound notes." By no means did it make her wealthy, but it kept her fed, clothed and housed.

"They had to reward you. You returned their most precious child to them." His statement was a mixture of approval and awe.

"Yes, in the end I understood the gesture and greatly appreciated their generosity."

"And still, you seek to make London a better place at the cost of your time and safety."

She didn't reply to this comment. She'd never shared so much of her personal history with anyone before, never mind a nob. Still, there was so much to tell, she'd only offered a thimble's worth. Nevertheless, she wasn't inclined to offer more.

"I haven't any connections to the underworld, this culture alive and thriving in London away from Mayfair where I suspect the man with the ruby ring conducts business." Aylesford filled the silence. He moved closer and didn't stop until he stood directly before her. With her shoulders against the bricks, she had nowhere to escape though she was profoundly aware of his attention. "And you need access to some of society's more exclusive events so you might discover this nobleman who entices women away from the brothel never to be heard from again."

"But isn't the man you mention one and the same?" She shook her head and raised her eyes to match his. "Aren't we both seeking the same person?"

"Of course. Perhaps. Maybe," he murmured, the air between them fraught with a strange combination of disguised emotion and unspoken words. "Maybe not."

They stood that way a minute longer and the mood changed. Precarious questions hung in the quiet. Their breathing paired in tandem. She relaxed by degree. The gaming hell was forgotten. When he placed his gloved palm on the wall at her back, she knew what he meant to do and despite her brain screaming an objection, her heart began to flutter a faster beat. A rush of anticipation swept through her. This was foolish. As foolish as throwing a knife blindfolded and having it bounce back and slice into one's brow. As foolish as she'd ever behaved. And yet still she didn't object.

He was going to kiss her and bloody hell, she wanted that kiss.

CHAPTER 12

Aylesford stared into Scarlett's face and decided he didn't just *want* to kiss her, he needed to. As much as his next breath. It made no sense, this foolish obsession he'd entertained, allowing her to intrude on his thoughts persistently, envisioning her in her trousers and without them as well. She represented something forbidden and yet so tempting, so far out of the realm where he spent each day, he couldn't deny himself. Not this time at least. He couldn't think clearly from wanting her. And when he'd watched her drink brandy from her flask, he'd envied the liquor and its heavenly task of warming her from the inside.

He leaned closer, inhaled her rosemary mint fragrance, remembering belatedly that she was deadly with a knife and could very well already have a blade in hand, but even that warning did not stop him.

There was no denying he was drawn to her. He could try to convince himself it was merely curiosity because of their vast differences. She was beauty untouched and elemental, raw and unruined by society and yet she'd known so many hardships. He represented perpetuation of heritage and title more than importance as an individual. A man who upheld his family's history and lived a prescribed future. Somehow, she brought out a freedom in him he'd never acknowledged before. He desired her for this and for a deeper reason. Something reckless that he refused to examine too closely. A reason he'd never be able to explore beyond this moment.

This kiss.

Emotion flickered in her silver-gray eyes. Did she mean to stop him? He lowered his head. Her breath feathered across his lips and he settled his mouth over hers.

A surge of desire radiated through him as soon as she met his kiss with enthusiasm. Did she feel it as well? With the wall at her back and his arm braced against the bricks, he sheltered her with his body. He raised his free hand and gently clasped her cheek, angling her head to gain the best access. The wind changed direction and a few silken strands of her hair brushed against his wrist where his glove separated from his coat. The smallest nuance seemed the greatest enticement.

Any leash he held on desire was quickly broken. She placed her hands on his chest, palms flat as if she sought balance or measured his heartbeat, the thrumming rush of blood through muscle like nothing he'd ever experienced. The air around them became charged, heated and vibrant, to create a spell, an alchemist's wicked concoction and now, having all the elements combined, proved a force overwhelming.

Nowhere else did their skin touch besides their mouths. Too many layers of wool and silk remained in the way. Even her leather gloves presented another barrier between them, and yet his body heated, consumed with sensation and an urgency he could hardly think to explain.

She gasped and he paused in anticipation of her resistance, rewarded instead by the touch of her tongue. He plundered her mouth as he'd dreamt of ever since first seeing her when he'd matched the challenge in her eyes and knew there was an unexplained connection there. He licked into her heat, the satin smooth glide of her tongue eliciting sensation so strong he fought against a surge of desire.

This wasn't typical behavior. He courted women honorably. He asked permission to escort a lady into the dining room. On occasion he bestowed a chaste kiss to a forehead if not the traditional buss to a gloved hand. Something about the darkness, the risk, and Scarlett caused him to abandon propriety and taste danger for a change. Kissing in public, never mind in a dark alley in a questionable neighborhood, was improper. Indecent. *Downright reckless*. The actions of a second son. Not a duke.

But damn, it was glorious.

She wasn't prepared for his kiss, and if anything Scarlett prided herself on being prepared for whatever life presented. She'd fended off attacks, survived hunger, poverty and sorrow, and yet one touch of his mouth upon hers and she was suddenly lost. For no reason she could explain, his kiss weakened instead of emboldened, the heated press of his mouth to hers a force beyond her control. She was out of her element now and the very thought terrified her. His interest was unexpected. *Unwise*.

Yet she didn't pull away.

Drawing a breath, she parted her lips and welcomed his tongue, each stroke velvet and silk, incredibly warm and enticing. Unlike the staid man who shouldered a lofty title, his kiss was composed of indulgent pleasure and welcoming comfort. His tongue chased after hers, curling and twining in a game of tag that had everything to do with desire and nothing to do with child's play. She sank into surrender unable to comprehend anything except her rioting emotions. Indecision vanished the moment their lips touched and despite the blood that roared in her ears, she could hear his breathing as uneven as her own. He wasn't unaffected. Something drew them together, more demanding than desire.

His mouth angled perfectly to capture hers, to give and take with assertive force. Yet for all its command, his kiss possessed tenderness. Almost reverence. And this caused her to doubt almost everything she believed true. He was one of the most powerful men in England. She was a person of no consequence. She represented a means to gain information, nothing more. Unless he was after a bit of the rough, though she doubted that motivated his actions.

Her heart squeezed, disliking the latter suggestion, and she abandoned thought and reason, opening to him, inviting his tongue to taste, find her secrets, discover temptation. Her never-ending restlessness ceased. Somehow, he brought her peace. And with that thought, some strange, unfamiliar emotion flooded her, coiling tight in her belly. She attempted to sort it out, but logic was of no use. She pressed hard on his chest, her fingers finding a wall of muscle beneath the cloth, the smallest movement capable of mesmerizing her.

They drew apart too soon. He initiated the separation and she suffocated her disappointment.

"You should go home now."

She scowled, her mind all at once clear again. "Now?"

"This is a dangerous area at night."

Of course it was. She aborted the laughter that rose in her throat. So he was suddenly an expert on crime in Greater London. They were both after answers, or so she thought. What was he about?

"I want to protect you."

Aah, so she'd appealed to his sense of duty. His assumptions were infuriating. All pleasure evaporated in another beat. "That is hardly necessary, Your Grace."

"You need to call me Ambrose."

His suggestion, or was it a command, stoked her irritation and riled rebellion within her. "And where will you go, Ambrose?"

He canted his head to the right and indicated the gaming hell door. "I'm going in there to locate the man with the ruby ring."

Her displeasure deepened. Damn the fact she was female and society judged a person's worth on gender rather than merit and intelligence. If she could only disguise her breasts, she'd masquerade as a man and enter the gaming hell herself, but once again nature schemed against her, her bosom too ample to be bound and hidden.

Perhaps he understood her frown. He offered an olive branch of sorts.

"There's no doubt we've crossed paths because our purpose and goal are one in the same. If you agree to work together with me on this, I will meet you tomorrow morning and share everything I've learned tonight."

It wasn't what she wanted to hear but it was more than she'd expected. "How early?"

A lot could transpire in a few hours if one was savvy to the operation of underground London and Scarlett still had several more leads to investigate.

"At dawn, if you prefer. You can determine the time and place."

She nodded and hesitated for only another breath; his kiss still warm on her lips, her conflicted senses only partially recovered. "Half seven. Rotten Row. Don't be late." Then she pushed aside her cloak and with a glance over her shoulder melted into the night.

What had just happened? Annoyance rippled through her, each step a little faster creating the distance she needed while too many thoughts barraged her brain. She'd been kissed by a duke. She had abandoned her surveillance and given power over to another. She'd made a series of detrimental mistakes. Aylesford had no right making her question things that were better left unconsidered. Her world was an unforgiving place, full of sharp angles and deep pitfalls while his was soft and accommodating, the path of nurtured comfort and blissful happiness, every desire met and fulfilled with abundance.

Why had he suggested she use his Christian name? *Ambrose.* It was a name befitting his person. His title. Like some immortal saint or mythological king. She shook her head and relished another breath of cold air. They were nothing to each other beyond unlikely acquaintances. *And yet his kiss.* She rebelled against the fluttery feeling in her chest.

Forcing her attention to the forked alleyway ahead, she chose the one on the left for its narrow bend. She knew this area well enough, although one could never be too careful in this part of the city.

Her heart still drummed against her rib cage and she willed herself to focus.

Ambrose.

Use of his Christian name made their relationship personal. *Intimate.* An odd twist of emotion lodged between her ribs now. She didn't like it. She clenched her eyes to force away the feeling. Too late she opened them. Ahead, a man dissected her path.

It was Felix. What was he doing here? Had Bow Street sent him to investigate something in the vicinity or was she his purpose and aim? Scarlett couldn't help but wonder about his frequent appearances. He was following her. Why? She didn't like that either. Too many coincidences. Too many unanswered questions.

"My lady." He moved forward and blocked her progression. Apparently, he meant to talk, not fall in stride beside her. His expression was difficult to decipher.

"I'm no lady and you know that well." A thread of ill ease prickled across her shoulders. Here in the shadowy backstreet she was no longer certain if she faced friend or foe. Surely her mind played cruel tricks.

"We meet again." He offered some semblance of a smile, then brushed at his nose with his gloved fingertip. He was wearing a low-brimmed beaver hat and coat. "Have you a moment to spare?"

Something wasn't right. Too many unsolved problems surfaced with his appearance this evening. She could hear it in his tone, see it in his eyes.

"But of course, if you don't mind walking while we do so." She made to move around him, but he stayed her with an open palm.

"No. I've business in this area so I'd rather we converse here before you move on."

He glanced over his shoulder as if to secure they were alone and Scarlett followed the path of his attention with her eyes. No one was there. Still, his behavior was odd. Unlike his usual jovial entreaty. There was an unnerving calm in his voice. Did someone watch from afar? Felix had appeared in her life often enough that she possessed a basic understanding of his usual behavior.

Two years ago, a string of ugly attacks in Mayfair brought about their acquaintance. Genteel ladies were no longer safe to ride in their carriages without extra tigers, the threat of being accosted causing London's female elite to shun societal events for fear of being overtaken on the roadways. Until the perilous spree was resolved and the criminals apprehended, the Maidens of Mayhem had watched and protected as an invisible force keeping the peace and defending those in danger whenever needed.

In one of those encounters, Felix and Scarlett crossed paths. The sharp-thinking runner quickly realized what Scarlett was about and how her associates worked toward restoring normalcy. Grateful for the assistance they lent without ever seeking notoriety or credit, Felix formed a casual bond with Scarlett. Not quite friendship, more a mutual respect. He'd once happened upon her as she'd held a knife to a miscreant's lower body and threatened him with castration. In the end, she'd handed the criminal over to Felix, but not without a lengthy discussion first. Proud of how she and her fellow Maidens had protected the thoroughfare, she'd let it slip about their little task force.

She'd regretted that conversation ever since.

Scarlett had always believed the runner trustworthy—except now something seemed off.

"What brings you into the London stews?" she asked.

"Misdeeds and the usual criminal activity." He waved away her question and turned the discussion around. "How is it I find you here in such a dangerous area? You should take heed of your safety. A woman prowling about alone at night is an easy target."

Was that a general bit of advice or a veiled threat? Perhaps her suspicions were getting the better of plain logic. She watched Felix closely. Whether he was seeking the same answers as she or baiting her, she didn't want him to discover Aylesford waiting in the alleyway across from the hell. That would be disastrous for the duke. If she could engage Felix in conversation a little longer it would secure His Grace more time.

"I rely on no one but myself. I need no husband or father to watch over my every decision." She purposely turned and angled in the opposite direction.

"Everyone needs someone to share their company." Felix leaned closer, his eyebrows raised in expectancy of her answer.

"That's not true."

"Isn't it though?" He smiled, but it didn't reach his eyes. "Your behavior seems unwise under the circumstances. I wouldn't want anything untoward to happen to you."

"Are you trying to frighten me?" She might have laughed under different circumstances, but she all at once wondered if perhaps he truly did seek to scare her.

"Warn you, Scarlett. Nothing more."

"It doesn't feel that way." And it didn't. Something about this meeting had become a confrontation and yet she didn't know why or what Felix wanted from her. Her emotions were running riot since Ambrose's kiss and now she couldn't think straight because of it.

"Everyone wants for companionship. We're friends, aren't we? More than friends, perhaps?"

What exactly was he asking her? Instinct poked at her brain, prodding her better sense. "What is it you need to know, Howell?"

She searched his face for some telling sign, a twitch of betrayal or disloyalty, but found none. He laced his hands together as he considered her question, the action bringing attention to his gloves and she was reminded of how difficult it would be to locate one particular man wearing a ruby ring in a city that housed over a million in population.

"Have you ever considered leaving this miserable city? You can't possibly find happiness among this squalor doing what you do. There are other places to go. Men who could offer you a better life. Didn't you once have wishes for a happily ever after like all young girls?"

"Not everyone has the same dreams. I never had the childhood you refer to nor would I waste my time on wishes."

"Fair enough. You may not need a husband, but perhaps a man's company now and then."

Felix leaned closer and she fought the urge to withdraw. What was he after? He couldn't possible harbor affection for her? They barely knew each other and she'd never given him cause to believe . . . not that it mattered with most men.

She forced herself to laugh and with a turn of the head maneuvered more space between them. "Why so much interest in my wants? My welfare? You didn't seek me out for that reason. Why don't we talk about whatever brings you here instead?"

Felix looked at her for several beats and the longer time stretched the more she realized he was stating his intention without words. When she thought she couldn't bear another moment of silence, he finally spoke, stepping backward as he did so.

"I merely wanted to remind you the streets are filled with peril at night and that you should take better care of your personal safety. The hour grew late because I had to wait until you were through with Aylesford."

Panic sliced through her with the speed of a precisely aimed blade thrown through the air to find its mark. How did he know? What had he seen?

"Good night, Scarlett."

He was gone before she managed a reply.

CHAPTER 13

Ambrose knocked twice and was admitted entry to the hell without question. Unaccustomed to Martin's type of ephemeral amusements, Ambrose considered all the reasons the system was inadequate and then abandoned that line of thinking. What did it matter? It wasn't as though he'd cross the threshold of this place ever again.

The interior was hazy with cigar smoke, the air too warm to feel comfortable, yet the crowd inside didn't seem to mind the dim lighting and unappealing atmosphere. Several gaming tables were scattered throughout the large room, men clustered around each. Errant yells of celebration and misery joined the slick toss of dice on the tables to provide ambient background amid the cacophony of conversation in the surround.

Hoping to appear out of place, Ambrose stalled in the middle of the hell floor as if in awe of the games at play. He was by no means a sharper, hardly skilled at cards beyond the perfunctory entertainment found in polite drawing rooms, but he could play the mark. His shrewd intelligence would serve him no purpose if exposed and he'd wager his entire dukedom few men within these walls possessed the same qualities. Ambrose searched for one person specifically. Let the man with the ruby ring note his polished appearance, from fine tailoring to Hessian boots. Any swindler would label him an easy target and invite him into a game. At least, that was Ambrose's plan. He had few other ideas at his disposal.

Unfortunately, the evening unraveled quickly. No one approached him. No one sought to empty his pockets or relieve him of his purse. After an hour of walking about the hell and appearing bewildered, Ambrose lost all patience. He dropped into a chair at the closest table and signaled for cards and brandy.

The hour was already late and while he'd expected to be fleeced, he quickly learned the patrons of the gaming hell were only interested in winning their wagers, their perspicuity focused on every roll of the dice or folded hand.

His mind began to wander. He'd kissed Scarlett. If it was meant to extinguish an urge, he'd failed by igniting a stronger desire to do so again. *What a kiss.*

He threw in his hand and surrendered more money, unsure of what cards he'd held. He would see her tomorrow morning at dawn. Hyde Park was not an ideal meeting place and yet she piqued his interest once again. With nothing to report to her he'd appear a bigger fool than she probably already thought him. She'd—

A male voice beside him jarred him from his thoughts and he forced his attention to the cards before him.

"It's your turn." The stranger shook his head with annoyance. "You must have more than cards on your mind to ignore that last hand."

Ambrose raised his eyes to the only other player at the table. Men must have come and gone while he'd mused about Scarlett. This man was impeccably dressed, much like he, and wore no gloves. He also wore no ring.

"I'm distracted, that's all." Ambrose discarded and accepted another card from the dealer. So far, nothing had gone as planned.

"I won't complain if you lose every hand as long as you have money in your pocket."

Ambrose nodded his head though he remained silent.

"Brokenhearted is better than an empty purse." The other player smirked as he continued his one-sided conversation. "If you're in the mood to forget your troubles there's a plum situation not far from here where the girls will do most anything you request."

"Is that so?" Ambrose continued to play, trying hard to focus on the cards and keep the conversation going. "Anything I request?"

The older man chuckled as if he shared an unspoken jest. "Well, if you've tastes that go beyond the natural, you won't find what you're looking for although I know someone who can solve that problem too."

A wave of disquiet washed through Ambrose as the man continued, his voice lower now.

"I've an associate who can supply exactly what you need if you have the ability to pay the price." He paused, but only to collect the coins at the center of the table. "You look well in the heel. The price is steep but well worth it. Better yet, once you find a situation to your liking, you'll never need to look for company again."

"And how can I meet your associate?" Ambrose's heart beat hard in his chest. Was it truly this easy? He doubted it, though this information was definitely worth his pursuit.

"My associate will contact you. Do you have a card with the address where a message can be sent?" The man began to collect his belongings. "From there a meeting will be arranged."

Ambrose's brain stuttered to a stop. He couldn't supply the information requested. No one could ever link the Aylesford name with any of this seedy business no matter he worked to better London. Perhaps his brother's apartment at the Albany could serve the purpose. Ambrose would intercept the message if possible. He'd alert Martin to expect something and not to open it. That plan might work. But would Martin listen? Ambrose had few options at the moment.

"Your indecision and silence tell me everything I need to know." The man produced a card and held it out in Ambrose's direction. "I'll tell my associate to expect you. The choice is yours."

Ambrose took the card. Could this be a pathway to find the man with the ruby ring? A criminal and miscreant who abused women? Or was he about to embark on another ineffective chase? At least he'd have something to share with Scarlett come morning.

Half seven. Rotten Row.

It was too early for the fashionable set, but not for the young whips who wished to race their horses against the wind free of intrusion by every landau and barouche out to flaunt their wealth on the promenade. Soon the park would fill with a crush of dandies while children begged for bread only a few miles away.

Scarlett dressed in a traditional gown of pale blue silk, with proper underskirts, a pelisse, bonnet and reticule to match. The ensemble was cumbersome and restrictive, hardly her clothing of choice. Heaven help her if she needed to crosskick someone in the chest or scamper up a drain onto a nearby roof. As always, she carried her knives. The security they lent her could never be replaced.

This morning she sought to blend in more than when she ventured into any other area of London. Society held a magnifying glass to most every female, at the ready to discuss their flaws. Meanwhile, any lord or lordling might wade in an ornamental fountain, cast up his stomach from excessive imbibement or parade across the tiles at the opera house with his paramour, only to be thought charming, roguish or elusive. The ironic double standard chafed and fueled Scarlett's irritation with better society as a whole. Still, despite the early hour, she needed to appear the proper lady's companion out for a morning constitutional.

Aylesford arrived promptly. She hadn't expected him on horseback and the sight of his broad physique atop a majestic black stallion caused her stomach to react in an odd, unwelcome manner. She spotted him several long minutes before he realized it was she.

Excellent. If she appeared unfamiliar to him when he'd kissed her so thoroughly, pressed against his hard chest so completely, she'd undoubtedly fool anyone else who might glance in her direction.

He stopped several yards away and watched her where she

waited under a sweet chestnut tree. After what she considered too long a time, he dismounted and gathered the reins, the large Arabian at heel behind his master as they approached.

No man should look as ruggedly handsome, as regal, as the Duke of Aylesford. What must it feel like to have all of London at your feet? His clothing was impeccably tailored to fit his broad shoulders and tapered waist. Buckskin breeches hugged his firm thighs before they narrowed into polished Hessians so shiny they reflected the newborn light of day.

When at last he reached her and tied off the reins, she'd become uncomfortable with his silence and the path of her wayward thoughts.

"Good morning, Your Grace."

"I thought we'd agreed you were to call me by my Christian name."

"Surely you didn't intend for me to use the familiarity when we might be overheard."

"There's no one about at this ungodly hour." He moved his eyes to the sky and back again, the action offering her a glimpse of his sharp profile.

"There's always someone to overhear." She canted her head to the right and left to emphasize her words. One could never be too careful. "What did you learn last night at the hell, Ambrose?"

His eyes sparked with pleasure and then heated with intensity immediately after. She'd shocked him with her boldness.

"I did not find the man with the ruby ring."

"It would have been too easy, walking into a gambling den and discovering the one person we sought."

"But I did acquire a name that garners my interest."

"In what way?" She couldn't help the spike of eager attention. Every clue gathered was another step toward locating Linie.

"A gentleman who can supply me with female company to suit my needs."

She smirked. "That isn't an uncommon offer, unfortunately." She fell silent a moment. "And what exactly are your needs?"

Their conversation was interrupted by the thunder of horse hooves, a trio of riders racing by close enough to give them pause.

"That question cannot be answered while we stand in Hyde Park." His gaze swept over her and her blood heated. He was dangerous in so many ways and she thrived on danger, enjoyed it actually, but some small voice inside her warned Aylesford was a threat from which she'd never recover. She'd best beware.

"I see."

"I almost did not recognize you." His words held a faint hint of revelation. "You appear the fashionable lady this morning. You have many facets, a diamond of the first water disguised by your own nature."

"Thank you, Your Grace." She needed to keep that barrier, the formality that reminded he was one of the most revered men in England and that she was nothing more than an ill-gotten bastard daughter.

"I prefer your trousers."

He smiled and she returned his grin before she thought better of it.

"So what will we do now?" Discussing their plans would help distract her from noticing the way sunlight danced on the waves of his hair, brown and black, streaked with light and dark.

"*We* won't."

His brow furrowed and she suspected he knew she wouldn't be happy with his reluctance to involve her.

"I have connections that will prove useful."

He wouldn't take kindly to being reminded of the incident in Wapping, but she was prepared to do so if necessary to convince him. She glanced to the bridle path where another trio of riders were set to race. Soon the park would fill with governesses and their charges, young couples out for a picnic or stroll in the sun. This place seemed a world away from the areas of London she called home, where she felt comfortable.

"That may be true, but until I know for sure what this man represents . . ." His words trailed off as the approaching pair of riders snared his attention.

This time the gentlemen slowed as they passed Aylesford and his magnificent horse beside the path. Scarlett had the good sense to step into the shadows, partially obstructed by the tree's trunk.

"Aylesford." The tallest man with the shortest hair spoke to the duke. "Good morning. This is a pleasant surprise."

"Gaines." Aylesford nodded. "Good day."

His forthright dismissal discouraged any conversation and the riders continued on their way. When they'd gone a reasonable distance, Scarlett stepped back into the light.

"I was curious as to your request to meet here. Soon this park will be crowded with the social set."

"And yet you didn't mind meeting me here." She watched his eyes, wondering at his true feelings.

"I am Aylesford. I'm a duke." He eyed her intently. "I do as I please."

She wasn't convinced in the least. Every noble was more concerned with society's opinion than with their own desires.

"I've obtained a name." Julia had sent her a message. With her friend's access to refined teas and gatherings, she often gained choice bits of gossip ordinarily off limits to Scarlett. Apparently, the man known as Clive to the ladies at the brothel was somehow connected to Lord Welles.

"And who is this mystery person?" Aylesford turned toward his horse and ran his hand down the stallion's neck.

"Viscount Welles." Scarlett waited, curious to see what Aylesford would do. She had no intention of being left out of the search.

"I do not know him. There is an event at the Earl of Pembroke's estate this evening. It may be the perfect opportunity to gain knowledge of this man and his connection to The Scarlet Rose."

"What time will you send the carriage for me?" Her stomach turned over, prepared for his immediate refusal. She was no fool to the way the world conducted relationships.

A series of emotions flashed in his eyes. Scarlett watched and waited.

"It would be better if I investigated this mention of Viscount Welles and a possible connection to our concerns."

He sounded uncomfortable.

"I won't be excluded."

"That is not my intention, Scarlett." He drew a deep breath and exhaled slowly. "It will be easier for me to ask questions. Besides, I can't accompany you to the event."

"Can't? Or won't?" All enjoyment of their meeting slipped away. "You only just mentioned you can do as you please."

"Within reason."

"How foolish you are to believe you are free of restraints when every act you take is another constriction of your title." She couldn't keep the sharpness from her words.

"I know no other course. I've been groomed my entire life by my father, rest his soul, to carry on the Aylesford legacy."

"I had no father." She said the words softly, unsure of what he'd say in return.

"Everyone has a father."

"I suppose there's a small degree of truth in that if one considers the science, although there the definition becomes murky." She stopped walking and looked at him squarely. "You had a father. Someone to teach you to read a map, take you fishing or carry you on his shoulders when you were a lad, but I knew no kindness in that manner. I never had a father and my mother . . ."

"Forgive me, Scarlett," he interrupted before she could say more. "It was shortsighted of me. I spoke foolishly and out of turn."

"It's of no consequence." She reclaimed her determination. "This evening is an ideal opportunity to ask questions."

"You would be in danger. I will not be the cause of placing you in harm's path." He sounded resolute.

"Are you protecting me from the waltz? From a randy guest or gossip-minded dowager?" She peppered him, unwilling to compromise. "I assure you I've survived much worse."

"I do not doubt it." His words were spoken with a sincere honesty that reached for her heart.

"I believed that we were to share information and work toward a common resolution. To discover if something nefarious is happening to the women at the brothel."

He nodded in agreement.

"You'll find I'm resourceful. You'll need my insight into matters like this."

"I'm able to ask questions, Scarlett. I'm capable beyond your belief." He had the audacity to smile in her direction.

"So what time can I expect your carriage?" she pressed, unwilling to give up easily.

"Scarlett." He said her name as if it contained his explanation. His tone brooked no argument.

"Goodbye, Ambrose." She had every intention of attending the earl's event and Julia would enable it to happen, but she needed to know Aylesford's limits and he'd just revealed his opinion of her whether he intended to or not. She might be desirable for a kiss in a shadowy alleyway, but he'd never acknowledge her in front of his peers. He'd hardly treated her as an equal.

She walked away and didn't look back.

CHAPTER 14

Ambrose stepped out of his carriage and toward the Earl of Pembroke's large estate. The gathering was held in celebration of the birth of their first son and rightful heir. All of better society composed the guest list. Ambrose had no doubt a crush would be in attendance too, unwilling to miss the event of the season and one so joyous at that.

Since he'd left Scarlett on Rotten Row earlier, he'd carried an overwhelming sense of dread and he strove for distraction throughout the day. He'd met with his secretary, discussed important estate issues needing attention and attempted to write a rebuttal speech for the next session of Parliament. When that failed, he instructed his man of business to gather available information concerning the almshouse charities and the state of their funding. He also instructed his solicitor to collect research on current laws and initiatives connected to reform bills presented to the House of Lords. This task offered a modicum of relief, but in truth nothing worked to clear his mind and heart.

He didn't understand his feelings. He was a duke. One of few noblemen privy to the prince's ear. Respected and revered throughout England and beyond. A man of honor, reputation and heritage.

But he was also a man. Beneath the weight of his family's history, he was still a hot-blooded male who yearned for acceptance and affection.

She'd saved his life. That could be the only reason.

When they'd kissed, she'd touched his soul.

She was an otherworldly combination of strength and softness, harsh reality and delicate fantasy.

Romantic rubbish. Since when was he prone to ridiculous thoughts like these? Hadn't he criticized Martin for the same?

Still, it didn't matter.

Martin had embroiled him in a mess that needed resolution and then he could let all of this go.

He would let Scarlett go.

Belatedly he realized he could have sent a carriage. Not one with his ducal seal, but some conveyance. He could have offered her the opportunity to attend. But how would that proceed? Would she be admitted? Embarrassed? He wished to protect her from such. The world where he lived was also harsh and often cruel in a different context. No one suffered from hunger or lack of a dry bed, but instead they were given the cut direct, gossiped about and slandered, mocked and labeled as undesirable.

Could their lives be so similar?

In some ways perhaps, but not all.

The look in her eyes before she'd stepped away sliced through his heart.

Now drawing a deep breath he stepped into the ballroom, his rambling considerations having accompanied him to the top of the stairs where he was announced, the ensemble below hushed into quiet tones at his entrance, the orchestra's melody lingering in the background.

This was the world he lived in. One of lineage and reputation. Where he belonged. Scarlett may have found her way into his thoughts, but she'd never be able to fit into his world.

Scarlett's silk slippers tapped a determined cadence on the Earl of Pembroke's polished tiles as she made her way to the ballroom beside Lady Julia. Having a widowed friend who'd married into the aristocracy had its benefits. Gaining entrance to an esteemed societal event was not a feat Scarlett would have accomplished herself. She'd have been left to skulk around the garden and trespass at best while wearing a makeshift disguise. Now she could explore without question as Julia's distant relative in the city for a visit. Of course, she couldn't reveal her real name, but that was a matter easily amended.

After meeting with Aylesford, Scarlett had returned to Linie's apartment to find it still remained unoccupied. This fact reinforced her determination to discover what might have happened to the seamstress. Frustrated by the odd collection of clues and emboldened by Aylesford's rejection, she'd knocked on Sally's door across the hall. Their brief conversation proved beneficial and Scarlett learned other girls at the brothel had recently been propositioned by Clive and that the man with the ruby ring claimed to be connected to some of the highest-ranking gentlemen in London, flaunting his power and status in an effort to convince the girls to leave The Scarlet Rose.

The odd collection of facts had yet to coagulate into a logical explanation, but she didn't despair. Every clue was another piece of the puzzle. This evening she would add more to her collection.

She'd dressed in a daring gown of plum silk and delicate ruffles. Her hair was twined in an elaborate braid tacked at her nape with pearly hairpins to showcase her teardrop earbobs, her arms encased in silky white gloves. While she usually abhorred the trappings of feminine fashion, tonight she had something to prove and her clothing enabled her to accomplish that. She'd locate the man with the ruby ring and discover his connection to the brothel. She believed something nefarious was happening to the girls and it was directly connected to the elite, many of whom might be standing in the very same ballroom. Aylesford relegated his search to a lower level. He'd have difficulty coming to terms with one of his peers acting reprehensibly. Once she located the wearer of the ruby ring, she would finally have proof and with that information could discover what happened to Linie. She didn't need Aylesford's assistance. He clearly didn't want hers.

This wasn't her first societal event, nor her first formal ball. But usually she was consigned to the shadows and tonight without hindrance, Scarlett stepped into the ballroom under the glow of dozens of chandeliers. The room was a crush, guests and servants maneuvered elbow to elbow around the perimeter of the dance floor. As expected the gentlemen wore formal gloves, their fingers obscured from view, but Scarlett wasn't deterred. She sought conversation and eyed the dowagers seated near the far wall. These ladies kept a vigilant watch on every discussion and interaction in the room. They were often ignored by the popular set and in that proved a valuable source of information. With a slight nod to Julia, Scarlett began to move in their direction.

Aylesford smiled cordially and turned away from the dance floor. He had no desire to dance with any of the debutantes paraded about for his benefit. He had no desire to dance at all. How was he supposed to locate someone with a ruby ring when everyone's hands were covered? Likewise, he couldn't begin a stir by questioning everyone in an attempt to locate Viscount Welles. He was out of his element in that regard. Perhaps he should have listened to Scarlett after all. She'd been correct in her suggestion he would need her to accomplish the goal.

Martin approached, his usual sly grin in place, a brandy in hand. In a rare moment, his brother's tomfoolery might be a welcome diversion. He turned to face the dance floor again.

"You'll scare the debs and dowagers with that scowl, Ambrose."

"I'm not scowling." He made an effort to transform his expression. "Do you know if Viscount Welles is in attendance this evening?"

"Can't say I do, although this ballroom is a crush. Every nob and bob is here, no doubt."

"Yes, and every unmarried female seems to be in attendance as well."

"Aah, and you're the prized duke who must fend them off or submit to a dance." Martin chuckled.

"You oversimplify the matter." A beat of impatience caused his words to come out stronger than he intended. "Everyone looks to me and the attention is not pleasant. They acknowledge what I say, what I do, as fundamentally observant of what I eat and drink. Conversations cease when I approach and swell when I depart, the content often produced with the intent to say what I wish to hear. The lack of sincerity is appalling." Perhaps that explained his attraction to Scarlett's refreshing candor. She had no expectations of him.

Martin had the good sense to remain quiet. The orchestra began a new number and a set of eager couples ventured to the floor. They watched the whirlwind of colors and motion before his brother broke the silence.

"Deuced situation to be in, even if it's only dancing. Although I wouldn't mind a whit if I partnered with a lovely lady tonight." Martin made a show of surveying the room. "Who is that fresh face near the dowagers? I wonder if she's new to London. I haven't seen her before and unlike you, I do make it my business to keep abreast of societal news."

"Do you now?" Against his better judgment, Ambrose followed Martin's line of vision. While his curiosity was mildly intrigued, he didn't wish to match eyes with anyone and give the impression of interest. He'd discovered the most subtle gesture would often invite a proud father or overzealous mother to misinterpret his attention and foist their daughter in his direction, and the very last thing he wanted to do was force polite conversation or dance with a shy newcomer this evening.

"She's stunning, isn't she?" Martin continued. "The lady there, in the silky gown, dark as nightshade and I bet just as lethal. She has a look to her that ramps up my interest."

Ambrose settled his eyes on the lady at last and his heart jolted with recognition. The female wasn't just another gentlewoman of society. It was Scarlett, polished and refined, as enticing as a rich glass of merlot. She was standing off to the side, in conversation with one of the oldest members of the *ton*, but despite her positioning near the corner, she was drawing attention from every male in the vicinity. Ambrose glanced from wall to wall, quick to notice the ladies leaned together in whisper, the men equally interested though they revealed that quality through sidelong glances and covert surveillance, their attention suddenly divided between their polite escort and the riveting new face across the floor.

"I do not know her"—Martin set down his glass on a nearby table—"but I may have dreamed her to life last night. This event just became enormously more interesting."

"Well, keep your eyes in your head and your head out of the clouds." His words came out in an angry grumble. "We're supposed to be looking for the perpetrator from the brothel. The one who committed the misdeeds you believe you heard. The complicated situation you created and embroiled me into when you summoned me to that same brothel. Remember? Your goal is to look at the men, not the women."

"Yes, but in the meantime . . ."

"No." Ambrose glared at his brother. "All of this trouble came about because of your randy interests."

"But she's a lady of the *ton*." Martin's tone turned just as harsh. "What rubbish. You're determined to waylay every bit of my fun."

Ambrose swallowed back his immediate retort. Scarlett wasn't a lady of the *ton*, no matter she might fool the collective crush around her. And with certainty, she'd never be Martin's bit of fun.

Every precious memory he'd tucked away came back in a rush of possessive temper. The silky brush of her hair against his cheek, the delicious lush taste of her mouth, the soft, enticing whimper she made in the back of her throat when their tongues tangled amidst their kiss.

And now she stood among his peers with no one the wiser. Except she was drawing attention by merely existing. The same way his body experienced the pull of longing, a firm tug of attraction, as if two forces yearning to be combined.

There was no denying she looked remarkable. He'd called her a diamond of the first water earlier this morning when she'd donned a day gown to meet in Hyde Park, but now she fairly glowed. And her hair, all that gorgeous hair she'd kept pinned back and hidden from him, was now arranged with intricate curls and petite braids in a style that made his fingers itch to unwind and explore every fetching wave and tantalizing length.

How did she manage to be here? He'd foolishly sought to protect her from rejection when she stood only ten strides away in conversation with some of the *ton*'s most perspicacious old biddies. All the while she probably had a knife strapped to her stocking-clad thigh and a dagger in her reticule. A stronger jolt of desire, intense and insistent, shot through him. She did strange things to his usual decorum and restrained demeanor. He'd attribute it to her being forbidden and a danger to his title, nothing more than sensual curiosity, and yet even that recognition didn't stop erotic suggestions from heating his blood as intensely as a fever dream.

He watched, as transfixed as his brother, until an unexpected lick of jealousy snapped him to cognitive attention. A young gentleman, one Aylesford didn't recognize, approached Scarlett and asked her to dance. He couldn't tell if she accepted or declined as, much to his annoyance, other guests milled about and interrupted his surveillance.

"I'm for it, Ambrose, and there's nothing to be done about it." Martin's voice reached his ears though he didn't turn to acknowledge his brother.

"Leave Scarlett alone." Unable to harness his displeasure, the words came out in a menacing growl and he gripped his brother's shoulder as if to nail him to the floor.

"Scarlett? So you know her." Martin gave a humorless laugh, his gaze skittering across the room and back again. "Of course you do."

Ambrose dropped his hold and turned. "Yes, and we'll leave it at that. Find someone else to dally with and stay out of her path."

"Because you want her for yourself?" Martin's voice acquired a cynical tone.

Their conversation was brought to an abrupt halt as Viscount Townshend approached. Will was a friend and, as Ambrose had learned the other evening at White's, the viscount was only just easing back into society. Ambrose would engage him in conversation and thereby clear his mind and dismiss his brother's annoying tomfoolery.

"Your Grace. Cross." Townshend filled the space between Ambrose and his brother, brandy in hand. "This time last season I was sitting alone in my drawing room staring at the wall coverings and reflecting on a series of poor choices. It feels good to be out and about again. I should have taken your advice, Aylesford. It would appear I need to make up for lost time."

Martin grunted a noncommittal sound, so unlike himself, but then again not, as he was likely still angered over their previous discussion. At least Townshend's approach offered the opportunity to move forward.

"Good to see you, Townshend." Ambrose nodded. "And even better to hear you've moved on."

"Indeed." Townshend smiled. "It's as if I can view things through a clearer lens having experienced what I did."

"I would imagine so," Martin concurred. "Nothing heals the heart like a new romance."

Ambrose followed his brother's attention and scowled. Apparently, Townshend noticed the whole of their interaction.

"Speaking of it, who is the lady in violet silk?"

Townshend's usual bland expression gained a lecherous quality Ambrose had never noticed before. Or perhaps it was his imagination that identified a leering gleam in the gentleman's eye. Emotion seemed to be winning in a war against logic. He clenched his fists at his side and purposely ignored the question though an intrusive hum rang in his ears the longer he waited.

"Never mind about her," Martin supplied. "Lovely as she is, she is spoken for."

"Aah, I am too late. Who's the lucky fellow?" Townshend glanced at Martin and then turned to Ambrose when neither of them supplied a response.

"I can't rightly say," Martin answered and Ambrose swore he heard laughter in his brother's reply.

Townshend returned his attention to Scarlett, who as if on cue smiled brightly at something her companion said. The gentleman had leaned too close to her ear. Did the fellow not abide by the rules of etiquette? Ambrose took a step, catching himself at the last minute before he stormed across the ballroom and yanked the man away.

"Well, the two of you are as quiet as tombstones tonight." Townshend's attempt to inject a bit of humor fell flat. "You can't blame me for trying to gain the lady's attention. It's only human nature for a hotblooded bachelor to seek the prettiest female in the room."

Ambrose looked Townshend in the eye. He was a younger man, fit and handsome enough for the popular set to twitter about as he walked past. His recent broken engagement marked him as eligible, open to commitment and willing to domesticate while also portraying him as an emotional victim of circumstance and fate. All the romantic tripe females cooed about and found alluring. He couldn't have Townshend sharing his unexpecting charms with Scarlett. Not that she would succumb to such nonsense. Not that she was even interested.

Still, he couldn't have it.

"You won't approach her, Townshend." Ambrose said the words quietly. From the periphery he noticed Martin's brows raise slightly.

"If that's a dare or challenge, Your Grace, you're bound to lose this time. No need to cajole me into action." Townshend offered a chuckle. "I'm not out of my game altogether and as your brother said, the best way to nurse an injured heart is with a fresh dalliance between the sheets."

"I think you misunderstand." Ambrose jerked his head around, at a loss to turn his attention away from Scarlett but willing to make the sacrifice momentarily. He spoke again, his voice low and lethal. "You won't approach her."

An uncomfortable silence punctuated his statement in which Townshend nodded slowly and took his leave thereafter.

"What was *that* all about?" Martin leaned closer. "I thought Will was your friend. You had no cause to chastise him. I scarce hardly recognize you tonight. That was not very kind of you, brother."

How dare Martin admonish his behavior and take him to task when Martin was at the top of the list in every mishap and complicated problem. Ambrose ignored him and searched the crowd to locate Scarlett again but she was gone. The moment of provocation with Townshend had caused him to lose sight of her. "Damn it, Martin."

He turned to his left prepared to unleash his frustration on the man, but he too had vanished.

CHAPTER 15

"Thank you for accepting, Lady Hammon."

Scarlett placed her hand on Lord Burton's elbow as he escorted her to the floor. She regretted the use of a fictitious name but the matter couldn't be avoided. Besides, after this evening she wouldn't again enter these circles so the lie would die a quiet death with no one the wiser.

She'd learned to dance at Wycombe and Company. The Maidens of Mayhem were adept in all sorts of avocations needed to complete their pursuits and whenever one of them learned a skill they were quick to share their knowledge. Scarlett never felt completely confident in her dancing ability. She rarely had the opportunity to put it to use although a sweeping spin or lively high-step did assist in her defensive maneuvers.

"My pleasure, my lord."

They fell into the flow on the dance floor amid a crowd of prancing couples. The style of dance and the throng of guests kept their movements limited and that enabled them to converse more easily.

"You are a very fine dancer, my lord."

"Thank you." The young gentleman beamed with a near blinding smile. "I've practiced at every event this season."

His guileless personality lent itself perfectly to Scarlett's intention. "So you've been attending a busy schedule of affairs. How lovely. I must say I was surprised Lord Welles wasn't in attendance this evening."

Scarlett waited, wondering if Lord Burton could supply her with the information she needed.

"I do not know him, my lady, or I would happily assist you."

Their dance continued in a gregarious, if uneventful, fashion and when it came to an end, Lord Burton chivalrously bid her good night and deposited her at the edge of the dance floor. The experience proved the precursor to all others and her evening progressed in the same fashion. She'd tried to elicit information from the dowagers when the musicians took their break and delicately questioned each gentleman when she was asked to dance, but the elusive viscount was not to be found.

Additionally, she hadn't noticed Aylesford in the ballroom. Part of her wished to advance to the cardroom or gardens in hope of seeing him in formal attire while another part of her, a stronger more independent part, insisted she attend to the task at hand and forget about the handsome duke, his velvety hot kiss and the intensity of her deep-set desire to experience it yet again.

Surely, he had forgotten about her after he'd dismissed her with succinct candor at Rotten Row. Reminding herself of the moment helped smother the desire to see him. At least she tried.

Every so often Scarlett would stroll the perimeter with Julia and they'd share innocuous conversation sprinkled with tidbits of information, but the sum of the evening as of yet amounted to little. Keeping up the pretense of expectation, she nodded toward her friend now and they joined at the corner to take another turn.

"Have you located the man you're looking for?" Julia acknowledged a passing guest, at ease in the very same atmosphere Scarlett abhorred.

"Not of yet, and with every gentleman's hands gloved, I fear this is an exercise in futility."

"Still, it gives you the chance to discover his identity. Have the dowagers and chaperones had any useful information to share?"

"I'm afraid not." Scarlett glanced from Julia to the doorway, her attention snared as a guest entered but it wasn't Aylesford.

"Your duke hasn't arrived."

"He's not *my duke*." Scarlett fairly hissed her reply.

"I don't wish for you to be hurt. You are my dearest friend and in that, I feel your pain as my own. Falling in love—"

"Love?" Scarlett scoffed. "I don't love him."

"Of course you do. Or at the least, your heart is considering it." Julia had the audacity to smile but her grin quickly faded as she continued to speak, her tone serious and sincere. "Your interest sparks in your eyes when you say his name. It's there in the tilt of your chin and defiant slant of your shoulders as you deny it. It's evident in each syllable of every word you use to protest."

"I can't love him," Scarlett lamented, shaking her head as if she could rid herself of the intrusive emotion. Love was weakness. It carried the power to crush her soul and suffocate her.

"That's another matter altogether." Julia patted her arm gently and they stopped walking near a tapestry on the wall. "Do you fear he will clip your wings and cage you? A good man will lift you up so you can fly higher. Remember that before you chastise yourself for allowing yourself to be open to love."

"I don't fear him. Emotions like love are complicated and debilitating. It has nothing to do with Aylesford." She knew in her soul what she said was a lie. She fisted her fingers. An equaled tightness knotted her chest.

Julia shook her head slowly as she spoke. "I worry over you."

"That's needless and uncalled for and I told you as much the other day at the offices." Scarlett's voice rang with resolve. She'd never jeopardize the Maidens of Mayhem and the valuable work they did throughout London. "I can protect my identity."

"Yes. I know. That's not what concerns me." Julia reached for her and touched a gloved hand to Scarlett's arm. "But who will protect your heart?"

*   *   *

Aylesford stood alone among the rosebushes in the Earl of Pembroke's garden and embraced the chilling night air. He'd forced himself from the ballroom after watching Scarlett's third dance. He could forbid Martin from asking her to dance, but there was little he could do about the other dandies who sought her attention. He couldn't appear the besotted, if not deranged, fool. Were he to give in to desire and ask her to dance, his interest would place Scarlett under a lens of perspicacious scrutiny and everyone who was anyone would employ rabid tenacity to vet out the mysterious *and stunningly beautiful* newcomer's identity.

How was it she'd become such a dangerous distraction? They'd only kissed once and yet he couldn't erase the memory of that kiss or forget her delicate scent of rosemary and mint, the lovely way light shimmered in her silver-gray eyes.

She'd asked him to help her attend Pembroke's event and when he'd declined, she'd appeared here anyway. She was unstoppable. A woman with strength and determination. Tonight, a woman of delicate femininity.

Combined the two were an indomitable force. And yet she didn't fight for herself, she fought for others. For the good of London. He needed to do better. With the power at his disposal he could accomplish matters with little resistance. What good were his wealth and influence if he couldn't utilize the two to better the lives of all citizens? The minx, through her determination and graceful strength, had taught him a lesson or two. It was no longer a matter of sustaining his title but of creating a legacy that perpetuated a habit of charitable deeds and meaningful improvements. He'd pursued these ideas with his man of business and now looked forward to turning discussion into action.

But now, Scarlett awaited. He strode toward the terrace doors. Logic told him it was foolhardy to allow this opportunity to pass. One dance was not a commitment. One dance was nothing more than an isolated memory. What harm could it cause? Their association was fleeting at best, as transient as sand through an hourglass.

Every moment another grain fell away into oblivion. He firmed his resolve and focused.

He would ask her to dance and discover if she'd gained any information. Yes, that was productive reasoning and not the weakness of some lust-driven urge. It made more sense than the thrumming desire to hold her in his arms, to hear her laughter and see her smile. Thoughts like that were a trick of shadows and light, for their relationship was nothing more than an unexpected anomaly.

He located her with little effort, his body drawn to hers, his eyes able to land on the curve of her neck and slope of her chin with keen accuracy. She turned in his direction as if she sensed his attention and the slight rise of her slender brows proved it true.

Another few strides and he stood before her, his gloved hand extended, hers warm through the silk as she accepted his escort. They walked to the dance floor without a word, but his body was strung tight, every muscle tensed. Who was this demure creature within his arms? The same woman who threw her blade into the shoulder of a thug intent on harming him? Who took up a cause that would improve London and better womankind though it brought danger to her doorstep? She'd overcome such a broken past and yet envisioned a paradisiacal future.

Scarlett was many extraordinary women embodied in one.

"Your Grace."

"My lady." *If only that were true.*

Awareness flared between them as they began to move, their bodies in perfect synchronization, the music flowing through them as if they were part of the melody.

"You've surprised me yet again, Scarlett." He looked down into her face, rosy from the heat of the ballroom, her lashes a dark fan on her cheekbones, her lips tempting and sweet, and he wanted to take her away from Pembroke's ballroom and carry her into his bedroom. He closed his eyes in a hard blink to ward off his eager imagination.

"In what way?" She smiled, the slightest tilt of her lips.

"In every way." He matched her grin, the abashed admittance words of truth.

"I suppose the same could be said of you." Her smile dropped away. "I did not expect your dismissal earlier."

He clenched his teeth against a ready apology. "I did not dismiss you. I meant to protect you. There's a difference."

"I'm here at this event regardless. You accomplished nothing more than . . ." She didn't complete what she meant to say and looked away.

He knew how that sentence finished. He'd hurt her feelings when he'd meant to protect her from the same type of rejection.

"Come with me." He stopped dancing, clasped her elbow and steered her toward the nearest terrace doors giving her little choice without causing a scene.

Still, she didn't resist though her spine went straight and her chin tilted at a defiant angle. Something in his chest sparked to life. Anticipation? The thought of their kiss haunted him still but that wasn't why he'd sought to remove her from the dance floor.

He shouldered passed a grouping of four men enjoying brandy and ushered Scarlett outside. He didn't stop walking until they were deep into the rose garden, away from the prying eyes of meddlesome guests. Belatedly he wondered at how many people had watched him leave, noted his determined strides to take Scarlett beyond the crush. The prying public was always at the ready to speculate and draw unfounded conclusions. The life of a duke was forever on display. At least they wouldn't sully her name. He doubted she'd given anyone her real one. She was far too clever.

"What are you doing? It's cold out here." She smoothed her gloved palms up and down her arms, her gown little protection from the temperature.

"You're right." He inhaled deeply. "I wasn't thinking." He reached for her. "Come this way."

Again they traversed the limestone path, this time taking a fork that led around the corner of the estate. He didn't stop until they reached the drive.

"Again, what are you doing?" Her eyes went wide as he signaled a footman and requested his carriage.

"It will be warmer inside." He motioned for her to follow his lead. "And private."

"I can't leave."

"I'll have you returned shortly." What was he doing? It was impulsive and reckless, but he ignored better sense and opened the carriage door, making quick work of handing her up the steps. Let someone question his actions. As a duke he could do whatever he bloody liked. Resolute in his actions, he spoke briefly to his driver and then followed her inside.

Once on the bench he drew another cleansing breath. Little made sense in the past few weeks anyway. He hardly knew himself. What he did know though was seeing Scarlett dance with another spiked a feeling of possessive anger within him that was wholly unfamiliar. And too, jealousy and anger tangled with reason. He wanted her with a wild need he'd never known and that singular realization warned him to back away, yet that option seemed too drastic and so he ignored that as well. The scent of rosemary and mint filled his lungs when he tried for another calming breath. He wanted her, but he couldn't have her, and worse he didn't want anyone else to have her either.

Apparently, he'd lost his mind and abandoned all ability to make decisions with sense and logic. Martin had finally broken him. No, he wouldn't place blame there. Perhaps his heart was the true culprit. Still, he was drawn to her whether he liked it or not. Best he get on with purging his irrational urges.

Scarlett watched as Ambrose settled on the seat across from her, his broad shoulders and height accentuated by the carriage interior. He took up space. Here in the carriage, often in her thoughts, but with careful intervention, never in her heart. She wouldn't allow it. She would fight against it. She would try.

Why were they in his carriage? Did he have information to

share? She needed to return to the ballroom and find the man with the ruby ring. As of yet her questions had revealed little.

"I didn't dismiss you or your concerns earlier." His voice sounded gravelly and she didn't know if he regretted what he'd done or the words he spoke now. His expression was partially lost to the shadowy corner.

"It doesn't matter." She reached across the interior and placed her hand on his arm. "You didn't need to remove me from the ballroom to tell me that."

"I know." He clasped her hand in his and tugged gently, then more assertively. She leaned forward. "But I couldn't do this in there."

His mouth came down on hers with unerring accuracy, firm and determined, strong and possessive in its intent. She yielded. She couldn't not accept his kiss. Despite a world of reasons she should push him away, she placed her hands on his shoulders and allowed him to draw her onto his lap.

She played with fire now. She would have to accept the consequences later.

As decadent as warm honey, the slick heat of his tongue caused all thinking to cease. Emotion was dangerous indeed. It made one weak, careless and vulnerable. Still, she returned his kiss, drowning in the sensation, seeking more. She'd only tasted honey once, when she'd stolen a sweet off a merchant's cart. She was young and just developing her skills of distraction and sleight of hand, but she'd never forgotten the euphoric taste of her daring that day.

Aylesford's kiss obliterated that memory and surpassed the joy. She held tight to his shoulders, the hard muscle shifting beneath his coat as he maneuvered them into a better position.

She wanted this. There was no denying it. It seemed like forever she'd carried her indifference as a shield, unwilling to allow a man into her heart because she'd witnessed the price her mother had paid. But deep down, in a corner of her soul she refused to examine, she knew someday she would like to know a man's affection, to believe she was worthy of love, and to lose nothing by doing so. Julia had spoken honestly, able to see in Scarlett the emotions she wasn't ready to admit. Kissing a duke would only lead to heartache. Their situation was impossible, their time so limited. Still, a smarter woman would make peace with the fact this wasn't meant to be.

At that moment, she wasn't a smarter woman.

He growled against her mouth, some low, throaty, appreciative sound that reverberated through her.

And still they kissed.

His hands spanned her back and held her to him. She cursed the weighty clothing required to play the part of a lady. She'd always found pleasure in her own skin, comfortable with her body and inhibited by the required layers upon layers piled upon a woman as if to diminish or disguise, to stifle their importance and quiet their existence. She wanted to feel and experience, to taste and discover every nuance of Aylesford's body.

Intense desire speared through her. She needed him to touch her everywhere. To feel his skin, inhale his citrusy scent, remember the weight of his body upon hers. She yearned for so much more than this. She'd give him her body, free to explore and caress, to evoke sensation and pleasure, but she wouldn't allow him to touch her heart. Not with any permanence, mayhap only this one time.

Shocked at the strength of this revelation, she gasped and pulled away.

What was she doing?

She made to scramble off his lap, across to the other side of the carriage, and the separation must have helped him find clarity as well because he assisted her immediately. They sat in silence for several beats and she pressed her palms together in her lap, her insistent desire a tangible thing she sought to crush away.

"Are you all right?" His voice indicated he was not himself either.

She nodded but it was a lie. She wondered if she would ever be *all right* again. Everything about him devastated her. His handsomeness. His title. His concern for her welfare. She focused on his hands where they rested on his thighs. He was strong and yet he held her with elegant grace, the same way he held his heritage and responsibility. The manner in which he conducted every part of his life. She was not special. She was not different. It was just his way, lest she believe otherwise.

"I will have a footman return you." He knocked twice on the carriage roof. "I'm leaving so there will be no confusion or scandal."

She nodded again, still a little bewildered by their intimacy. She had not a hair out of place. Her gown was only a tad wrinkled. She could enter the ballroom through the terrace doors and step right back into her role.

"Good night, Ambrose." She swallowed, telling herself it would be the last time she uttered the words, but he didn't understand. He smiled at her use of his given name and then the door opened and she left.

CHAPTER 16

Scarlett hurried along the path and up the three marble steps to the outside terrace. Pembroke's estate was so large she easily accomplished the task of skirting the shadows and returning undetected. Her body still reeled from the emotion in Aylesford's kiss. Why would she open her heart and invite hurt inside? She couldn't consider that problem at the moment, her reason to attend this affair far and removed from a romantic interlude. Realigning her purpose, she rounded the corner to approach the doors and nearly collided with a gentleman out alone on the terrace.

"Pardon me, my lord." Smoothing her syllables, Scarlett offered the stranger a gentle smile and attempted to pass him so she could reenter the ballroom.

"Lady Hammon?"

Scarlett paused. She'd only given her fictitious name to a select few. The gentleman must have sought her out specifically.

"Yes?" A thread of discord rippled through her as she matched the man's eyes. His were keenly focused on her though they projected malevolence, not pleasure.

Eyes don't lie.

"I'm Viscount Welles. I was told you were looking for me. Shall we walk for a turn?"

He offered his elbow and she was inclined to accept his escort though she wondered at his intent. "The evening air is cooler than I originally thought and I haven't brought my wrap with me. Why don't we return inside and find a private corner?"

"This will only take a moment." He laid his gloved hand over hers, locking her to his side as he continued to lead them across the terrace. "My words will be brief but meaningful."

Scarlett swallowed the questions that immediately came to mind, prepared to hear out Lord Welles before she spoke. Anything she might say could inhibit him from offering information leading to Linie's recovery and the resolution of why girls seemed to go missing at The Scarlet Rose.

"A lovely young lady as yourself must keep busy with social calls and tea parties."

Scarlett had no desire to discuss minutiae. She remained silent and waited for the gentleman to continue. He paused beside a far balustrade and turned to peer into her face. She could only surmise he meant to speak directly and desired to be out of earshot of the other guests in the ballroom. This would not be a friendly conversation.

She shifted her stance and purposely brushed her fingers to the outside of her leg. She carried two knives this evening. One strapped to her thigh beneath a ridiculous amount of skirts and a small dagger in the reticule that dangled at her wrist. Smaller blades were useful deterrents in crowds. Her long knife, secured above her stocking, was a lightweight yet lethal weapon, which sailed silently through the air when thrown.

"Of course, men have their preoccupations as well. The two domains are distinctive and exclusive."

He paused as if waiting for her to interject, but Scarlett remained silent.

"It would behoove you to stop asking questions, my dear." A hard glint showed in his stare. "Talk of brothels and the like is unbecoming. Nothing but malice finds those who don't mind their own business."

Scarlett's heart kicked into triple time. She'd mentioned none of this to anyone inside Pembroke's ballroom. Lord Welles, and with certainty other gentlemen, were aware of her interest and discussed her beyond this event. Coupled with Felix's unexpected observation outside The Pigeon Hole, she wondered at just how deep and dark the problem ran at the brothel, or wherever these gentlemen interfered. An uncomfortable and forbidding sense of trepidation chased her suspicions.

"I'm not sure I understand you, my lord." She would play the innocent despite she wished to know more. If only she had the ability to follow him. But Lord Welles had proven elusive. This could very well be her only interaction with him.

"I'm sure you do. You're far too intelligent to convince me otherwise." He patted the top of her hand as if reassuring a young child. "It is rather chilly tonight. You were correct in your observation earlier. We should return to the ballroom." He continued, his expression forbidding. "Enjoy the party, but after tonight spend your time with watercolors and embroidery. Further questions about ruby rings or missing girls will result in a dangerous outcome, one that will most definitely lead to an unfortunate end."

He left her at the door and reentered the ballroom, swallowed by the crowd almost immediately though Scarlett had no desire to follow him through the room. She'd never mentioned her interest in a ruby ring to anyone inside. However discreet she'd believed herself to be, somehow her actions were known. She was being watched.

With no other option but to confront Madam Violet and hopefully gain the woman's permission to speak to a few of the girls, Scarlett knocked on the back door of the brothel the following day. She refused to consider Ambrose's kiss and the state of her emotions. If she forced herself to focus and pushed all thoughts of what occurred inside his carriage into the dark recesses of her soul, she might be able to discover something she'd overlooked. The duke was becoming a distraction and, with her interest in the problem known to others, men who threatened her with harm, she needed to find Linie and resolve the situation without further interruption.

Now on the threshold of The Scarlet Rose, she knocked again more forcefully. The same burly protector answered the door and ushered her inside only this time Scarlett had no need to skulk about in the shadows or wait for someone to attend. The madam was already in the vestibule area, her expression shrewd and determined.

"If you're here about employment, you're a day too late. I've all the girls I need. I've recently released my entire house and filled the rooms with a lovely group of new women. You're a pretty one though. Check back with me at the end of the week. I might still have a place for you."

Scarlett allowed the woman to finish before she disabused her of the assumption. All information was valuable. The fact that Violet fired every working girl in the house didn't ring true as a sound business decision. Brothels always wished to offer new faces. It kept customers returning and the house culture lively, but to sweep every girl from the establishment indicated it as an action meant to start fresh and perhaps avoid a greater problem. Some gentlemen made it a point to return to the same girl every time they visited. Those same gentlemen would be disappointed with Madam Violet's deliberate turnover.

What really provoked Madam Violet's decision? Had one of the girls complained too much about abuse or mishandling? Had a few banded together to push back on Madam Violet's convenient memory lapses whenever they voiced their concerns?

Some of the girls depended on their earnings for the basic necessities of life, most importantly food and rent. Violet's decision was cruel and likely a shock to the girls when they discovered they were all without employment. Granted, they had little recourse. Violet's well-organized bawdy house, disguised under velvet drapery and silken linens, perpetuated a veneer of respectability that overlapped class boundaries and kept a highly ambiguous relationship with Bow Street. Hadn't she seen Felix exit one afternoon?

She doubted he had visited to serve a summons or demand justice in response to a complaint. If Felix found pleasure at the brothel, he most certainly wouldn't condemn any of the practices therein.

Her stomach roiled at the conclusion. The entire situation was all interwoven and tangled into a complex knot, the man with the ruby ring at the center of the disturbance. Additionally, Linie's disappearance remained an odd component. And now, with all the girls gone, any truth Scarlett might have uncovered was absent as well. It was like starting from scratch with nothing at all. She bit back the curse that was quick to her tongue.

"Thank you for your time." There was no reason to explain the truth of her visit now. Better it appeared she'd come for employment and left peacefully. She exited through the same door and waited near the hedges in the area where she'd first eyed the brothel all those weeks ago. She had a few hours before she would visit Linie's apartment again. Something might come of watching the door. One could never be certain.

Aylesford rapped soundly on the front door of Wycombe and Company, an apparent place of business, though after setting his solicitor to the task of determining exactly what that business was and having the search yield little, Aylesford decided to venture to Mortimer Street himself. He'd noticed Lady Wycombe speaking to Scarlett more than once last evening and since he had no idea where Scarlett lived, at times wondering if she wasn't a figment of his imagination altogether or some fairy able to materialize from the early morning mist, he decided to act on the one solid fact he possessed.

He dropped the brass knocker again and followed the action with another series of knocks. He wasn't accustomed to waiting and his impatience threatened to get the better of him. Of late he possessed a restlessness he couldn't explain. He couldn't foist blame on anything in particular, not even his brother's entanglements. Everything about the situation Martin had embroiled him in was difficult and inconvenient, yet he believed in the cause and wanted, no, he needed to help Scarlett resolve the issue.

At long last he heard two female voices on the other side of the panel. He leaned in and listened closely, mildly amused when he heard one of the ladies declare, "There's a duke on our doorstep."

Indeed.

At last the panel opened and Lady Wycombe greeted him. Another woman stood in the background, her sagacious watch unwavering.

"Lady Wycombe, please pardon my unannounced call."

"Your Grace, welcome." Lady Wycombe widened the door and gestured for him to enter. "It is a pleasure to see you again."

So she'd noticed him at Pembroke's event as well. Or mayhap Scarlett had pointed him out. He wondered if it was in a positive or negative light? Everything about Scarlett was mutable.

He stepped inside the hall, quick to note the downstairs rooms were not lit and no fire burned in the hearth in the front drawing room. "I won't occupy much of your time. I have a simple question and then I'll be on my way."

The woman in the background aborted some abrupt sound before it left her mouth. She turned on her heel and went upstairs, seemingly assuming she was of no consequence.

"Don't mind Phoebe, Your Grace. She's suspicious of everyone. It's not just you this morning."

Believing this was sufficient explanation, Lady Wycombe indicated the same stairwell. "Shall we go upstairs? I can make a pot of tea."

"Thank you, no." He had only one purpose and hoped to keep his visit brief, the information gathered his true intent. "I'd like your help in locating our mutual friend."

"We've a shared acquaintance?"

All notions of things proceeding easily evaporated. Was every woman outside the ballroom guarded and wary of conversation? Or was it the circles Scarlett kept? He was accustomed to most everyone acquiescing to his requests, bending to do his bidding and supplying whatever he desired. Yet another reminder that this was not his world.

"I'm certain we have many as we were both in attendance at Pembroke's social last evening. I'd prefer to speak straight to the point. I wish to find Scarlett." He paused, momentarily stunned that he didn't know her last name. How the minx maneuvered through conversation without revealing the most fundamental facts of her person proved mind-boggling. She was stealthy and in that incredibly more desirable. She outfoxed him as a matter of habit.

"Why would you want to do that?"

Perhaps he should accept her invitation for tea. "I need to speak to her."

"Have you disappointed her in any way? Angered her? We regard her safety before anything else."

Apparently, Lady Wycombe preferred to speak directly as well.

"As I've stated, I need to speak to her." He was Aylesford. His family had shown exemplary valor and loyalty to the crown. His heritage and reputation were pristine. In that, he needn't explain his reasoning to anyone aside from the Prince Regent, but here he stood in the modest front foyer of a business on Mortimer Street asking for a personal favor. The irony of the situation amused more than angered him. Perhaps he'd proven fairly mutable as well. "Will you at least forward a message?"

"Yes, I can do that, Your Grace." Lady Wycombe arched a brow. "I will fetch you a piece of paper and pencil at once. Please come into the drawing room."

CHAPTER 17

"I'm not sure why you'd insist on meeting like this." Scarlett moved her eyes about the masculine room, wall to wall, corner to corner, her curiosity rivaling her confusion as she examined his study. "Your reputation is at stake."

It was blatant proof of the chasm separating their two worlds when a female was concerned with a male's reputation and not the other way around.

"No one knows you're here." Ambrose waved his hand toward the table where a coffee service waited along with several plates of tidbits, cheese, biscuits and fruit.

"I hope not." She stared into his dark eyes, oddly unable to read his emotions, his note requesting they meet having surprised her. "For your sake."

"It's imperative we compare notes and understand the information we've gathered. In the long run it will help us avoid redundancy and could instead lead to the solution. You'd previously suggested we join in a collective effort in the outside world. By sharing the facts here we'll expand our options."

"If you think so." Scarlett doubted His Grace had discovered anything she hadn't already investigated, but she'd humor him. One afternoon wasn't too high a price to pay. Besides, there was always the chance he might have garnered a clue she interpreted more clearly, he being unfamiliar with the complex culture of thieves and miscreants. "So what do you know?"

He laughed. A deep, rich chuckle that startled her for its potency. It rippled through her and she smiled, her grin provoked by the mere sound of his amusement.

"Oh no you don't." He moved to the table and poured two cups of coffee. "I suppose you expect me to tell you everything while you withhold all the useful facts you've learned." He laughed again and she smiled wider. "We'll trade information."

He offered her a cup and she accepted, settling deeply into an overstuffed chair, but not before she removed her skirt. He watched her with his brow furrowed and she was compelled to explain.

"I'm more comfortable in trousers." She slid a knife from the band of leather at her calf. "As this is bound to be a lengthy conversation, I thought to put myself at ease." Besides, she couldn't help but tease him a little. He did prefer her in trousers, even if he wouldn't admit it. She withdrew a small dagger from the back of her waistband and placed that on his desk beside the other blade.

He watched as if transfixed. "Are there any other dangerous weapons hidden beneath your clothing?"

He may have belatedly realized how his question charged the air between them because he cleared his throat and walked to the window and back again as if he hoped she didn't read the obvious innuendo in his words, whether intentional or not.

"Nothing you need worry yourself over." She enjoyed baiting him further. "You may share first or ask me a question. I'm not sure how you'd like this to proceed."

Didn't that speak to a number of things? The investigation . . . their relationship.

From where she viewed him he was limned in sunlight, his broad frame and classic features reminiscent of the heroes she'd seen chiseled from marble in the National Gallery. Not only was he devastatingly handsome, but he was good of heart. He might have dismissed his brother's concern over the working girls at the brothel believing their problem beneath him, but instead he'd committed himself to resolving the issue and dirtying his hands, all the while risking his reputation and personal injury. Lord, he'd been set on by thugs in a dark alley and still he hadn't complained.

Despite she had her heart locked tighter than a fortress under siege, she couldn't help but admire his strength and conviction. He was magnificent, and incredibly handsome, more the pity.

"Have you gained a description of the man with the ruby ring?"

His question jolted her into clear focus. She gave her head a shake and met his eyes as she answered. "I spoke to Missy. She worked at The Scarlet Rose before Madam Violet cleaned house and replaced all the girls. She's seen the man we're after twice and said he's a tall, thin man in his early thirties with light hair, so blond it's almost white. The fellow possesses striking blue eyes and while she couldn't recall any specific scars or qualities that would make him easier to identify, she mentioned he was a dandy from his fine tailoring to his cultured tones. The girls all knew him as Clive. Obviously, men who frequent brothels aren't apt to supply their last name or even their true first name under the circumstances." She took a sip of coffee. It had grown cold and she didn't want it anyway. Waiting for his reply, she idly ran her fingertip over the scrolled design on the handle of her long blade.

"Interesting."

"And why is that?" She hoped that didn't count as her question. Surely, he wasn't that sly.

"When I spoke to my brother about the gentleman he'd wagered against and lost, Martin described the man with the ruby ring as a heavyset middle-aged man with dark hair and dark eyes. These descriptions are as opposite as possible and little help to our investigation."

"Could it be there are two gentlemen involved in luring women away from the brothel?"

"There's likely an entire network of disreputable men feeding on the innocent hope of girls in dire situations, but I can't imagine two men wearing the same ring. A piece of jewelry so distinguishable no matter who we question, he or she notices the gemstone piece and remembers it. What are the odds of something like that happening?"

What are the odds that I, the illegitimate daughter of a destitute commoner who prostituted herself and ultimately died at the hands of her lover, would be seated in the personal study of a duke?

Scarlett couldn't dismiss anything. Predictability was rare and strange things happened in the world where she lived on a daily basis.

"I believe it's a nobleman, perhaps more than one. Some toff who uses influence and title to dazzle the girls into complacency. Once they leave the brothel, a number of fates may await, but not for a minute do I believe the tale told to the girls. No affluent nob is setting these girls up in a cottage with servants and the like. The sex trade is an ugly and often fatal undertaking." Again her thoughts flitted to her mother and the price she paid for her decisions. She rose from the chair and paced to the window.

"I'm going to contact Bow Street. The runners may have taken complaints concerning these same types of occurrences at other brothels. It's an option we haven't pursued."

"And not a good idea." She would speak to Felix if it warranted a discussion. "The fourth Duke of Aylesford inquiring with Bow Street concerning missing whores from Southwark is just what the newspapers feed upon. You can't possibly believe anyone will be discreet where your name is concerned."

"I can disguise my request with intentions to write new parliamentary law, which by the way is not a lie. I'm invested in making improvements and working for change. But for the time being, there's no need for anyone to know our true intent."

"It won't work." She shook her head to emphasize the point, although his intent to employ his position and influence piqued her curiosity. "It's a mistake to involve the law. Most times, they look the other way to crimes that happen beyond Mayfair and besides . . ." She paused, remembering how the runners dismissed her mother's death as deserved and unimportant while Scarlett's entire life had upended. "I've no doubt the same men from Bow Street whom you would seek to resolve the problem visit the brothels for their own pleasure. They're not likely to upset the very places where they indulge their entertainment. Unfortunately, they are a part of the complication as much as the resolution."

"That is a rather cynical way to view things, Scarlett." His soft-spoken tones were possibly meant to gentle the insult. "I understand what you're saying but I still believe in the course of law."

"The law works for some but not for all."

"As that may be true, it doesn't erase the fact that at times it does work."

His tone implied he'd do exactly as he pleased, whether she agreed or not. It was hard to get the duchy out of the duke, she supposed.

She nodded, although she still knew it to be a poor idea. "So, who has the wrong of it? Missy or Martin?" Scarlett sincerely hoped Ambrose wasn't keeping a tally on questions because she'd asked far more than she'd answered.

"I don't know." He blew out a breath of exasperation and settled in the chair across from her. "Did you make any progress during the Pembroke event? Were you able to learn something from the dowagers?"

She looked away and back again, hoping he would assume she was carefully recalling the facts, all the while regretting her omission, but she wasn't about to share the threat Welles issued. Ambrose would become protective and angry. Those emotions served no one and he might confront Welles in haste before she could determine how involved the viscount proved to be. She planned to learn his address and watch the property as soon as she obtained the information.

"Nothing that aids in our search. It's difficult to steer a conversation into a jewelry discussion, never mind one specific gentleman's ring."

He waited but she said nothing more.

"What else do we know?" he prodded.

"I know you're asking all the questions." She slanted him a glance as she spun her dagger in small circles on the desktop with her pointer finger.

"You're right." He placed his hand atop hers to stop her fidgeting. "It's your turn."

"Why haven't you married?"

She'd either touched a nerve or took him completely by surprise because at first he didn't move at all, frozen in thought or otherwise immobile, but then he raised his eyes to hers, a wry grimace on his face. She didn't know if he would answer and he still hadn't released her hand, but after another beat, he began to speak.

"I've plenty of time to beget the obligatory heir."

"I see."

Apparently, he viewed marriage, and perhaps any kind of intimate relationship, as dangerous, just as she. For her, fighting a gin-soaked vagrant in a secluded alleyway was just another Tuesday morning. Ferreting out a liar, chasing a thief or interrupting a robbery were pedestrian compared to the risk of baring one's heart and trusting emotion.

"And you?"

How foolish to open this line of questioning and not expect him to reciprocate. That was poorly done of her. Too often he blurred her focus.

"I doubt any man would have me. Regardless, I've no need of a keeper." She slipped her hand from beneath his, bereft as soon as she completed the action and touched her fingertip to the blade of her knife where she traced the edge carefully. "Unlike you, I don't have decades of history haunting my past and dictating my future."

"It isn't as horrific as you make it sound." He shook his head, an expression of amusement fast to replace his earlier seriousness. "It's my turn to ask a question."

She *was* keeping a tally and he was wrong, but she didn't correct him, her curiosity too invested now.

"How long is your hair?"

He caught her by surprise. She wasn't aware he'd noticed. Why did he care? Could it be he thought of her as often as she considered him whenever they were apart? Only a fool would believe such sappy tripe. She reached up and unpinned the bun at her nape, her hair dropping past her shoulders to skim her rib cage.

His eyes darkened and she saw his jaw clench. She swallowed whatever words she might have said. A strong frisson of desire, sultry and demanding, replaced the casual mood in the room.

What were they doing?

Playing with fire. Again.

Why?

Why, indeed.

CHAPTER 18

He might try to fight against it. For whatever that was worth. But he bloody knew it was a waste of time and energy. He hadn't stopped thinking about their kiss since . . . since they'd kissed. And having her here in his study with the door closed and the curtains drawn offered him an opportunity to repeat that piece of heaven. He wasn't fool enough, or strong enough, to resist.

He closed the distance between them, his body tightening with anticipation every step he took. When he reached her he threaded his fingers through the penny brown lengths of her hair, its decadent strands like spun silk, and skimmed it over her shoulder as he arranged it behind her, loving the texture as it slid beneath his touch. It was longer than he'd imagined and he'd spent a lot of time wondering about it.

"I haven't stopped thinking about our kiss." Her skin colored, a rush of soft pink that confessed she liked his admittance. "Have you?"

"No." She breathed deep with her answer. "Ambrose—"

He suspected she would qualify their last kiss, erase the absolute loveliness of their embrace, and he wouldn't allow it. Instead he swept her into his arms, flush against his body tense with need, and angled his mouth down to hers.

She tasted better than he remembered. Soft and willing in his arms despite she was the strongest woman he knew. He inhaled deeply and was rewarded with rosemary and mint. This was too much pleasure at once, too much joy. He'd kept his feelings locked away for so long and now they rushed back with vehemence. He was woefully unprepared.

He angled his head, realigned their kiss, and fit their mouths more tightly together. He swept his tongue inside her lips to rub and parry with hers in a playful game that quickly turned more sensual. His cock throbbed in his breeches and he growled, lust at the forefront but some other deeper emotion, something more powerful and dangerous, all the while urging him on.

Sliding his palms down her slight frame he settled them at her waist while she swept her hands upward, wrapped them tightly around his neck where her fingers splayed through his hair and held tight, her eagerness an additional aphrodisiac.

He was a duke, a pillar of decorum and respectability and a prime example of the gentleman's code of honor, but all he could think of was stripping Scarlett bare, lying her down on the plush carpet in his study and finding sweet bliss between her creamy thighs. He would go mad from wanting.

His heart beat a dangerous rhythm in his chest. He yearned for more and smoothed his hands to cup her hips, her trousers composed of temptation, the fabric unable to disguise the softness of her curves.

Still, he needed more and pulled her forward so she could feel the extent of his ardor, his erection hard and eager beneath his falls. Someday they would satisfy this aching desire. Someday they would see this through. That singular thought created the strongest longing and anticipation of all.

He kissed across her jaw winding a pathway to her ear while he played at her neckline. He heard her gasp as he swept his hand inside, his fingers brushing over the tip of her breast, the warm bud tight beneath his touch. She shuddered within his embrace, always so strong and at the same time so fragile. He would keep her safe always. *Always*.

The determined honesty of that thought startled him. He'd become too involved, fallen under her spell completely. And when a second realization struck him, that any harm could come to her, take her from him, it ignited a spike of anger too hot to ignore.

He broke their kiss, his words of promise urgent as he stared into her eyes. "Let me protect you."

"Protect me?" She immediately stiffened and pulled from his arms, her voice a strange mixture of surprise and indignation as she backstepped toward his desk. "I don't need your protection. I can take care of myself. Don't you believe I can protect myself?" She brought her hands behind her back in what he assumed was a serious pose meant to emphasize her point. Then in a lightning fast flick of the wrist, she threw her knife. His eyes shot to the other side of the room where the blade was buried in some unfortunate ancestor's portrait, right between the eyes.

"Not like that." He glanced to the painting and back again. "Definitely not like that. But I can protect your name, your reputation. I won't allow anyone to say something untoward of you. To disparage you in any way." *To hurt you. There will be no mercy for the fool who ever hurts you.*

But he couldn't tell her that.

"You can't control the words that leave other people's mouths, Ambrose, no matter how noble and"—she paused, her voice tentative as she continued—"generous you are. We may reside in the same city, but we don't live in the same worlds." She straightened her shoulders and her chin hitched a notch. "And what's all this talk of always and forever? I'm nothing more than an interesting diversion, unlike the polished highborn ladies who grace the salons of the *ton*. Despite this wild spark between us it can never be more than what we have now. It is a firework, explosive and entertaining, but fleeting and destined to burn away before one realizes its full beauty."

"That's not what this is." He narrowed his eyes and pinned her with his attention. "That's not what we have now."

"A more appropriate label escapes me," she answered softly, then continued in a stronger voice. "Besides, a label is unnecessary unless you're taking out an ad in the *Times*."

"You're behaving contrary on purpose." He didn't wish to argue.

"You assume I need your protection when I've managed for nearly twenty years on my own."

"I don't discount that, but why continue to carry the weight of your past when I'm offering you support? Nothing more."

"Of all people to talk about carrying the weight of the past. Your heritage and reputation take up room in the carriage. Your title is a living, breathing participant in this conversation."

"And what of your past? If you wish to erase your heartache, I'm offering you a way forward."

"You know nothing of my past."

"Because you haven't told me yet."

"And I never will." She faced him with resolve in her expression. "Our lives were never meant to intersect."

"I disagree." He reached forward and pushed a loose lock of hair behind her ear, trailing his fingertips across her cheek as he withdrew.

"My past is nothing but secret upon secret." She inhaled deeply though she didn't say more.

"There's no sense looking back when there's so much to look forward to." He shook his head, her comments and complaints unexpected. "I can't change my history, Scarlett, any more than you can."

"Exactly. You've just proven my point. Still, that is no excuse for being insistent and overbearing." She strode across the room and retrieved her knife. "I apologize for the painting." She blinked hard. "I'll see myself out."

Holding tight to his declaration and unwilling to reflect on how holding tightly to Scarlett had startled her into retreat, he'd sent a missive to Bow Street and now awaited the arrival of an agent in his study, brandy in hand. He moved his eyes to the portrait Scarlett's knife had skewered. Her aim was infallible. Uncle Demetrius must have a splitting headache in the afterworld.

Downing the liquor left in his glass, he considered how brave Scarlett must have been to survive all those years of independence while he lived a very comfortable life in the fold of his family with every convenience and luxury. Her desire to excel and risk personal harm to help others was brave and admirable. She was an example of what was missing in the world. Honest integrity, innate goodness and so much more.

His mind quickly abandoned that thought for the next, Scarlett's soft body within the circle of his arms, her slick, delicious tongue in his mouth, her warm, sweet breast in his hand. His groin immediately reacted, but there would be nothing for it. At least not at the moment.

A soft knock sounded on the door and at his bid, Jamison, the house butler, entered.

"Mr. Felix Howell from Bow Street has arrived. Shall I deposit him in the blue drawing room and call for refreshments?"

"Thank you, Jamison, but that won't be necessary. Please show Mr. Howell to my study." No doubt the runner would appreciate a fine brandy. Lord knows the job was one to be admired.

"Your Grace."

Mr. Howell entered and approached. He was a stout man with dark hair and Aylesford immediately experienced a sense of familiarity. He sifted through every incident from Martin's past, wondering if somehow he'd crossed paths with the agent at another time when his brother had found trouble and he'd been called in to extricate his sibling and smooth over the mess.

"Mr. Howell, thank you for coming." They shook hands and Aylesford indicated the sideboard where several crystal decanters waited. "Can I offer you a brandy?"

"No, nothing for me." Howell walked toward one of the chairs. "I save my drinking for after hours."

"A wise habit," Aylesford agreed as he took the opposing seat.

"I asked you to meet with me because I've a concern over an establishment an acquaintance has visited. He believes a dangerous force may be at work, someone who means to do harm."

"Then you've made the right decision." Howell reached inside his coat and removed a folded paper and pencil. He settled both atop his lap. "If you will explain your concerns, I'll take notes and investigate. From there I'll write a report and have it sent to you straightaway unless you'd rather we meet again. It's not often I grace the streets of Mayfair. My usual visits tend to be in different areas of this great city."

"Indeed." Aylesford watched the runner closely. The more he conversed with Howell, the stronger that same nagging feeling returned. Had he met the man before? It didn't seem likely.

"Whenever you're ready, Your Grace."

"There's a brothel near Vauxhall called The Scarlet Rose." Aylesford paused, uncertain if the runner meant to write the information down, but as of yet the man made no indication to do so. "Some of the working girls have gone missing and no one seems to know their whereabouts."

It was the leanest description of the problem because something didn't feel right about confessing everything he'd learned to Howell. Aylesford had nothing upon which to base this feeling, but he was too smart to ignore it. Now he wondered if Scarlett had been right all along and involving Bow Street was an outright mistake.

"Have you had complaints of any kind or reports of missing persons connected to the brothel?" Ambrose probed, hoping for more details, anything to open a new avenue of information.

"With all due respect, Your Grace, we at Bow Street aren't inclined to share our findings with others. We usually ask the questions. That's our purpose."

The runner replaced his pencil and paper before he leaned back against the upholstered chair. He cleared his throat and reached up to wipe at his nose twice. He wore no gloves and Aylesford was momentarily distracted with the man's fingers but of course,

no ruby ring was found there. He might have laughed at his misplaced foolishness. Scarlett had his thoughts disassembled and divided, his emotions all out of place.

He hadn't liked the way they'd parted. She was angry with him
and rightly so. Hell, he didn't even know how to reach her unless
he visited Lady Wycombe in her late husband's building. That
was one fact that must be remedied immediately. Where did she
live? How did she live? Was she lonely? He had to have a way to
contact her. *He didn't even know her last name.* Damn it all but she
was distracting when she wanted to be.

He might have continued down this convoluted rabbit hole if
Howell didn't clear his throat a second time, apparently assuming
their conversation was at an end when Aylesford had fallen silent.
They stood up and began to walk toward the door.

"Thank you, Mr. Howell." He didn't like the look in the runner's eyes as they exchanged a cordial farewell. Scarlett hadn't
wanted him to involve Bow Street and now Aylesford was inclined
to agree, but it was too late for that.

Scarlett sat on the floor of her apartment and crossed her legs,
the warmth of her small fire a balm to her restlessness. She picked
up her knife from the floorboards where it lay beside her and
watched the firelight glint off the metal in a dance of orange and
silver.

When had her life become complicated by too many emotions?
The moment she'd laid eyes on the Duke of Aylesford.

Hoping to work away her frustration, she positioned the honing
stone in her grasp and began to sharpen her blade. Every purposeful slide down the edge helped ease her tension, but she knew it
was little more than distraction.

What had she expected? That he would make her a duchess?
A bitter laugh tripped up her throat. She wasn't duchess material.
She never would be.

But she'd given him her heart. A gift. To herself or to him, she
wasn't sure which meant more. No matter, it was time she was rid

of it. She had no use for romance and was meant to be alone. No father. No true mother.

Liar.

Her mother had done the best she was able. Had whored herself to feed Scarlett and clothe her. Yet it had led her mother to her death.

The stone slipped and Scarlett had to shake her head to refocus on the blade before she sliced off a finger.

If only—

No.

If only was a game for fools. *If only* was a path to heartache. True, a sliver of hope countered, but she'd survived heartache before. Long days of hunger and lonely fearful nights. Her mother's violent, far too early death. Scarlett had become stronger because of it.

No.

No, no, no.

This time it would cause irreparable damage. This time she would be weakened beyond repair.

Despite her childhood and her mother's choices, or the path she'd chosen for her own life, she yearned for a trusting bond, an intimate closeness, some slim sense of security. She couldn't quell these feelings. They lived in her as much as their counterparts of independence, determination and resilience.

Satisfied with the condition of her knife, she polished it with a strop and laid it on the floor beside her.

She'd become enamored of a man who was as unreachable to her as the stars in the sky. Why had she done this to herself? She protected everyone and failed herself.

A shiver swept through her no matter she sat beside the hearth. When one played with fire, one invariably got burned. She would heal, but the scars would always remain. What a fool she'd become. When the first tears fell, she didn't wipe them away. She deserved to cry.

She hadn't intended to let Ambrose into her heart. She'd tried to be strong and yet the force of his affection was like quicksand. The more she fought against it, the more it sucked her in, deeper and deeper, until ultimately, she'd drown in it altogether.

The memory of his precious kisses and irreverent touch squeezed her lungs until she could hardly exhale.

She needed to speak to Julia. While Diana and Phoebe were her friends, Julia was her sole confidant and Scarlett had no idea how to sort the chaos of emotions coursing through her. Julia had fallen in love and lost that love by death far too early. Julia might be able to understand the knotted mess of Scarlett's feelings.

CHAPTER 19

"It's nigh impossible to find one man in a city this large."

"Where the gentlemen wear gloves and the thieves do as well."

"Or to locate one specific piece of jewelry when the best jewelers are reluctant to speak of their clients and the worst lot won't reveal the criminals."

"I agree." Scarlett sighed in frustration. Everything the other Maidens said was the exacting truth. Perhaps her search to find Linie was nothing more than an exercise of futility. It could be the seamstress left on her own accord or ran away on a flighty whim. There was no way to know. Still, Scarlett couldn't discount what the other girls at the brothel had told her. Or the mess she'd embroiled Ambrose in. Once one picked at a scab it would likely become infected and she'd gone ahead and done just that.

She'd come to Wycombe and Company this afternoon in hope a discussion with the other Maidens of Mayhem could help generate new ideas. Any avenue to investigate would be welcome. And then later tonight, when she met with Ambrose, at least she'd have something new to share.

She dropped her head back against the chair rail and closed her eyes, the conversation around her swarming with ideas suggested and discarded with alacrity. She'd rather just listen at the moment. Her usual intuition hadn't surfaced, too many emotions clouding her vision. She had her best sense of perception when her mind was completely clear but it hadn't been in some time now. Her sleep was restless too, interrupted with maudlin tableaus and haunted images of her worst fears.

She suspected that was mostly due to her interactions with Ambrose. It was more than her mind that was preoccupied with His Grace. More the pity, her heart was entangled in the mess as well.

"I'm having tea with a few ladies of the *ton* who enjoy sharing the popular gossip of the week," Julia added. "I'll ask a few questions and make a note of anything worth investigating."

"If these girls are being lured away into a better situation, why haven't any of them returned to help a friend or share their good fortune? It's as though they cease to exist once they accept Clive's offer." Phoebe's tone expressed both anger and exasperation. "It doesn't make sense."

"And exactly who is this person Clive? Could it be Viscount Welles? Is there a real Clive or is it just a random name the man uses when he entices women away? We could be chasing after a person who doesn't even exist by this name and so all our questioning is for naught."

Scarlett concentrated on the conversation as her friends attempted to unriddle the flimsy facts she'd collected, focusing on Viscount Welles and his approach at the Pembroke affair, his comments and how he'd tried to warn her away. What if she and the other Maidens of Mayhem were working too hard? What if they were the ones complicating the matter? She lifted her head and slapped her hand flat on the tabletop.

"Perhaps we're going about this all wrong." The discussion skidded to a stop and her friends turned to face her.

"What do you mean?" Julia voiced what they all were likely thinking.

"Maybe the way to find the man with the ruby ring is not to search for him in a city of one million." She nodded, a feeling of certainty taking hold. "Maybe the way to find him is to make him come looking for me and not the other way around."

"You're not suggesting you become some type of bait, are you?" Phoebe stood up, her face drawn in a frown of disapproval. "Without knowing his identity, you could become his victim without ever knowing the threat. It's far too dangerous."

"I don't like the sound of this." Julia shook her head, visibly displeased with the suggestion.

"Hear me out." Scarlett waved at Phoebe, shooing her back to her chair. "The man with the ruby ring doesn't wish to be caught, but he also doesn't want me or Aylesford nosing around and asking questions. I think that's why he or one of his associates approached me at Pembroke's estate. The more chaos and mayhem I create, the more likely he'll want to silence me."

"And that's why I don't like how this sounds." Diana moved her gaze around their circle until she settled on Scarlett. "I know we challenge danger and fight for what's right, but I can't help but think this man will stop at nothing to have his secret kept, even if that means dumping another body into the Thames. This idea puts you directly in a perilous path."

This assertion kept the room quiet for several ticks of the longcase clock.

"Aylesford will never agree to it anyway." Julia's tone invited a new vein of discussion. "He's far too noble to allow a female to put herself in danger, most especially one he cares so deeply—"

"He's not my keeper, Julia." Scarlett sprang to her feet, a sense of panic causing her response to come out louder than necessary. "He doesn't allow or disallow my choices."

"Of course not." Julia appeared taken aback. "I didn't mean to imply any such thing."

Scarlett took a deep breath and reclaimed her chair.

"He cares for you, that's all." Phoebe leaned in, her voice slightly above a whisper. "And just because we've experienced pain in the past, doesn't mean any of us deserves less than a happy future."

Coming from Phoebe, this was an unexpected and optimistic observation.

"While that is true, I don't think we need to expand any further on that subject." Scarlett looked to each of her friends. "I'm not sure what I'm feeling right now. My emotions are as confused as this matter with the brothel."

"We all care about you, Scarlett," Julia persisted. "More than Aylesford. Sometimes talking through emotion is the best way to find sense in it. We're here for you and always will be, especially when you're troubled."

Diana and Phoebe turned toward Scarlett, their eyes wide with an imploring look of expectation.

"You must tell," Diana insisted.

"Yes, you must," Phoebe seconded.

"There isn't much to tell." Scarlett scowled at Julia, who appeared inordinately amused.

"Indulge us then." Diana smiled. "Just a vague overview. No specifics are necessary if it makes you uncomfortable."

"You may as well," Julia encouraged. "You're always the one with the astute intuition, but your eyes tell a story that's too easy to read."

Scarlett settled back against the chair rail. It would be difficult to explain to the Maidens exactly how Ambrose regarded her when she didn't understand her own feelings on the subject, but she knew better than to fight their inquisitiveness. If there was one quality they all had in common, it was a relentless curiosity. There would be no peace until she explained and if it helped her sort her feelings toward the duke than it was well worth the risk.

Scarlett mentally sifted through her tasks and errands. She'd visited Linie's apartment and found no change. Sally wasn't at home and the building looked otherwise undisturbed. She also sought out Madam Ivory on Bond Street, but that too was nothing more than time wasted. By the end of the day she had a collection of unrelated facts and an overdue apology.

Ambrose deserved a better explanation than she'd provided. He didn't know her past or understand her resistance. Taking advice from the other Maidens of Mayhem, she considered revealing at least some of her history the next time an opportunity arose. Yet a wavering desire to bare her soul wasn't enough nor was it very productive.

She knew he was wrong in involving the authorities. His assumption stemmed from a predictable tendency brought about by being overbred and overbearing. He'd been raised to be that way and much as her history had foretold her future, his did the same, at least until one worked to change the course.

She smiled as she walked in the afternoon sun toward his property, her boots in cadence with her heartbeat. He might be all those insufferable things, but he'd somehow managed to win her affection. Not that it meant anything in the wide scope of things. But she'd allow herself this pleasure. He spoke to her somehow without saying anything at all. Their connection was real no matter it was temporary. Memories of their time together would be welcome in the future when they'd both moved on.

She reached Aylesford House and eased around the side, over the fancy wrought iron fencing, below the glowing gold of the windows in the drawing room, beneath the elaborate metalwork that composed the supports for his bedroom balcony. She'd enter through the back even though she'd never been looked upon as anything other than a visiting guest by Aylesford's staff. They'd either been informed or instructed to treat her with every politeness. She pushed back against the belief she could ever fit into Ambrose's world, but in his home she at least felt welcomed.

She climbed the three stairs that led to the kitchen, prepared to work the lock and enter undetected if necessary, but a fair-haired slip of a maid opened the door before Scarlett had a chance. The servant stood in unwitting surprise for only a moment before she recovered her sensibility.

"His Grace says you are to always enter by the front door."

So plainly put, Scarlett's heart tripped a beat. He wasn't ashamed of her. Nor would he hide her existence. What did that mean? Her presence here could cause irreparable harm to his distinguished reputation. No doubt decades of ancestors were spinning in their graves at this very moment.

"Thank you."

The kitchen was warm and quieted for the night. A large pot sat over the fire and two more simmered, steam rising from their lids. Everything seemed in its place with only one footman moving boxes into a large pantry at the right. Engrossed in his task, he didn't spare her a glance and Scarlett followed the maid down the hall toward the front of the house. The servant paused when she reached the hall.

"I will inform His Grace you are waiting."

"There's no need, Cora." Ambrose appeared near the second-floor railing. "You may go. I'll attend to the lady."

How did he know she'd entered? Was he looking out his bedroom window when she'd passed? Or had he sensed her presence? He possessed an uncanny intuitiveness that at times reminded her of her own. Half a smile emerged at his use of the words *the lady*.

He took the stairs and stood before her. He extended his ungloved hand.

"Let's share what we know in my study."

That statement held more clues than any issue they'd investigated, but she didn't say a word and simply placed her hand in his. They climbed the stairs in silence. Mayhap they both knew what would happen next. She did and her heart applauded the decision.

Ambrose led Scarlett beyond the door to his study. He may have misread her. He may be volunteering for another argument, but from the look in her eyes and the way his body seemed in tune to her every breath, he didn't believe so.

They entered the sitting room attached to his bedchambers. If she realized this, she didn't make it known. He walked to the hearth and poked a few logs to stir them into a more vigorous flame and then turned, bracing one shoulder against the mantel. She'd come here to talk to him about something.

"I apologize for my behavior earlier."

To his chagrin, pride not regret colored her words.

"You've said as much earlier and I don't blame you for becoming upset." He pushed away from the hearth. "I had no right behaving so obstinately."

"You have every right. You're a duke."

"That I am."

"Nevertheless, you have to view this with detached clarity."

Did she speak of the situation they sought to remedy or the strange relationship they'd forged? At the moment, all he could think about was her delectable mouth. He watched her speak but it wasn't to hear what she was saying.

"You're right."

His agreement stopped her from continuing. Her brows lowered and her eyes narrowed, as if she didn't expect him to comply so easily. He approached her slowly. She was brave and strong and so damn enticing, yet in her eyes, eyes that told the truth, he detected a flash of uncertainty. Was it fear of him? The bold sensuality that wove through the room? Or of her personal feelings? There was only one way to find out.

"Scarlett." He stood in front of her, her lovely gaze fixed on him though defiance still shimmered in their gray depths. "We may disagree on the path to the solution, but we both yearn for the same outcome."

She swallowed and canted her head the slightest at the ambiguity of his words. "What exactly are we discussing?"

He pressed his palm to her cheek and slanted her head upward. "The undeniable pull between us." He lowered his mouth and waited. He would never take what she wasn't willing to give.

She moved the slightest bit closer. "Life rarely frightens me, Ambrose. I've seen things, experienced trouble, that I wouldn't wish for anyone to confront, and so I've tried terribly to harden my heart. . . ."

He listened, emotion welling within him despite the palpable sensuality of her whispers against his cheek. Her life was shadowed by secrecy and yet he couldn't bring himself to ask more of her.

"But you've somehow reached inside me and wrapped your hand around my heart."

She didn't say another word. Instead she went up on her toes and closed the distance between their mouths, moving into his embrace at the same time.

CHAPTER 20

Ambrose couldn't think straight from wanting her. When she moved within his arms he deepened their kiss, licking into her mouth and at the same time struggling to keep a leash on his desire. She tasted exactly as he'd expected, like adventure and desire and every wild fantasy he'd dared dream when he wasn't embroiled in work and life's drudgery.

Still, by degree the kiss slowed, transformed and became more. A promise. *A bond.* His heart hammered against the wall of his chest and, as if she knew, she smoothed her hands over his shoulders, down to lie over the furious beat. He pulled back and broke their contact, but only by a hairsbreadth of space.

"When I am with you . . ." He inhaled and was rewarded with her rosemary scent.

"Everything is better," she finished, her words against his mouth as she continued their kiss.

He pressed her tighter to him, his hands skimming down her back and up again, restlessness winning out over control. He eased his hands to her ribs, angled his mouth so he could taste her, tease her, all the while knowing she could feel his arousal against her belly.

He wanted her and there was no disguising his need.

"You're so brave and strong, always so strong," he murmured, reluctant to leave her delicious mouth. "Let me give you the pleasure you deserve."

She speared her fingers through his hair and tightened her fists, the slight tug an unexpected inducement.

"Is that a yes?" He nibbled across the turn of her jaw while she nodded, and whispered against her ear, "I'm heartened you wore skirts today."

He didn't give her a chance to respond and reversed her with succinct efficiency, unlacing the back of her gown. She breathed deeply and he suspected she appreciated the freedom as much as he did, but this wasn't about him.

Clasping her waist, he turned her to face him. Slowly he lowered her bodice, the creamy skin found beneath the fabric causing his arousal to grow harder. She was beauty from the inside out, composed of layer upon layer of loveliness. Her skin heated under his perusal, tinged pink in the candlelight.

"Come with me." He laced his fingers in hers, guiding her to an elongated chaise near the fireplace, the longue buffeted with a multitude of pillows. She sat and he captured her mouth in another long kiss that professed how much he wanted her though he knew he'd not be satisfied tonight. He'd always want more of her, want to offer her more. Gently, he lowered her to recline on the cushions.

"My intent is to give you pleasure upon pleasure, Scarlett." He ran his fingertips along the neckline of her gaping gown, his eyes matched to hers intently. "And while I kneel beside you, you are in control. Every kiss, every caress I offer, is to bring you the joy you deserve." He noticed she drew a shuddery breath, this beautiful warrior in front of him, draped on his bedchamber chaise as if a gift of the gods.

He admired her courageous spirit and independent strength, but while he willingly relinquished control tonight, he hoped to bring her to her sensual limits, touch her vulnerable soul and open her heart.

"You don't always have to be strong, love." He nuzzled her

neck and whispered against her ear, "With me you can let go for a while."

"Yes. Yes, Ambrose." She reached her hand out and then just as quickly dropped it to the fabric pooled in her lap. "I want you to pleasure me."

He dragged her neckline down farther, capturing fabric in the process to expose the lovely swells of her breasts. He was captivated momentarily by the ribbons on her corset, belatedly realizing she managed independently with no maid to help her dress. A grin of wicked satisfaction itched at his lips and he pulled the ribbons free.

She sank deeper into the cushions, her head flung back and her eyes fluttering but not completely closed. Instead she watched as he loosened the ties near her clavicle and bared her luscious breasts. Cool air kissed each rosy nipple and caused them to tighten. He inhaled her sweet fragrance and captured an anxious bud between his teeth, his mouth scorching a trail across the curve of her silky, smooth skin. He reveled in her indrawn gasps, her tense muscles, though she hardly moved until she pushed her fingers through his hair and held him to her. He drew her nipple deep into his mouth and laved his tongue across the tip, her ardent response ramping his desire another notch.

He pulled away, managed a shaky breath and rolled his shoulders, wanting so much more and yet unwilling to ravage her despite the furious drum of need in his blood.

"Touch me, Ambrose." She pulled him closer, his chin skimming over the softness of her breast, her delighted reaction to his whiskers another shot of fire in his veins.

"I am yours to command." His murmur was nearly lost to the rustle of fabric as he gathered layer upon layer of her skirts in his fist. She truly looked like a mystical goddess, her shoulders bare and her lovely long legs exposed. The slightest turn of her ankle caused his cock to twitch. Now with her creamy skin displayed before him, he thought he would lose his battle with control, his arousal hard and anxious.

He traced his fingertips over the top of her stocking, pausing to linger over the delicate skin of her inner thigh. She moaned and he repeated the delectable torture, experiencing the pleasure-pain in much the same way.

"Please, Ambrose." Her whispered plea cut into him deep. He wanted to give her everything she desired. Not just this interlude of pleasure, but so much more. A future, security, happiness and a family.

His mind spun with myriad ideas that had nothing to do with their intimacy and everything to do with time beyond their reach. A future filled with obligation and expectation . . . rife with com-plicated uncertainty. But his ardor won out, pushing against thoughts of the days ahead and firmly demanding he embrace the moment in front of him.

He brushed the pad of his thumb along her thigh as he rose up to kiss her, drinking deep from her lips, all the while stroking upward, his fingertips gently teasing the sweet heat between her legs. She parted for him and invited him to explore, the opening in her pantalets damp as he slid his touch beyond the lace.

He groaned, unable to hold back. She was all silky wetness, hot and ready. He wanted to break from her mouth and kiss her sex, lick into her, taste her with the same fervent desire that composed their embrace.

With more control than he believed possible, he smoothed his finger between her slick folds, a shiver of delight passing through her, the wriggling clench of her muscles a sign she enjoyed every caress almost as much as he. Tamping down desire as his body hummed with need, he eased his finger across her tight core, stroking back and forth, back and forth, until at last he delved into her heat. She trembled and gasped, restlessly shifting on the chaise. He paused and broke away from her lips.

Kissing a path along her jaw he nibbled at her chin, the skin soon abraded by his whiskers, but she enjoyed the sensation, her soft murmurings an enticing inducement. All the while he teased her, worked her higher, faster, plunging deeper into her wet heat and out again, the brisk slide of his fingers causing her to squirm, her breathy pants a sign she was so very close.

At the very last minute, when he feared she would shatter if he waited even one breath longer, he replaced his fingers with his mouth and sank his tongue into her sex, tasting her sweet, sweet climax, kissing them both into oblivion.

It was much later when Scarlett left Aylesford House. She wasn't comfortable in Mayfair and while she knew the streets and the thoroughfares well enough, she was more accustomed to traveling rooftop to rooftop in Southwark or through a maze of back alleys in Wapping.

Hacks for hire appeared frequently at each corner but she didn't wish to ride. Walking helped ease the melancholy that replaced the emptiness in her heart. How would she let Ambrose go when this was all over? How would she forget his tender kisses? His lovely dark eyes and handsome smile? His genuine compassion? The way he teased her body to respond with undeniable passion?

He somehow caused her to feel alive in ways she'd never imagined and that elusive sense of security, of a safe haven where she was loved and cherished, tempted like an exquisite treat just beyond her reach.

But someday soon she would need to say goodbye. Their shared intimacy and the liberties she'd allowed complicated the matter tenfold. They both knew from the start their unlikely partnership was temporary. Neither of them behaved fanciful in collecting thoughts of happily ever after. She paused for a breath to help choke down regret. So much regret.

Frustrated with the path of her thoughts she hailed a hackney and directed the driver to Southwark. He almost refused, but after the promise of a few extra coins, agreed to take her there. She needed to visit the streets of her childhood. It would serve well to remind herself she was nothing more than the bastard daughter of a Southwark whore. Any ideas, however cunning their temptation, of becoming involved romantically with a duke, needed to be purged with swift efficiency. She'd never been one for fairy tales and had stopped wishing on stars when she was barely five years old. This false reality that unwittingly crept into her to stir up hope needed to be extinguished promptly or she'd be left in the cinders of its wake.

She rapped on the roof when she neared the corner of Webber Street and overpaid the driver. Then she set out on foot down one dank alley after another until she stood across the roadway from a dilapidated tenement building covered in soot and unpleasantness. This was her history. She didn't need to get closer. The old, ugly memories reached for her with their sharp cutting tentacles no matter the distance she put between the past and present.

Disgusted with herself, she turned and headed north toward her home. What was she doing wandering aimlessly in the night? Even she knew she challenged fate out alone in the most dangerous area of London. She'd allowed emotion to overtake her. She was losing her edge. It was Ambrose and his kisses. He made her think thoughts that were better left alone.

Walking faster now, she turned another corner and passed the maze of alleyways that led to Earnshaw Street. What had happened to Linie? She'd disappeared. Didn't anyone miss her? Did anyone care? Was the girl's life so insignificant?

Where were all these confusing emotional thoughts coming from? Scarlett breathed deeply forcing the bracing night air to bring her clarity.

A noise from above broke through her melancholy and alerted her better sense to use caution. She had her knives though she was in no mood to use them. Her body was tense and her mind restless, the combination ill-fitted for efficient combat. A trickle of gravel rained down the side of the building to her left and she hurried her steps. She was being followed. Tracked. Any thief or murderous vagrant would mark her as an easy target.

She loosened the ties at her waist and discarded her overskirt to the ground. Come morning someone would make good use of the fabric as a blanket or article of clothing. Her underskirts and boots were now exposed to offer the most efficient attire and she broke into a run, her cloak flowing behind her in silent undulation.

Her enemy dropped from above and she remembered Felix's attack all those weeks ago, when he'd mentioned he aimed to test her skill. Had he been measuring her ability? Did he already see her as a threat? And was that him standing in a menacing stance several yards away? It was too dark to be sure. The moonlight was fickle this evening and shadows chased each other in a relentless game of tag.

The stranger advanced, the hollow tap of his bootheels in tandem with the thrum of her heart. It could be Felix. The man's size and posture appeared similar. But why would it be? Did he mean to challenge her? Hurt her? Yet he'd intimated at a possible relationship between them on more than one occasion. She couldn't unriddle these answers. A fight awaited and the stranger at the end of the alley appeared impatient.

CHAPTER 21

"Who is she?"

"Who is who?" Ambrose startled to awareness and almost spilled the liquor in his glass, a scowl fast to replace his vacant expression. He'd come to White's and now regretted the decision.

"Whoever it is who has caused you to forget how to drink brandy and converse." Galway shook his head slowly. "You've been sitting here motionless for the better half of an hour. I've watched from across the room."

"You've watched?" Ambrose took a healthy sip of his drink. "And then you thought to come over and check on me? Are you gauging my sanity?"

"Something like that." Galway settled in the opposing chair and signaled to a footman for a drink. "So is it brother troubles again?"

"You remember where we last left off. No, this time Martin is not the cause of my confusion."

"Merely confusion?" Galway accepted his brandy and took a swallow. "And here I thought you were lost to us all, driven mad by Martin's nonsensical antics, the way you sat staring at the wall without blinking an eye."

"You really *were* watching me."

"And?"

"And what?"

"Honestly, Aylesford, I've known you for several years and I've never seen you so distracted, but if you don't wish to talk about it you may as well just say so."

"That was the point of me sitting quietly for the last forty minutes." Ambrose set his glass down on the table between them. "Besides, nothing's wrong that I can't mend myself."

"You're having me on." Galway chuckled. "Maybe you don't see the angst in your expression whenever you look in the mirror, but I see it now. Something has you turned inside out."

Ambrose swallowed and remained silent. He wasn't sure he wished to discuss the battle between his heart and mind with Galway. They were good friends, but their companionship would end badly if the viscount said something unthinkable in regard to Scarlett. And just having that thought, that someone could insult her or impugn her honor without cause, without knowing her, was the exact reason he struggled with his emotions now.

"There you go again." Galway *tsk*ed his tongue and feigned mocking disapproval. "Lost to the conscious world."

"I'm involved with someone and I'm concerned for her welfare."

Galway's brows raised so high they nearly disappeared in his hairline. "Now we're getting somewhere." He leaned forward and dropped his voice lower. "Anything you wish to say remains between the two of us. I would never betray your trust."

Ambrose knew this for truth, though he still hesitated. For reasons he could not explain, his interactions and most especially his feelings as they pertained to Scarlett seemed intimately personal and precious. Every nuance of their relationship, however secret and private, was a treasure he didn't wish to share. The way she rubbed her fingertips together when she fought to keep her hands at her sides, the way her pulse fluttered like a trapped butterfly at the base of her neck, her enticing fragrance and the entrancing gleam in her lovely gray eyes . . . the list was endless. And still, it was some kind of unnamed betrayal to admit his misgivings to Galway no matter the viscount sought to help.

"It's your noble nature, Aylesford. Whoever she is or whatever the problem she's caused you." He waved a hand in the direction of the room where pockets of gentlemen engaged in conversation. "Everyone knows how honorable you are, how strong your desire to protect and do right by your title. She must be someone very special to have you thinking thoughts of the future."

"I haven't said anything on the subject."

"You don't have to." Galway continued enthusiastically, "I've known you long enough to read your mood. Some very special woman has captured your heart and you're contemplating how you'll propose and secure her as your new duchess."

"How many drinks have you had?" His question held no humor. Galway's assumptions were almost correct although the missing pieces were the most important. Ambrose wanted Scarlett but he couldn't have her. It was a simple, if not painful, equation.

Instilled at birth, Aylesford's sense of duty had always been there, a constant reminder and part of his life like the portraits of his ancestors that lined the gallery hall at his country seat. Dukes didn't marry commoners, most especially a wild, fearless, knife-carrying temptress like Scarlett.

"Mind you, all this deflection only proves I've determined the cause of your quandary."

Ambrose finished his drink in one swallow and stood. He needed fresh air. "Aren't you the clever one?" He nodded his farewell and strode from the club, restless and anxious to return home. Even the wait at the curb for his horse to be fetched from the mews seemed interminable.

Life was nothing more than mundane tasks strung together under the guise of obligation and duty, but Scarlett had opened his eyes to so much more. She represented freedom and bravery and a long list of things he didn't know quite how to identify except she made him feel good and notice things and embrace life instead of marching through it as if half asleep. She'd had no intention to change him and yet she had.

For the better.

And he wasn't about to let her go.

Nevertheless, the dukedom was nothing to ignore. His responsibilities as a peer of the realm were not to be besmirched. Conflicted emotion coalesced in his chest and he rode hard, eager for the peace and quiet to be found in his study, except he found Martin there instead.

"You're not in trouble, are you?" Ambrose rounded his desk and dropped into his chair, tense and unsettled by his own ambivalence.

"Shouldn't I ask you the same question?" Martin countered.

"Why would you?" Would the questions never end this evening?

"You're in love with her and you're too thickheaded to do anything about it?"

An eerie silence ensued. His brother knew him better than he'd anticipated. Either that or Ambrose had misjudged his staff and their desire to spread rumors assuming Scarlett's visits were romantic in nature. He doubted the latter was true.

"I can't have her, so this conversation is moot."

"And why can't you?" Martin leaned in, his elbows on his knees as he continued. "You're Aylesford, a duke, as you're so fond of informing me whenever it suits your needs. You can do whatever you like and London will have to accept it. They have no choice."

"I don't care a whit about London's opinion, but society would ostracize her, give her the cut direct and treat her cruelly." His voice softened on the last bit. Scarlett was proud and confident, but inside she would ache from it all. And she would be pained on his behalf. She possessed such magnificent empathy for others. Their relationship would be crippled with doubt and regret from the very start. "I couldn't see her hurt more than life has forced her to endure already. It would be selfish on my part."

"More selfish than keeping your love from her? Telling her how you feel and allowing her to decide her future?" Martin leaned back into the chair. "From what you've shared it sounds as though little has been in her control up to this point and yet you've decided to take this decision away from her as well."

"It's not like that. Stop twisting my words," Ambrose groused. "You're giving me a deuced headache." *Christ, he sounded more like his brother and less like himself every minute.*

"So, then." Martin paused as if choosing his words carefully. "You're ready to let her go? To never see her again for the sake of some dead ancestors and their blue blood? Is that worth the price of love and happiness?"

"No." He stood and heaved a breath, annoyed with just about everything at the moment. "No." He said it again louder.

"Then what is it?"

"I'm always in control and the things around me that I can't control are managed with sound decisions and methodical plans of action. This is different."

"Honestly, it's a personality flaw. You're . . . what's the word I'm looking for?" Martin made a circular motion in the air as if by doing so he could force his brain to work faster.

"Composed?"

"No."

"Staid? Rigid? Dignified?"

"No, no, no." Martin snapped his fingers and grinned triumphantly. "It's whatever word means all of those things combined."

"If that was your attempt at levity, I am not amused." The last thing he needed this evening was counsel from his devil-may-care brother.

"What you are is closed off. At least most of the time and this female is forcing you to open up." Martin stood and walked to the sideboard where the liquor decanters stood patiently in wait. "I think she's good for you."

"Not if I'm losing myself."

"It seems to me like you're finally finding yourself." Martin returned with glasses, each with two fingers of brandy.

"I've always considered myself reliable and consistent."

Martin cast a glance around the room. "Like an ottoman."

Like an ottoman.

"And she's all energy and wonder, constantly in motion," Ambrose continued, a bit of awe in his voice.

"Like a shooting star," Martin added. "Well, I'd say this conversation has been very productive."

"Has it?" Ambrose supposed, if pressed, he'd have to admit talking to Martin did clarify his feelings more so than when he'd ridden home from White's.

"And that's worthy of a toast." Martin raised his glass, a scoundrel's smile across his face.

"How is it we're brothers and so completely adverse in personality?" Ambrose ribbed, tapping his brandy against his brother's.

"I suppose between the two of us, one offsets the other to create an equal balance."

"Indeed." Ambrose nodded. "That could be it."

He came at her with one intent, a narrow blade in hand, a mask covering his face. This was not a simple thief or convenient robbery. The air was fraught with a tension that told her one thing only: He meant to kill her.

As the stranger neared she noted his height and frame with better perspective. It wasn't Felix. Disappointment washed through her as she realized the strength of her attacker was unknown, his skills untested, though she wasn't fearful of a fight. She had her knives. She had her wits and a heap of frustration to work out. She was ready.

With only a few seconds to spare, she drew her blade and dropped low to roll away from the oncoming thug, jumping to her feet on the other side of the narrow alley. He pivoted with unforeseen grace, his hulking form bearing down on her with barely three strides between them. A slant of moonlight caught on his weapon's edge, warning her of his position in the otherwise black confines where they both blended seamlessly into the darkness, two shadows at war with each other.

He advanced again, a grunt of dissatisfaction escaping his face hidden by a dark cloth where only his eyes were revealed. He was too large to withstand a long fight and Scarlett intended to exhaust him and gain another advantage. She dodged the arc of his arm, the knife blade less than an inch from her nose and then she pivoted fast to set into an erratic run, darting from left to right, in case he thought to bury his dagger in her back.

Yet despite his size, he kept pace, one narrow passage after another, the warren of alleyways and alcoves a labyrinth of confusion. Unable to pause long enough to distinguish her surroundings, she rushed to the right with blind hope she hadn't confused her bearings but it took less than a heartbeat to recognize her mistake.

This lane ended in a stone wall twenty paces ahead. She'd need to fight for her life or she'd never see Ambrose again. The startling realization, that he was her first thought, that he was worth fighting for, *that they were*, flooded her with determination. She wanted to feel his kiss again, his arms wrapped tightly around her, the weight of him atop her as they made love.

No, she wouldn't die tonight.

But someone else would.

She stopped running, shed her cloak and flattened her body against the wall melting into the inky blackness, as lost as the morning mist at dawn. His heaving grunts of exertion and flat-footed tread alerted his arrival seconds later and she sprang from the side, looping an arm around his neck, her body supported on his back as she leveraged her knife against his throat. The collar of the hood he wore provided him with protection but not so much he couldn't feel the bite of her blade. He rolled his shoulders and attempted to dislodge her but she held fast.

"Drop your knife. Don't move."

He shrugged again, hoping to gain the advantage and drop her from her perch, but then she heard the clatter of his weapon as it fell to the cobbles and echoed in the dank air. Maintaining pressure with the knife at his throat, she ordered him to the stone wall so his mask-covered cheek lay flat against the stone.

"What do you want?" She pressed harder on the blade to ensure he understood she possessed no patience. He was a big man, heavyset, yet it was hard muscle not soft excess that gave him his size. He'd kept pace with her and she didn't doubt he was already regaining his endurance and plotting how to reverse their positions. "Answer me."

"You ask a lot of questions, Scarlett."

His voice was gruff and she didn't recognize the tone. He could be any hired thug carrying out someone else's specific instructions. But he knew where she'd be tonight, which meant he'd watched her and tracked her habits. That thought alone made him dangerous indeed.

"Who sent you and what do you want?" She tightened her grip on the hilt of her knife and angled the blade deeper. She had no qualms about slicing through the fabric to pinch at his skin.

"I wonder if they've gotten to your duke yet. Informed him that your body was found in the Thames. Do you think he will be upset? Mourn your passing? Or will he move on to another whore and forget all the trouble you've caused him?"

Alarm, icy cold and sharp, sluiced through her veins while the frightful image she dreamed a few nights ago, of Ambrose's corpse facedown in the murky waters, a knife protruding from his back, flashed to mind with vivid alarm. What did they want with Aylesford? Did they mean him harm? What would they gain?

Silence.

It was her fault. She'd stirred up a hornet's nest with all her questions. She'd invited him into a world he barely understood. How was it all connected?

"Close your mouth or I'll make a new hole in your neck." She noticed her voice shook and steeled herself against emotion, unwilling to allow him to see how his words affected her.

"I'm sure they've dropped him in the river to feed the leeches by now. It's high tide and one less duke matters little in my world."

Not in mine.

Her heart pounded though she could hardly breathe, her pulse in a furious sprint. Too many thoughts pressed in on her. It was a novice mistake to be distracted by a criminal's guff. It only took the slightest hesitation to allow the upper hand—

He jerked free, wrestling for her knife before it went flying, landing somewhere in the darkness far from where they stood. She acted quickly but he overpowered her, shoving her against the same wall, one bare hand pressing down on her temple to keep her head turned, the other wrapped around her throat.

"You've run out of warnings, Scarlett. You've asked too many questions and turned over too many rocks. You should have minded your own business. But you didn't, did you, Scarlett?" He squeezed tighter. "Such a pretty name. I imagine your face turning the same color right about now."

Without the moon, they were drenched in darkness. The stale heat of his breath struck her face and the sensation was ominous, as if death itself had come to claim her. His body prevented her from moving her arms, but she still had a small dagger in her pocket. Just a two-finger blade. If she was going to die, she would fight first. She squirmed in an attempt to reach the blade, but couldn't gain any space. Kicking at his legs she managed to shift slightly and free one hand to claw at his fingers where he held her neck. She gripped his knuckles, attempting to peel them away, skimming over a large ring on his fourth finger. The knowledge propelling her to fight harder. She had to warn Ambrose. She had to break free.

Grabbing hold of his pinky finger, she forced it backward at an unnatural angle, the sudden pain enabling her to shrug free for a gasp of air, twist and delve into her pocket. Her fingers wrapped around the blade and without another thought she pulled it loose and blindly thrust it forward.

He howled in pain, gripping his crotch and backing away with a string of curses, but she didn't wait to reclaim her knife or issue further pain, the temporary distraction was just what she needed for escape. All she could think about was Ambrose and the fear that someone was sent to kill him.

CHAPTER 22

Jamison showed her to the front drawing room without hesitation. His expression showed no shock considering her state of disarray. Apparently, he'd been specifically instructed in regard to her visits. The knowledge pleased her and at the same time elicited a prod of concern. What did their relationship amount to anyway?

Ambrose entered before she could consider the problem. He looked wonderfully disassembled, his shirtsleeves rolled back to reveal strong forearms and his collar agape at the neck. She might have admired him further, noting every masculine detail, but the situation was too dire for that.

"What happened? Are you all right?"

The alarm in his voice prompted her expedient explanation. "I was attacked. The stranger told me they were coming for you." A tremor ran through her words and she hated the show of emotion.

Ambrose thrust his fingers through his hair. He did not take the news well. Purposefully striding toward her, he stopped short and looked her over twice before he dragged her into his arms, his mouth coming down on hers with unerring accuracy. The kiss began rough, an affirmation she was unharmed and safe within his grasp, but it soon gentled into gratitude and something she couldn't label but caused her to feel precious and cherished.

Even after the kiss ended, he kept her pressed to his chest, her ear to his heart, for several long minutes. Then he carefully pulled away and threaded his fingers through the loose strands of her hair. Her body was already synchronized to his every movement, whether rash or subtle, and she noticed how the further rumpled he became, the stronger her desire grew.

Seeking to reclaim some semblance of clear thinking, she shifted the subject back to where it should be. "I didn't get a clear look at his face. Not for lack of trying but between the darkness and his concealment, I never saw him although his body shape and movements are another matter."

"No. I need you to leave this entire matter in my hands now." His words may have been phrased with concern, but all she heard was ducal command accompanied with a firm shake of his head.

"What?" Shock overrode anger for a beat.

"This back-alley miscreant—"

"You mean, the clever cunning nob," she countered. "He was wearing a thick ring. No common petty vagrant can afford the luxury of heavy gold and gemstones."

"Whoever it may be, the search for this man has put you in harm's path and I can't have that."

"You can't have that?" Annoyance laced each word despite she sounded like a bloody parrot. She couldn't believe he meant to remove her from further inquiry when she was the one *who'd saved him* in Wapping. Too many conflicting emotions beat at her now.

Did he think she and the other Maidens of Mayhem were frivolous females who pursued justice for entertainment, ready to abandon the cause when the situation grew difficult? It was more than insulting. Didn't he have confidence in her? Anger lit her temper as she stared right back at him. Her mulish expression and stony silence invited him to continue.

"There are times when I don't even think you're careful." He'd softened the words, though that made the matter no better.

"Careful is what gets you killed." He would add insult to their discussion and criticize her as well?

"Scarlett." His cultured voice rang with derisive authority. He closed the distance between them and she was overwhelmed by his heat and the masculine scent of his shaving lotion.

"The very fact that you're using the word *killed* proves my point. I can't have you in danger more than you already tempt fate."

The sincerity in his words spoke to her heart, still there was no excepting he meant to dismiss her involvement. Raising her eyes to his, she asked him an important question. "Why?"

"Because I care about you," he answered at once, reaching out to stroke the pad of this thumb across her lips. "It would be better if I call the authorities—"

"No." She stepped away from him. "You're going about this all wrong." Annoyance laced her reply though she fought against it. She didn't wish to be contrary, but he wouldn't listen.

"My word carries weight with Bow Street. They won't ignore a duke."

She'd just escaped a harrowing violent attack where the perpetrator taunted her. Aylesford was already a target, and yet he insisted she step aside. She would agree to placate him, but she wouldn't obey. That would be a fool's decision.

He pulled her back into his arms while she muddled through these thoughts, relieved he didn't press her for an answer, apparently convinced his ducal authority extended to her as well.

The pleasure of feeling his hands unpin her hair, fan through the lengths, and gently rub the base of her neck was near mesmerizing.

I love him.

Thoughts like that were too dangerous to entertain and she blinked hard against the emotion.

"I couldn't bear if anything happened to you. If you were to disappear or be injured." He kissed her temple and she raised her eyes to his. "Do you trust me?"

"Yes." She stared at him, a struggle of emotion passing through her before she continued. "But trust isn't the issue here. It's just . . ." She paused as she collected the right tone. "I was worried about you." She'd never told him about her dream and she wouldn't do so now. Her intuition never failed her and yet in this, it was unthinkable.

"I won't allow anything to happen to you, Scarlett. And they won't be coming for me either. Those are empty threats meant to scare you into compliance. My home is a fortress and my servants infallible. You have nothing to fear."

Confidence firmed his voice and practically radiated from him. Command and control were in every aspect of his bearing, but in this he was beyond comprehension. Criminals ignored law and wrote a code all their own.

Still, she had too many feelings for him. She'd told herself not to love him. She'd tried to lock her heart up tight, but she'd failed. And now he made it worse by wishing to protect her and keep her safe.

Ambrose kept a stranglehold on his temper in an attempt to keep calm and carry on his conversation with Scarlett, but what he really wanted to do was find the person who'd attacked her and pummel the man into oblivion. He took another evening breath and matched her eyes.

She might have been taken from him.

She might have been killed.

Belatedly he realized he needed to put aside his anger and offer her what she truly needed. He walked to the bellpull and summoned his butler, instructing Jamison to have a hot bath delivered abovestairs along with a hot meal.

He was a selfish bastard, consumed with rage on her behalf and in that he'd neglected the horrific trial she'd experienced. A wash of pride swept through him to know she'd returned directly to Aylesford House. She'd come to him.

Now he needed to show her she'd made the right decision. At the moment, arguing over the process was a poor choice. He'd reacted poorly, but he'd make it up to her.

"You've been through a horrible ordeal." He returned to her side and gathered her within his arms again. "It's well past midnight and you need to rest." When she remained silent, he continued, "I've instructed the staff to prepare a guest room. A hot bath and meal will be waiting for you abovestairs. It's the least I can do after you worried on my behalf."

He sensed her indecision, felt her tense for a fleeting moment in his arms. She was independent and strong, so unlike the delicate, often frail women who decorated the *ton's* ballrooms. He hoped she would see reason for practicality, if not any other justification.

"Thank you."

She settled her head over his heart and for a few blissful moments he held her, not knowing where the future would lead but grateful for this night they shared together.

Somehow, she always knew she'd end up in his arms, despite her better sense or determination to avoid the situation. Her intuition knew. Her heart did as well. And now she was here in his bed at Aylesford House. In wait of a duke. She'd accomplished the opposite of her plan and fallen in love with a man who was off limits. No good could come of it. Except this one night.

As he'd promised a wonderful meal and decadent bath awaited her abovestairs. She'd sunk into the scented water, closed her eyes and eased her muscles, allowing the flighty and fanciful thoughts she long ago abandoned to dance behind her closed lids. This was the life genteel ladies lived. Rosewater baths and delicious hot plates, too many to choose which one tasted best.

There'd been strawberries under a glass cloche. She had no idea how he'd managed that. But her experience with dukes was limited to one. She'd dipped each ripe red berry in a saucer of thick cream and savored the taste on her tongue. She never envied the life led by ladies of high society, she never wished for more than what was her due, but it was hard not to imagine the security found in such an existence.

She had no way to repay Ambrose for his generosity. She knew he expected nothing. Long before she rose from the bath, she'd decided to give him something she'd never relinquished to anyone before. *Control.* Or at least, in a matter of speaking.

Once her decision was made, she reveled in anticipation. For her gift was just as much for herself as Ambrose. He couldn't be hers forever, but he could be for just one night.

She dressed in her chemise only and padded down the hallway to his chambers. Her heart pranced in her chest. Her pulse skipped along with it. Then she'd climbed into his bed and waited, every tick of the ornate gilt clock on his mantel a reminder of how precious this evening would be.

At last, the snick of the door latch told her he'd entered. Only the glow of two candles lit the room though a fire roared in the hearth on the opposite wall.

She watched him undress, first his coat and waistcoat, his cravat and then with a masculine roll of his shoulders and flex of his biceps, his shirt. One by one he stripped away his fine tailoring and esteemed heritage until she saw only the man, all heated smooth skin and hard muscle. Her heart pounded with hope, appreciation and too many other emotions. She wanted this. She wanted him. But just for this one night.

He didn't speak as his fingers set to work on the buttons of his falls, though his eyes never left hers, their language not one to be heard, but felt. Silence blanketed them, the room fraught with a lovely quiet. He couldn't have expected to find her in his bed and yet he made no objection, said no words, as if him coming to her was the most natural action in the world. Purer than drawing air and breathing.

When he discarded his smalls, he came to the bed and she rose on her knees to welcome him. He clasped the hem of her chemise and raised it over her head to accept her invitation. Watching his every movement, she allowed him to look her over thoroughly, seeing the flare of desire spark in his eyes, the hard set of his jaw. He didn't hesitate and leaned in to capture her mouth in a deep kiss.

He murmured something and she murmured back, her fingers

finding his bare shoulders, delighting in the shifting play of muscle as he settled on the bed and they lay back on the mattress. She inhaled, a surge of emotion welling within her. She loved him. The despairing condition gripped her so violently her exhale seized in her lungs. She forced herself to breathe. She couldn't love him. That choice promised pain. This night could only be pleasure. Nothing else. Pleasure for both of them, enough to last a lifetime.

He gathered her to his chest and kissed her tenderly as if she was precious and cherished. She tucked the feelings away to keep in her heart. She might never experience the same again.

Ambrose hardly recognized himself, the desire to devour Scarlett so great he feared he'd frighten her if he didn't tamp down his ardor. Bared before him, she was more beautiful than he'd imagined and he'd spent an inordinate amount of time doing just that. But now she was in his arms. In his bed. He wouldn't waste a moment more.

He kissed her with the reverence she deserved, this lovely, strong, intelligent woman who'd come into his life under the most unlikely circumstances and changed him forever. She made a soft noise in the back of her throat, part gasp, part moan, and he swallowed both, wanting to have her breath inside him. He'd become nothing more than a randy scoundrel, anxious for any taste of her and yet she'd awakened a freedom in him he didn't know he'd possessed. She made him feel alive.

Her hair, gloriously long, fanned out across the linens in silken strands that begged for his attention. He didn't know where to touch first, so many temptations lay before him.

"Is this what you want, Scarlett?" He suspected it was her first time and was unquestionably impacted by her gift. He had to be sure she wanted him as much as he desired her.

"Yes." She reached up and stroked her fingers down his cheek, placing her palm there before she gently pulled him into another long kiss.

He'd never bedded an innocent, his mistresses of the past were all women of experience and yet none of them ignited his passion as Scarlett did. And while she was likely more knowledgeable than a debutante that didn't detract from the discomfort she might feel. He would need to go slowly and bring her pleasure upon pleasure. He wanted her to experience only joy. She'd already had enough pain to last a lifetime.

He eased beside her and while their kiss continued, he smoothed a hand down her shoulder, lower to skim over her full breasts, the tips tight against his palm. Over and over again he traced back and forth until she arched into his touch, hungry for more. He trailed tender kisses down the curve of her neck, across the gentle skin of her collarbone to the slope of her shoulder. For a woman who was always so strong, who yielded a knife with lethal grace, fought for dignity and valiantly withstood life's hardships, she was silken and soft in his arms, tender and loving.

He traced his other hand down her rib cage, skimming over the curve of her hip, barely touching though he reveled in her response, the noises she made in the back of her throat erotic and enticing. He broke their kiss, bit her chin and then lowered his head to her breast. She shivered as his exhale teased the rosy tip before he took it in his mouth. This woman who was all strength and will allowed him to explore her body, pliant and supple beneath his mouth, tempting and delicious with each sweep of his tongue. Her hands gripped his shoulders, her fingertips digging into his muscle as she embraced sensation. Tonight he would claim her, bury himself deep inside her heart for always.

CHAPTER 23

Scarlett knew the physical workings of intercourse. She'd grown up in a house where sex was a matter of business, not love, and had seen too much as a child though she had little experience with the emotions entailed. But every kiss and nuance, every tender touch Ambrose offered her, demanded she believe otherwise. When he slid his fingertips over her nipples, a shock of pleasure arrowed straight through her as sharp and keen as a knife's blade. Then her body rebelled against her. Yearning for more. Yearning for him to touch her again, soothe away the pain and kiss away her worries. Anything to cease the strange restlessness inside. Her breasts grew heavy and aching while below, between her legs, she grew wet with want, an unanswered pulse of desire and greed taking hold. She wanted more. She wanted him on top of her. His body pressed to hers. Inside her. Filling her. Claiming what she'd given to no other man.

He stroked over her hip, a dotting of gooseflesh fast to race over her skin, and she wriggled with impatience. Why did he torture her so? Why didn't he climb on top of her and push himself inside like she'd come to understand the process?

His body was beautiful. All strong sinew and hard muscle. His gaze intense and dangerous. He was a man with one intention. She was his. At least for this night.

I love you. No. She couldn't say it. How ridiculous and naïve he'd think her to profess her love because a duke took her into his bed.

He leaned down, his hair brushing under her chin to tease her further, his exhale hot against her skin and then, his mouth, liquid fire, nipping and sucking at her breast until she truly believed she would die from the wanting, the constant drum of impatience and yearning, sparking over and over in the very depth of her soul.

She reached down, clumsily brushing against his hip, seeking some kind of retribution for the ecstasy and agony he wreaked upon her. He released her and pulled back, his hair a tousled mess, his eyes determined and dark.

"Are you all right?" he asked, his voice low and gravelly. Proof he was affected as she.

"I want to touch you."

A wicked gleam lit his eyes. As if he never considered *she* might wish to explore *his* body. It both delighted and annoyed her, but no emotion could take hold as long as she stared into his eyes.

He leaned back on the bedpost, devastatingly handsome, in a masculine pose that she knew she'd remember forever. "I am your servant, my lady."

Again, his answer should have angered her, but she experienced only pleasure, the heat between her legs too demanding, the surge of her pulse and thrum of her heart too insistent to bother with words.

She rose up on her knees before him, kicking the bed linens out of the way as she leaned in to press her lips to his. Her breasts skimmed across his chest, the dusting of hair there another layer of sensation. His erection pressed between them, large and hard, and as she slid her tongue into his mouth she encircled his cock with her fingers, the skin velvet smooth and hot in her grasp.

He jerked at her first touch and she paused, unsure if she'd hurt him, but he murmured encouragement with a humbling *yes* that rumbled from his chest.

Still, he was not one to be tortured alone. He placed a hand on her hip, around to her bottom to slide her closer still and then, when she'd nestled against him, he slipped his fingers into her sex. They stayed that way together on the mattress, their bodies intertwined, each feeling the other's heat, and she realized she'd never forget this moment. Never live another that would ever compare.

"You are mine tonight. All mine."

"You say that as if I'm your possession." She breathed deeply, unsure how he would receive the words. "I'm my own woman."

"Of course." He spoke against her mouth, unwilling to break their kiss. "But you own my heart. I am yours. Completely. Implicitly."

His confession took her by surprise and humbled her into silence until need demanded she act. She was anxious and curious, desperate to alleviate the fierce yearning. He took advantage of her position, sliding his fingers farther into her heat, finding the very spot that pulsed and demanded attention.

This was what she wanted. To be touched and adored. To be loved. She was vulnerable, weak with need, and anxious for more. Every time he slipped his fingers into the slick wetness of her body, she experienced a heightened tremor. More. She rocked against his hand, wanton, driven by impatience. *More.* And he stroked her faster, insistently driving her toward release, caressing her until the sensitivity was too much to bear.

Her climax came fast and with such startling intensity, she cried out. It was shameless the way she bore down on his hand, easing the ache and at the same time prolonging the sensation, not wanting it to end and begging for it to stop all the same. She'd never experienced such freedom and, at the same time, utter vulnerability. Limp with pleasure, she collapsed against his chest and they stayed that way while she reclaimed herself. He stroked her back, threading his fingers through her hair, and waited as if he knew what she'd just realized and he wished to give her all the time she needed to reassemble.

But she wasn't so easily fooled. If her body could revel in utter ecstasy, so could his, and she sought him out with the intension of driving him into sensual madness. Life taught that practice

helped one hone a particular skill, but she suspected her innocence and curious exploration is what undid Ambrose's discreet
decorum. She reached up and mussed his hair. She liked when he
looked less than perfect, like he did the evening he was attacked
in the alleyway. It helped blur the lines separating their worlds.

She gently pushed against his broad shoulders, the skin smooth
and hot beneath her fingertips, the play of muscles an enticing
temptation. With him on his back on the mattress and her kneel-
ing at his side, she continued her study, wanting to learn every
nuance of his body, each indentation and scar that embodied the
glorious man in front of her on the bed linens.

He closed his eyes and she would have given all her personal
belongings to know what he was thinking but now wasn't a time
for questions and words. She wished only to bring him to the same
breaking point as he'd driven her moments before. Drawing on
ill-gained knowledge and generous imagination she raised herself over him and settled across his thighs, straddling the muscles
and allowing her complete access to every part of his body. She
glided her fingertips over his well-defined chest, skimming over
his tawny brown nipples, and was rewarded with the immediate
jolt and flex of his pectorals, his jaw held tight.

Threading her fingers through the hair there, she marveled at
its coarseness, drawing little circles and lines with her index finger, which seemed to please and torment him at the same time.
Then she traced the kite-string of hair, down, down, lower, over
the ridges of his abdomen, tense and motionless, passing his navel
to his pelvis where his erection jerked in a bid for her attention.

He was large, but she never expected him not to be. He was big
in all ways, powerful and strong. He was hers for this one night.
She wouldn't waste any more time with looking when she could
be feeling and tasting. She lowered her mouth to his, kissing and
at the same time rocking slightly, the lengths of her hair drawing
over his shoulders and upper arms, his hands settling on her hips
as if to stop and encourage her all the same.

She didn't allow her body to come in contact with his just yet.

To settle over him would be to miss out on so much pleasure and anticipation, and she wanted better for both of them. Still, he was accustomed to commanding and slid one hand away from her hip and around to nestle between her legs where she was drenched with wanting. She gasped, breaking their kiss and sitting upright.

"So wet and hot, soft as mink and twice as decadent."

She wasn't accustomed to fancy words and compliments. She'd never considered her body desirable. She almost lost her way for a moment.

But no. She meant to drive him wild. To etch into his memory a sensual experience so untamed and gratifying he'd never replicate or replace it, no matter what his future held. Sliding backward she escaped his tender caresses and moved her sex against his thick erection, sliding down the length and up again.

He seized, his thigh muscles hard as rock beneath her.

"Christ." He spoke the word through clenched teeth and she was secretly pleased at his distress. He hardly cursed. To drive him to take the Lord's name in vain was quite an achievement. "If you do that again, I warn you, I will ravish you completely. There will be no more play in this game."

She laughed, soft and husky, as she repeated the same movement, brushing her sex against the top of his erection and then sliding down the hard, pulsing length with just enough pressure.

She'd called his bluff and he was having nothing for it.

With one swift movement he had her on her back and beneath his delicious weight. It felt so good she reveled in it, the action somehow forcing her to acknowledge how real the moment had become. Her face must have displayed shock because as they matched eyes he smiled, that handsome grin that made her insides quiver, and then he laughed, a deep, rich baritone, that made her want to laugh in kind, the sound reverberating through her entire body. If only she could capture the sound in a jar to cherish, to take out and listen to when her loneliness returned.

Her heart drummed against her rib cage, demanding she take notice of it. She loved this man. It served no one any longer to deny it. She could never share those feelings with him, too dangerous and precious. But she knew it with every shred of her consciousness. She loved him. If only this night could last forever.

His upbringing had been staid, traditional and inflexible. From the moment he'd drawn air on the day of his birth, his life was planned, enhanced and accomplished. Surrounded by rules set forth by his heritage, he'd become the duke and fulfilled his purpose, but what if he'd sacrificed too much? Being the fourth Duke of Aylesford meant leaving Scarlett behind. Saying farewell and never looking back. The idea slayed him, pierced his soul and cleaved his heart.

Yet if they could not have a future, they would have this one night. A memory to be replayed over and over when he wished he'd been born a regular commoner, not a nobleman who owed England loyalty and duty, not a peer with an obligation to protect even when the recipient of his protection believed herself indifferent.

He looked into Scarlett's face and that wish multiplied a hundredfold. She was beautiful, composed of strength and resilience, hope and generosity. Was it any wonder he'd become captivated? And tonight, she was his.

He settled between her silky thighs and she opened to him without hesitation. Braced above her, his weight supported on his arms, he couldn't wait to drive into her wet heat, his body anxious though his mind chastised that fervent need.

She stared back at him as if she divined his thoughts, knowing the struggle of his emotions. Perhaps feeling the same. She wriggled beneath him and he discarded his maudlin remorse. They could share this one night. One night that neither one of them would ever forget.

She reached up and placed her hand on his jaw. He swallowed, touched by her desire to assure him. He dropped his head down to hers, nuzzling kisses across her cheek, finding her mouth to deepen the gesture, his body strung tight.

He nudged his aching erection against her sex, slick from her climax and deliciously wet. She wanted him as much as he wanted her. Her hand fell to his hip as if to hurry him along. He wouldn't disappoint.

Her lids closed as he pushed himself inside her. She murmured something lovely and he was enchanted for several beats of his heart, but the need grew too great and he pressed forward, her body yielding though she was hot and tight. He struggled with his own need as he allowed her time to accommodate his thickness. Sweat beaded his brow as he gave way to a solid rhythm, sliding in and out, her body accepting him now, soft and willing.

Sensation raced through him with the speed of a lightning strike, over and over, the delicious friction almost too much to withstand. She began to move with him, matching his pace and arching upward to drive him deeper. Her fingers gripped his forearms, her nails biting into his skin. He wouldn't last very long if she continued her unknowing torment. Thrust after thrust notched his hunger for her higher, weakening his resolve. She had him tied in knots and aching to spend inside her, but he couldn't. The past had already treated Scarlett so unfairly, he would never steal her future away. She rolled her hips forward and urged him to sink deeper still. He complied without hesitation. Deeper, as if he could forever remain inside her.

Just one more stroke, he promised himself, and then just another until her body clenched and trembled beneath him, his name a whisper of pleasure on her lips.

With a growl of regret to accompany the sweet agony, he rolled to the side and spilled his climax in the sheets. Time seemed to cease. He relished the absolute intensity until sensation subsided. He took a minute to clean himself and move the linens aside before he drew her closer, nestled against his heart.

"Ambrose?"

Her raspy murmur teased his skin and he nodded, unwilling to break their perfect moment.

"I had no idea."

This time her voice held a note of wonder and he smiled, pleased he was her first, although with that conclusion came the implication there would be others. Some unfamiliar and ugly emotion twisted inside him like a dagger to the gut. He wanted to keep her all to himself.

He couldn't keep her.

He gathered her closer as if by doing so he could ward off reality. Yet with that same intuitiveness that at times caused him to wonder if she wasn't otherworldly, she sighed against his chest and whispered in not too quiet a voice, "You are Aylesford. You can do whatever you like."

"If only it were that easy, love."

He drew her closer, nestled beside his heart and held her until her breathing evened and she lay fast asleep in his arms.

CHAPTER 24

"How is it you are acquainted with the widow, Lady Wycombe? I knew the late viscount. He was a good man and shrewd negotiator. It is a stroke of sadness he was taken from her at such a young age."

They were cozied together in bed, her head resting on his broad shoulder and Ambrose couldn't think of a time when he was ever more content to do absolutely nothing, unworried of the hour or goings-on beyond his home. This time was an unforeseen gift. He played with her hair, fascinated with the length and silkiness, enchanted by the feel of it strewn across his chest.

He narrowed his eyes and looked down his nose to confirm she was still awake. She hadn't answered or moved since he'd asked the question and he could only assume she was either sifting through truth to determine what she would reveal or fabricating what she believed would be a suitable lie.

Another moment and she huffed a soft breath. Apparently, she'd come to some sort of reluctant decision.

"Julia Wycombe and I met through unlikely circumstance several years ago when she visited Chelsea Old Church. We met in the churchyard. She was visiting to bring donations and I was caught unaware."

Apparently more comfortable with the subject, Scarlett turned and propped up on her elbow, her head supported on her flattened hand. Silky strands of her hair whispered over his chest as she moved. The sheet covered most of her though one creamy smooth shoulder remained exposed.

"I was collecting candles."

"For the church?" He was sadly remiss at ladies' charitable works. While his mother was active in organizations for the less fortunate, he'd been groomed to be a duke from the day he first drew air and had no experience with the female responsibilities in his household.

"To sell."

She must have sensed his confusion. She placed a hand on his chest, weaving her fingers through the mat of hair there and smoothing over his heart. She went still, as if measuring his heart-beat before she continued. "I would collect the wax stubs left be-hind when visitors lit a candle in the name of a loved one and sell them down at the docks. The few coins I managed bought my food for the day."

He hadn't expected that. He hadn't expected anything that involved Scarlett from the moment they'd met. He wondered if beneath her palm where it lay over his heart she could feel the tremor of unsettling emotion moving through him. Her struggles were real, tangible and sorrowful and yet she was buoyant . . . utterly beautiful, her gray eyes bright with happiness.

"Anyway," she continued seemingly unaware of his awe, "Julia knew right away what I was about and approached me with an of-fer to join her for lunch. I suppose she thought me an extension of her charitable works. Either way I'd be foolish to turn away a meal, so I agreed. We became friends after that. She introduced me to two other ladies with exacting ideas about the female situation and we formed a little group. I thought of the name for it.

"At first, we truly caused mayhem as society has a problem accepting females as equals. No one welcomed us or our inter-ference even if it aided in a dangerous situation. But we quickly realized we were managing the problem incorrectly and we adjusted. Greater society prefers to remain blind to the poverty-stricken and destitute."

She stopped abruptly and he assumed she'd either admitted more than she ever intended or purposely held something back. It could be both for all he knew. So much was left unexplained and yet he wouldn't pry into that part of her life unless she wished to share. He could feed her, clothe her, though. Anything she desired. That he could do.

"Aylesford House has the finest chef in Mayfair. What would you like for dinner tonight? I will have Jamison inform the staff there's been a change in menu and we'll dine here in my bed-chambers, that way we need not get dressed."

His outlandish suggestion provoked a giggle that pleased him. She smiled, a sparkle in her brilliant gray eyes. Lord, she was delightful. He'd received lesser reactions when he'd presented sapphire necklaces and diamond earbobs to mistresses in the past. How was it she had so little and yet gave so much? She protected others and sacrificed generously when her life had been nothing but hardship from the start.

"Food never mattered much." She wrinkled her nose. "As long as I had *something* to eat."

"Come now, there must be a particular dish you'd like this evening." He reached below the coverlet and tickled her abdomen. "I swear I heard your stomach complain when we were making love."

Aghast, she swatted at his arm though laughter accompanied the assault. "You're terrible."

He watched her. No one dared ever insult him. Except Martin and that didn't count for much. He grinned, unable to explain the joy her words gave him. She was an eternal surprise and by that she brought out qualities in him he didn't know he possessed or at the most they'd been long forgotten, buried under duty and obligation. Anxious to continue their banter, he prodded her in a stern tone. "I'm waiting."

"I have all I want at the moment, thank you." She laced her fingers with his beneath the sheet and pulled his hand to her side.

He swallowed whatever clever quip he might have shared. Her confession warranted he be completely in the moment.

"I've always wanted to try a sugarplum though."

She shifted on the pillow and he needed to turn now so he could see her. Their conversation was about food and he couldn't deny the sense of closeness it provoked. It rivaled the precious intimacy they'd shared making love, this getting to know each other time.

"I doubt a platter of sugarplums would make for a very good dinner."

She laughed again and he wanted to devour her for she was far more delicious than any sugary confection.

"Well, you asked." Indignation underscored her words.

"Indeed, I did." He wondered at her daily fare. At her habits. All at once a million or more questions bombarded his mind and he wanted all of them answered immediately so he would know everything about the enchanting woman in his bed. An image of her in Pembroke's ballroom came to mind and his thoughts spun in a different direction. He yearned to see her befitted in the same majestic manner he regarded her.

"What is it that you dream of when you allow yourself to dream?" He would learn everything thing about her. Every wish and fantasy and then he would provide them for her.

"Not what you might expect."

"Tell me and let me decide."

"It can't be purchased." She shook her head slightly. "And this is a ridiculous conversation."

"Humor me then." He wasn't always successful at evoking a personal response from her, often abandoning his question when it caused her ill-ease, but this time he was determined to succeed and obtain an answer.

"Security."

She didn't say anything more and he allowed time to stretch, the answer to settle.

"To feel safe. No matter how much I train myself to be prepared for the world, the luxury of security evades me."

The gravity of her admittance held the room in somber contemplation a few beats longer. Then he was fast to change the subject and bring about her smile again.

"I'd like you to have new gowns. You deserve lush velvets and exquisite silks. Gemstones around your neck and in your hair." He knew her mood had shifted before he'd even finished speaking. He reached for her chin and gently turned her to face him, the pillow partially obstructing his view. "What have I said wrong?"

"I am here because I want to be. I want nothing in return."

Some unidentifiable tone colored her words. How had he upset her?

"No." Angry she'd misinterpreted his offer, he attempted to make amends. "As gifts, Scarlett. You'd look beautiful in a wardrobe of expensive fabrics."

"There's no need to try to change me." She did her best to disguise her disappointment but he saw it there in the depths of her eyes.

"That's not what I meant or would ever intend. I sought to give you a gift. You must want for something tangible."

She remained silent and he wished he could read her thoughts, divine her emotions. When at last she spoke, her voice had a serious quality that wasn't there before.

"I do want something."

Relief washed through him. Perhaps he hadn't hurt her feelings after all.

"Anything. Just ask."

"Never stop fighting for what is right for the women in brothels. If you could voice your thoughts for the betterment of females in society, people will listen. No matter what happens between us, what happens to me—"

"Nothing will happen to you." He said the words to blot out the unsettling foreboding that accompanied her statement.

She went quiet and he pulled her into his arms, holding her tighter than necessary as he kissed her hair and inhaled her delicate scent. He couldn't relax, his mind too busy with everything they'd discussed. He offered her gowns and jewels and she asked him to improve society. She was magnificent and selfless. If only she could be his—

"Ambrose." She twisted from his hold and turned so she could face him.

He looked into her eyes and saw such sincerity there an ache blossomed in his chest. What was she going to say? He wasn't sure he wanted to hear it.

"Nothing can ever become of us. Of this."

She gestured between them at the space that separated them. As if it somehow explained what they'd created and excused it from being real.

"All I know is how I feel." He couldn't let her walk away, out of his life never to be seen again. He was too selfish to allow that to happen. How could he go through his days not knowing if she was well? What she faced? Where she went? What color she wore? He would go mad from the wondering.

When the evening began, he'd convinced himself he wanted only this one night. That it would somehow satisfy the enduring craving that wouldn't go ignored. But he was wrong. Terribly wrong.

"This isn't about feelings. If it were, our decision would be much easier."

So, she felt it too. The bond they'd formed. The connection of their hearts. "Then what is it about?"

She'd be hard-pressed to dismiss what they'd experienced as casual or inconsequential. Besides, wouldn't that push against everything she'd regretted about her life? About the girls at the brothel?

"Please don't ask me to define our relationship. The more we talk about it, the more real it becomes and we both know how this will end. Someday you will marry and make a lucky woman your duchess. She will provide you with a family. You will be happy and your title will be secure and you'll forget about me and that's all right. I give you permission to do so."

Tears rimmed her eyes by the time she was finished and he pulled her into his arms, unable to speak. He could never forget her. He didn't want to talk about the future or the duty he knew accompanied the dukedom. She was breaking his heart when she'd only just filled it with love.

"That doesn't have to be our future, Scarlett." He threaded his fingers through her hair but kept her tight against his chest. "We've only just found each other and you're already talking about walking away. It doesn't have to be one night, Scarlett."

Scarlett startled, surprised by his words and alarmed at what his next sentence might be. She turned away, nestled against the beat of his heart so he couldn't see her clench her eyes, willing him not to speak the words that would ruin their evening, spoil the precious beauty of their lovemaking.

"What do you mean?" With eyes still closed she sank her teeth into her bottom lip. Her heart pounded a furious beat. He couldn't say it. *Please don't say it.*

"I could arrange an apartment. We could have many nights like this. You would have somewhere safe to live independently, a place to call your own."

How easy it would be to pretend and live the life of a highborn lady, to create an illusion that tempted with promises of glorious pleasure and endless sensual gratification. How lovely to believe she could be cherished by a duke. Indulged with silks and satins, ribbons and gemstones, but also how temporary.

Inevitably temporary.

The aftermath would leave her with nothing but shame. She couldn't live that way. A depth of unfathomable desolation yawned inside her despite his attention had filled her heart the same way his body had filled hers and eased the emptiness that always existed. "But it wouldn't be mine, would it."

"Of course it would be."

"But you wouldn't be mine, would you?"

He waited too long to reply and whatever infinitesimal sliver of hope had survived in her withered away.

"Like everything in life, there are conditions."

"So in this situation"—she drew a long breath—"I would wait for you, when you wished to come by. When you found time for me . . ."

"It wouldn't be that way. I would see you frequently, but if you wanted me to stop calling, I would. No questions asked. No conditions."

"And we would stay in some apartment. Just the two of us. We couldn't go out." *Like a bird in a cage.*

"Well, as you know all too well, society is ruthless and there are conditions we would need to follow."

His grip tightened as if he knew his words would displease her. And they did. When she remained silent, he went on.

"You've said you never wished to marry, that a husband is not in your future. This offers us a chance to be together."

"Good enough to tup," she whispered more to herself than him, and exhaled deeply. She looked into his eyes, hers finally wide open. She knew their paths would diverge. She just didn't anticipate the pain that would accompany it. She hadn't wanted her last memories to be this uncomfortable, painful conversation. "But that's all."

"Scarlett, the duchy has expectations I cannot ignore."

He placed a hand on her bare shoulder and she shrugged it off, turning her face away and into the pillow so he couldn't see her teary-eyed struggle.

Ambrose knew better than to try to speak further of it. Yet what had she expected of him? He was certain she cared for him or she wouldn't have become angry. Still, he couldn't imagine never seeing her again. That fact alone proved how deeply he cared for her. Eventually fatigue willed out and she fell asleep on the pillow beside him, but his mind was too conflicted to allow him to find rest.

It was half four when he heard a determined knock on the front door. Having released all the servants, he strode to the bedchamber windows overlooking the drive and saw his brother's conveyance there.

What could Martin need at this time of night? Had he found himself in dire trouble again? Ambrose glanced toward the bed where Scarlett still slept. He didn't wish for her to startle awake with the havoc his brother was causing. Drawing up his trousers and nabbing a shirt as he left, Ambrose made his way downstairs and across the hall to the front door. He swung it open ready to wring his brother's neck if this call might have waited.

"I came as soon as I could."

"Come in and stop your jabbering." Ambrose adjusted his shirt, pulled on in haste and half askew. "Why are you here? What couldn't wait until morning?"

"The man with the ruby ring. I know who he is and what he's doing. I learned everything this evening and came here straightaway. We need to act fast. You're in danger."

Ambrose heaved a long sigh to diffuse his initial concern. Scarlett was asleep in his bed upstairs. Their lovemaking was glorious and when he booted his brother out, Ambrose intended to wake her with kisses and caresses to erase away any poor feelings. Then they would make love again before dawn.

"Couldn't all of this wait until the hour is respectable? Why was it necessary to come here now?"

"Because they know. They know that you know and that you've been asking questions. We all might be in danger. Scarlett too."

"Martin, I can assure you no one has anything to fear." He wanted to smile. He couldn't wait to kiss her again. "Scarlett is safe. I'm confident no harm will come to her."

"But how can you know this? Aren't you the least bit worried?"

Martin scowled, his voice heavy with accusation. "I thought you cared for her."

"I do." He gestured toward the door in a hurry to see Martin out. He more than *cared* for Scarlett and had other wonderfully sensual duties to attend. "Stop by later this morning at a civilized hour and we'll talk about everything you've discovered."

"Are you sure? Is this what you want?"

"Absolutely. Now go." Ambrose waited until the door was closed and locked, then climbed the stairs, anxious to return to Scarlett's side, but he never got that far. When he opened the bedroom doors, the terrace doors slammed shut. The bed was empty and Scarlett was gone.

CHAPTER 25

Bound and gagged, Scarlett fought against the strips of linen that held her captive. She had no weapons, no blades, and the irony of that fact cut worse than the cravats that kept her immobile. She'd awoken gasping for air, her mouth covered and her eyes blindfolded. Then, trussed with amazing efficiency, wrapped in a blanket or other soft fabric, she was lifted from the mattress where she'd slept beside Ambrose.

Where was he? What had happened to him? She knew with certainty he'd never allow something untoward to occur, so had they knocked him unconscious? Hurt him? Anything worse sliced into her heart so keenly she couldn't consider it.

Making love with Ambrose last night had opened her eyes to new beginnings. Changed her heart. *Her mind.* About so many things. It caused her to confront her fears and embrace hope, an emotion lost to her when she was a child. She wasn't foolish enough to believe it could ever be more than what they had, but in knowing that she cherished the memory. She would always remember him. And she forgave his unintentionally hurtful suggestion she become his mistress. She forgave him everything because although they could never have more than last night, she loved him. *She loved him fiercely.*

Empowered by that realization, she twisted her wrists in an effort to loosen the knots keeping her tied. She was on the floor in a carriage traveling at a swift pace, that much she could tell, but otherwise the interior was quiet. She had no way to know if someone sat on the bench and kept watch or if her captor had foolishly deposited her and climbed to the driver's box. She would gain her freedom. It was only a matter of how long it took. Unclothed and without her knives she was at a distinct disadvantage, but she'd faced harder circumstances and survived. She needed to return to Aylesford House and save Ambrose. He'd released all his servants. No one would discover him if he lay bleeding on the floor.

Like her mother.

That alone caused her to fight harder against the silks that bound her. She arched her body in an attempt to wriggle free from the heavy cloth imprisoning her. It was difficult to breathe and yet she could gain air, so there had to be an opening somewhere. Rocking to gain momentum, she initiated a roll. The action met with a swift kick to her rib cage. Apparently, she wasn't alone in the carriage. Circumstances just became significantly more complicated.

Someone was going to die.

By his hand.

The someone who had stolen Scarlett.

He cursed an oath, his sharp words heavy with torment and rage as he rifled through her discarded clothing strewn across the floor, a reminder of their night of lovemaking. He reached for her coat. She always carried weapons. Frisking through the pockets he found only her slender flask, his annoyance mounting when her underclothes and gown yielded nothing. In a delayed moment of recollection, he grabbed her boots and withdrew a long knife.

A light knock sounded on his bedchamber doors and he bid Jamison to enter, the loyal servant roused from a sound sleep. The butler eyed him crouched near the foot of the bed with a sleek silver blade in hand and to his credit didn't react in the least.

"Yes, Your Grace."

"Dispatch the messages I've left near the windows." He indicated the walnut drum table across the room with a wave of his hand. "And have my horse saddled and brought from the mews. I'm going out."

Ambrose moved with swift efficiency as he finished dressing, the blade now tucked neatly into his left boot.

"It is almost dawn, Your Grace."

Jamison spoke in a noncommittal tone, though Ambrose knew the man's voiced observation came from a place of concern.

"Secure all the doors and windows. Don't allow anyone in except my brother or Galway. I've explained everything in the messages you're to send to them."

"Yes, Your Grace."

"My horse, Jamison." Ambrose brushed passed the butler, anxious to set out after Scarlett. "Now."

Less than ten minutes later, Ambrose rode hard into the new light. Inside his pocket he had the business card with the address of the contact he'd secured from The Pigeon Hole. The missives he'd sent urged Galway and Martin into motion, and too there was his one additional note to Lady Wycombe. He suspected she knew most everything Scarlett was involved in and could possibly help locate her now.

At least that was his plan. Nothing had followed a sensical course since he first listened to Martin's concerns weeks ago. But he couldn't regret that either because that had brought him to know Scarlett.

He had to find her.

He would find her.

Still, until he spoke to Martin and learned the information his brother had attempted to share, time was his worst enemy.

How could he allow this to happen? One moment Scarlett was wrapped securely in his arms, aglow from their lovemaking, and the next she'd vanished from his bed. She was unclothed, unarmed and vulnerable, and it was his fault. He hadn't considered her theories or suspicions.

He'd kill the man who harmed her.

A rage like he'd never known, primal and raw, filled him so intensely his ears rang from it. He kicked his horse into a harder gallop unsure of every decision, ruled by emotion more than logic.

He hadn't trusted her insight and judgment. Reacting with the same authoritarian command utilized in every ducal exchange, he'd sought control and thereby left her unprotected. He'd failed her.

Failed the woman he loved.

He brought one hand up to pound the center of his chest in an attempt to unknot the ache coiled there.

Someone was going to die today and it wouldn't be Scarlett. Or him.

They had a future to build. There was no need to deny it any longer. He would find her and apologize. He would confess his feelings and somehow convince her to believe him, believe in the two of them. Together.

On any terms.

He was hers to command now.

But first he needed to get her back.

Scarlett was carried and dumped unceremoniously in a cold dark place. Her landing was buffeted by whatever she'd landed on though she still felt the impact on her rib cage where the abductor's boot had connected. She hadn't worked free far enough to be able to view her surroundings, but she was confident if left alone she could wriggle from within the heavy layer wrapped around her. Not wishing to invite further injury that could impede her escape, she decided to wait and be sure she was alone.

Closing her eyes, she envisioned Ambrose as she'd last seen him, propped over her in bed, his handsome face all angles and shadows cast by the fire as he bent to kiss her. Their lovemaking had exceeded any expectation she'd secreted away in a belief she'd never find such a glorious connection. Not in the expected manner of reaching climax, even though the sensual way their bodies fit together transcended her dreams. No, it was the absolute rightness she experienced when she with him. From the very start, when she saw him enter The Scarlet Rose through the rear door, whether she was ready to acknowledge it or not, he'd touched her soul and at some point, stolen her heart.

She blew out a slow breath and avowed she would see him again. If for no other reason than to tell him she loved him. She had no illusions they could be together. Their relationship was an odd one. But Ambrose needed to know the honest emotion in her heart. And just as important, she needed to know what was in his.

Sensing no one, having heard only silence and the heated whisper of her own breathing, she squirmed and wriggled until she eventually inched her way out of the wrapped bindings. From there she maneuvered the gag downward and freed her mouth. Another few minutes and she'd used her teeth to loosen the knots at her wrists. She was free. She was also naked and the room was bare of anything that could cover her. The air temperature was ice cold, a single candle lantern her only source of light and heat. She'd been dropped on a bed, bare of linens, and the one window on the far wall had been boarded up from the outside. A limp length of drapery hung from a crooked rod on one side of the casing. She grasped it tightly and pulled, bringing the panel down with a sharp snap.

She jerked her eyes to the door and wondered if someone waited in another room or had heard her moving about. Nothing happened and after another beat of hesitation, she wrapped the curtain around her body and tucked it in like a strange but somewhat sufficient cocoon.

Being without clothing was a trap in itself but at least she was covered. Still, she had no weapons and with no idea where she was and why she'd been taken or the intentions of her abductors, she'd be foolish to harbor hope.

She sat on the edge of the mattress and clenched her eyes. Where was Ambrose now? Had the men who'd climbed into his bedroom window and taken her first harmed him? Had they left behind any clues that would lead to her recovery? Hope waned.

Just like the man with the ruby ring, she was one person in a city of over a million secured in an unknown location.

On that realization, hope died.

"Tell me where Lady Hammon is being kept." Ambrose slammed Viscount Welles into the ornate mahogany bookcase a second time, the man's head bouncing forward with the jarring strike.

"Don't know," the viscount repeated, his eyes imploring mercy. "I was never part of that plan."

Ambrose loosened his grip around the younger man's neck the slightest degree, his temper on a short leash though he remained cognizant enough to realize he'd get no information from a dead man and Welles was his only connection to the people who'd snatched Scarlett from his bedroom.

When he'd entered Welles's study, he'd shocked the viscount, the man sprawled atop a young girl with her skirts up. She was young and immediately struck with an expression of fearful wariness. In an instant, Ambrose decided she posed no threat and was likely a servant or an acquaintance Welles used for his own gratification. They two jerked upright on the chaise, the gentleman set in motion to object for the intrusion until Ambrose spied the ruby ring on his finger. Then all hell had broken loose. The dark-haired miss hesitated only a moment to right her clothing, before she slipped out the door and beyond his grasp. But it didn't matter. Welles was who he sought for answers, not his paramour.

Scarlett's information had proven true. Welles was tall with a head full of light hair and a medium build. He was a peer and not some back-alley criminal. He shouldn't have doubted her insight. He wouldn't do so again.

The viscount had a lot of explaining to do. Yet for all the man's accounting of a sex trade business where working girls were promised a better life and ultimately sold as gratification slaves to noblemen and customers on foreign lands, Ambrose still hadn't learned Scarlett's whereabouts, and each ticking minute of Welles's bloody longcase clock reminded how time was fleeting and precious. Un-doubtedly Scarlett would fight against her abductors and Ambrose worried what would become of her were the ruthless bastards who'd taken her to use violent force.

Fueled by this rage, he turned his attention back to the lord in his grip. "What do you know? Start talking and speak quickly. My patience is at an end."

"Milord? Your Grace!" A servant stood in the doorframe, his eyes widened in alarm.

"Tell your man to leave off." Ambrose tightened his hold on the viscount lest Welles get the harebrained idea to make use of the distraction. Ambrose had pushed past the stern butler at the door, the element of surprise to his advantage as he'd stormed through the entry hall.

Voices could be heard at the rear of the house so he headed in their direction. Then he'd entered Welles's study with no an-nouncement or hesitation. He was a duke, by God, and he would do whatever the hell he pleased. Especially in regard to Scarlett.

To his credit, Welles had hardly startled once he'd risen from the chaise and actually maintained a modicum of decorum until Ambrose had gathered his cravat in his fist and hauled him against the expensive water silk wall coverings.

"That will be all, Dorster." Welles cleared his throat before he continued. "Release me, Aylesford, I owe you nothing."

"Depending on what you say next, you may owe me your life. I'm not playing lightly here." This seemed to bring about a change of mind in the viscount.

"I'll tell you all I can but I must reiterate I know nothing about the woman you've described. I haven't the slightest idea of her whereabouts. My involvement with my associates and the busi-ness we conduct is a financial investment only."

"How convenient. You reap the profit but keep your hands clean in the process." Another minute passed and Ambrose loos-ened his hold enough to allow Welles freedom. He clenched his teeth against the urge to pummel the viscount for his indifferent complacency. "Go on. Get straight to the point or when I wrap my hands around your neck the next time, I won't be so gentle. Be assured we will discuss your unlawful habits at a later date after I speak to the Prince Regent. But now, I want answers. What is your associate's name and where can I locate him?"

"My investments are my own business and no wrongdoing can be proven." His tone remained assured and cocky.

"Then you should consider your immediate health and well-being as motivation."

"I've already told you I know nothing of where my associate transports the disposable whores—"

Ambrose's fist connected with Welles's jaw, the blow snapping the viscount's head to the left at a sharp angle hard enough to leave him momentarily stunned. Then Welles's eyes lit with rage and he came at Ambrose full force.

The two men fell to the carpet in fisticuffs though it ended quickly thereafter with Ambrose seated atop Welles's abdomen, his palms flat on the viscount's shoulders and arms pinned. He kept himself from drawing Scarlett's knife from his boot, his anger too unpredictable. "Tell me where I can find your associate."

Immobile beneath Aylesford's weight, Welles realized the futility of resisting. "Howell keeps an old shack on a pier in Wapping. The women are taken there and eventually put on a ship to be transported to their final destination. It could be France or Italy, anywhere the customer prefers to keep his new pet."

Ambrose leaned closer, his patience all but run out. "Where? What direction?"

"Thirty-seven Stoney Street."

As soon as Welles uttered the words, Ambrose connected with another sharp jab and put the man to sleep.

CHAPTER 26

The door latch rattled and the panel swung open, the harsh scrape of wood against wood enough to override Scarlett's gasp of surprise.

"Miss Wynn."

"Felix!" She'd been found. She heaved a breath of relief and rushed within a few strides of where he stood, mindful of her nudity beneath the threadbare curtain. Ambrose had had the right of it all along by involving Bow Street. Somehow, the authorities had located her.

"Felix," she repeated, her voice tremulous from the ordeal. "Thank God you're here."

He didn't react immediately but turned and secured the door. Had he subdued the miscreants? Was the threat already eliminated and they were safe now or did he worry for their welfare? When he turned to her again, she wasn't sure it was concern she perceived in his expression. He looked her up and down once, then again.

"For all your adventures, Scarlett, you're still quite innocent, aren't you?" He canted his head as if considering a serious subject. "That will bode well for us in the end."

His comments were strange. He seemed unbothered by her

state of distress and mistreatment, but he spoke again before she could remark on it.

"I brought you clothes." He indicated a bag at his feet she hadn't noticed in her relief to see his face at the door and he handed it forward. She almost reached for it, but a shiver of apprehension skittering down her spine as she noticed he wore a ruby ring on his fourth finger, exactly as described.

Had he taken it from one of the criminals? She marshalled her expression, forcing a grin of gratitude until she understood the situation more clearly. She needed to think, to gain time and sort the circumstances, because something was very wrong. She sensed it as surely as if a wild animal had entered the room, her instincts honed by experience and intelligence that most men underestimated.

"You should get dressed." His tone had become matter-of-fact and she stared at him as he tossed the bag closer to her feet.

"Yes, I need to." She waited for him to take his leave. He couldn't think to stay in the room while she changed. There was no screen for privacy. Even if he worried over her safety, he should at least turn his back. "Did His Grace commission you to find me?"

"No, although Aylesford was quite accommodating. He invited me into his home and allowed me the convenience of learning the floorplan and assessing the staff. I'm told you're very pretty when you sleep. I understand the duke's attraction. My men weren't too rough with you, I hope."

Any remaining doubt evaporated. She took another step, one hand useless as it held the curtain tightly in place. She needed to determine which type of weapon he carried and how many he concealed. She was already at a severe disadvantage. Keeping him talking would provide her with much needed time. "I thought you and I were friends."

"More the pity we couldn't stay that way, Scarlett." Felix shook his head slowly, his laugh hollow and humorless. "But you insisted on asking questions and nosing into things you shouldn't. I tried to warn you it would lead to no good. I've established a lucrative business that turns a pretty profit and I'm not about to allow you to interfere, nor Aylesford for that matter."

"What type of enterprise? Something that harms young women?" He wore a long coat that prohibited her from knowing if he concealed a pistol. Without her knives, she was limited to surprise and cunning as her most effective weapons.

"There's that suspicious nature again." He nudged the satchel on the floor harder with the tip of his boot. "Stop stalling and change your clothes. We won't be staying here much longer."

"You plan to kill me?" Scarlett fought to keep her tone even.

"No one is in danger unless the rules are broken. Everything in life is a choice and decisions have consequences. It's a fairly simple transaction actually."

"You sell women?" She struggled to fit the pieces together and provoke him, anything to throw Felix off guard until she could determine how to escape.

"No." He exhaled loudly, as if annoyed she continued to pester him with questions. "I sell sex. Females, males, it's all part of the operation and depends solely on the predilection of the client. My customers are discreet and particular. You'd bring a very high price if I was inclined to sell you, but I haven't decided exactly what to do with you, Scarlett. You are a rare breed."

She swallowed the black curses that sprang to her tongue. Angering Felix would complicate things. It was better to keep him talking and gloating.

"How do you manage to operate this business within the boundaries of society without being detected? You must be very cunning."

"It's easier than you think. Welles makes contact. He's got a naïve little helper who selects the likeliest girls and then he visits the brothel and convinces the gullible creatures they're bound for a better life. We have a jeweler in Wapping who assists with the transport at the docks. Everything proceeds swimmingly or at least it did so until you started poking around."

"Why are you telling me this?" She knew he meant to kill her. Otherwise every word he'd just uttered would serve to incriminate him, most especially as he knew her association with the duke.

"Not for the reasons you're considering. I've had another idea that may prove more appealing."

Than dying?

"Keep talking." She may as well stall for as much time as possible.

He moved closer now and stared intently into her eyes. She fought the urge to back away. Had she been clothed she would have attacked, kicking and fighting, but she still didn't know if he was armed and any attempt on her part would prove futile while she was wrapped in nothing more than a flimsy curtain.

"Become a part of it."

"What?"

"You'd never again want for money, never go to bed hungry, never watch the nobs have what you do without." He reached forward and wound a loose length of her hair around his finger before he released it. "You can transfer the girls, help them understand how much they'll benefit in their new arrangement, and all the while earn an unholy profit."

"You're suggesting I help you transport girls to supply deviant men with sex slaves?"

"You make it sound so tawdry." He scoffed a harsh sound. "It's hardly different than an arranged marriage or wedding contract."

"That's not true."

"Of course it is." He sneered. "You only wish to see what you want to see. Parents barter their daughters for top dollar and a dowry all the time. Women choose to work in brothels." He shrugged, undeterred. "Your mother traded flesh for coin."

"Don't talk about my mother."

"Have I touched a nerve?" He grinned. "I'm offering you an

opportunity to erase history and embrace a new future. You know you want that."

"You don't know anything about me."

"You'd be surprised what I know. You can consider my offer while we travel." His smile dropped away and his eyes glinted with anger. "Now get dressed."

"What you do is reprehensible, Felix, and I would never be a part of it."

"We'll see about that." He advanced another pace. "I provide a service. My associates and I have taken a more novel approach than most, but there's a demand for what we offer. The women are desperate to leave their work in the brothel and find a more secure life. Most of the girls are settled and happy."

"I don't believe that." She backed away. "You lie to them. You promise them security and a compatible relationship. And what if they are unhappy? What happens to those women?"

"They learn to like it or suffer an unfortunate accident. No one misses them and keeping the client happy is our most important priority. The gentlemen who come to me don't want trouble. Confidentiality and secrecy are of the upmost importance."

"And since you work for Bow Street, you conveniently ignore the unspeakable disappearances, the women promised a better life and sold into a distorted reality. It's horrible and inexcusable."

"It sounds like you painted a pretty picture of a false reality." He grabbed the satchel and pushed it toward her chest. "My patience has run out, Scarlett, and so has this conversation. Get dressed or I'll strip you myself. I'd take pleasure from the task if we had more time."

The way he leered at her caused gooseflesh to dot her skin. She swallowed the words that were fast to her tongue, unwilling to provoke him further. Once clothed she would be more prepared to fight and escape. She took the bag and moved to the farthest corner, turning her back as she carefully removed the day gown and drawers from its contents, all the while keeping Felix in her peripheral vision.

What had happened to Ambrose? Would Felix and his associates act so boldly as to murder a duke? Being he was connected to Bow Street and able to interfere in investigations, her speculation could easily prove true. A sickening feeling drenched her, threatening to derail her determination with self-pitying emotion, but she resisted. She discreetly dropped the curtain and stepped into the cotton drawers, drawing them up as quickly as possible and securing the string. Then she maneuvered her way into the gown, the laces at the back left gaping.

"Don't get any brilliant ideas in your pretty head. It will only bring you to harm in the end."

His shadow shifted on the wall in front of her. *The lantern.* She'd forgotten about the lantern. It was her only means of defense and a useful weapon.

A knock sounded at the door and his attention was divided. She turned, sparing the lantern a fleeting glance as she moved closer. Felix spoke in low tones to someone she couldn't see, his voice a mixture of anger and smugness.

"How foolish he is." Felix closed the door on whoever conspired with him on the other side. "Aylesford must hold you in high regard to stir up so much trouble. Maybe you're worth more than I originally believed. It looks like you've found a nob that enjoys a little slumming now and again."

He was alive.

"Time for us to go." Felix came across the room, his meaty hand reaching for her at the same moment Scarlett grabbed hold of the lantern.

It was only a single candle but in minutes it instigated a magnificent blaze. The well-worn curtain fabric provided ideal tinder and with the fisherman's shed little more than a stack of rotted wooden planks, the hungry flames flourished with voracity. The shed was perched on a rickety pier over the water and used for expedient transport. Now Scarlett knew the reason she'd been held there.

She only looked back once. Felix was inside, knocked unconscious by her hand, the metal lantern useful in striking the blow to his head. If the heat and smoke revived him then he would live. Otherwise, the inevitable fall into ice-cold water could do the trick once the shed collapsed. She'd seen no other person as she'd escaped. Either way, she had important plans that kept her moving forward. Felix's deceit and evil manipulation of the working girls he'd used and sold brought him to this end, not Scarlett.

She scrambled over a low-lying stone wall and down the embankment near the edge of the Thames. The stench of rotting fish replaced the acrid scent of smoke behind her. She searched the shoreline for an empty skiff or abandoned rowboat to move her to safety faster. While she wasn't being pursued at the moment, circumstances had a tendency to change rapidly.

Struggling to discern a vessel in the darkness, she followed the water's edge in hope of finding some kind of transport. The streets weren't safe and the water would be faster. She needed to send a message to Aylesford House. She needed to see Ambrose. To know he was alive and well. To tell him her true feelings before she took her leave.

She stilled and gulped at the air, the pain in her chest acute, stark and sudden. She must have run too fast or pulled a muscle in her struggle for freedom. It couldn't be the thought of never seeing Ambrose again. He was never meant to be hers in the first place. She was too intelligent to attach her future to an illusion of happiness, more fleeting than the puff of her breath in the cold.

Shoving emotion aside, she clambered over a series of knotty ropes holding a lopsided skiff to its mooring. It wasn't much but it would have to do. If she could manage the boat with a single oar and steer to the same culvert where she'd questioned Willie, she'd be able to send a message and regain use of the streets. She wasn't far from where she needed to be, but dawn was fast approaching and she'd rather keep to the cover of night.

Maneuvering along the shoreline with careful haste she eventually reached the culverts at the base of the London Bridge. Abandoning the boat, she hurried toward the street just as the new day dawned. She had no money and nothing of value to barter with a hackney driver. She was on foot with only the ill-fitting boots from the satchel Felix had provided. She ignored how her heels rubbed raw and blistered and instead focused on her one intent, to find Ambrose and secure his safety. Too, she needed to wrap her arms around his strong build and get lost in the comfort he provided. He had to be alive. She would consider no other possibility.

Saying goodbye to him would be the most difficult and heart-breaking task of her life. Harder than finding her mother bled out on the floor of their single-room apartment. Harder than running away and surviving alone in London for a decade.

Again, she pushed troubling thoughts aside and aimed for the street with determined strides. It took over an hour to reach the Wycombe building on Mortimer Street. It was the closest location where she could seek help.

She climbed the stairs and knocked on the door, hoping one of her friends had had need to stay the night as they were often apt to do. Both Phoebe and Diana were involved in ordeals that could lead each of them to remain here. Without her key, Scarlett relied on chance, unlucky as her recent evening had proven.

It was Phoebe who answered, fully dressed and awake despite the ungodly hour. Scarlett watched her friend's unsurprised reception with skepticism. It was almost as if Phoebe had expected her.

"Hurry. Come in. We've all been worried sick over you." Phoebe widened the door and moved aside. "I have distinct instructions from Julia, who received a message from Aylesford."

Another pulse of anxious hope swept through Scarlett. A dead duke couldn't send missives. He was alive. At least, at the time of her abduction, he'd been so. Scarlett stepped over the threshold and followed her friend up the stairs, Phoebe anxious to share what she knew as they moved briskly.

"Are you hurt?"

"I'm fine." Scarlett nodded and waved her hand so Phoebe would continue.

"I have clothes, money and a weapon waiting for you."

They'd reached the drawing room, where on the center table Scarlett could see her friend spoke true.

"I'm concerned for your welfare. We all are. This issue with the brothel has placed you in harm's way too many times. You take too many chances with your own safety."

"We can talk about that later."

"I knew you would say that, so Julia is waiting at Aylesford House."

Scarlett made to change, her movements hurried though her fingers were steadier now. She turned so Phoebe could assist with the ties at her back. "She is? I'll leave straightaway. Why are you here, Phoebe?"

"I've just come from Seven Dials." Phoebe finished the last tie and tapped her lightly on the shoulder. "I'm involved in a hunt of my own, yet it proved fortuitous that I was here to help you as well."

"As soon as this is all resolved, I'm anxious to hear more." Scarlett slipped the smaller of two knives into her cloak pocket and the other in her boot. "I will assist you in any way I can."

"I know that." Phoebe didn't elaborate beyond her answer and shadowed Scarlett to the back door. "Godspeed."

"Thank you." And with that Scarlett left.

CHAPTER 27

Ambrose maneuvered Odin, his horse, through the narrow streets of Wapping, his pounding heartbeat in cadence with the urgent force of the animal's hooves. He could see smoke rising on the horizon in the murky light before dawn though he didn't know if it had anything to do with Scarlett, the view obscured by the incline and elevation.

Within the next few minutes he managed a clearer line of sight to the water where atop a narrow pier, the remains of a fisherman's shack burned brighter than a May Day bonfire. He urged Odin closer until the horse defied his command and Ambrose slid from the saddle and ran toward the flames. Was Scarlett inside? Left bound and helpless to die within the blaze? His heart resisted and mind rebelled.

No.

No. She was too valiant, strong and vibrant. She wouldn't meet her end this way.

Still, he needed to know for sure.

Without hesitation he ran toward the blaze, the dancing flames quick to flare whenever the wind kicked up. The small shack was nothing more than a burning fireball now, there would be no entering or leaving, the entire structure engulfed and aglow.

He wasn't too late. This wouldn't happen. He scanned the few locals who'd heard commotion and gathered in a safe area to watch the unlikely spectacle. The fire had nowhere to go and eventually when the floor burned through, the pier planks would fall into the Thames and extinguish themselves. It proved no real danger to anyone except someone trapped inside.

As he approached the lingering spectators, he caught the stench of burning flesh, strong enough to make his muscles clench in objection and yet he refused the ready assumption.

Scarlett was a survivor. He loved her. Deeply. And he hadn't told her as of yet. Their story would not end this way.

"What happened here?"

The aching crack of wood caused a magnificent show of sparks as one wall collapsed, the fiery slats falling to the water in a hissing cry before they went completely black.

"Fisherman's shack's on fire," a lanky man answered with obvious interest as he hadn't turned from the blaze. "Some poor fool was trapped inside. A bloke over there said he could hear painful cries before the fires silenced everything."

Painful cries?

A man or a woman? Had Scarlett been gagged? Unconscious? Left to die and consumed by the fire without a chance to fight for her life?

His gut twisted with the ugly possibilities and again he forced the suggestions away.

"Did anyone see a woman?" Ambrose called out over the gathered group, his eyes scanning the onlookers the best he could considering the hour and lack of adequate light. No one answered. He waited, his heart still thrumming a furious beat. "A woman?"

One man toward the back made fleeting eye contact before turning away and Ambrose pushed through the growing crowd to stand in front of him.

"What did you see? Tell me, damn it." He grabbed a handful of the man's sleeve in his fist. He was accustomed to commanding and receiving what he wanted, but the people of Wapping and their kind didn't begin to understand the hierarchy of the world where he lived.

"I was the first down to the pier," the stranger boasted. "The high-pitched cries were hard to listen to though they stopped quickly enough. The fire must have taken the poor soul. Some say they saw a woman brought in, but I don't know if there's truth in that tale."

Ambrose released the man's coat and turned away, rage the only emotion strong enough to extinguish the pain this accounting suggested.

He was too late. He hadn't kept her safe. He'd failed to provide her the security he'd promised.

She couldn't be gone.

He'd only begun to love her.

Fleeing the pier, he mounted Odin and turned toward the closest street, not sure exactly where he meant to go. Welles had no answers. He could beat the man senseless. He could do worse. But it would change very little. If the viscount was to be believed, he was involved with the financial end of things only.

Perhaps Martin would know what to do. How the tables had turned. Surely there was a lesson in that realization somewhere.

Scarlett was admitted to Aylesford House and shown into the front drawing room without delay. Julia was pacing near the hearth, and entering the room brought with it a rush of emotion that had nothing to do with her friend and everything with the handsome duke who called this property home.

If he was safe, if he returned, she would confess all the feelings of her heart. It would be one gift she could offer him before she took her leave and allowed him the natural path of his future. To find a wife. His duchess. To father an heir. To continue doing all the myriad ducal things he did through the day when she was elbow to elbow with London's fellow commoners.

These conclusions twisted her heart tighter and her voice came out like a sob when she finally greeted her friend.

"Julia."

"Scarlett!"

The alarm and relief that flashed over Julia's face was a balm to her soul. She would always have her friends. She would always have the other Maidens by her side no matter the clenching anguish winding through her ribs at the thought of saying goodbye to Ambrose. She was hollow from it, withered and empty, and it wasn't due to her recent ordeal. Still, it was the only logical path forward.

Julia rushed across the carpet and embraced her so tightly Scarlett mustered a slight smile. She wouldn't cry. *She didn't cry.*

"I couldn't believe you were safe until I saw it with my own eyes."

"You're here."

"Aylesford insisted. Not that I wouldn't have come, of course. I've brought you a change of clothes and other things you might need. Someone has placed them abovestairs." Julia motioned toward a nearby sofa and they both settled. She clasped Scarlett's hands as if she still needed confirmation Scarlett wasn't a figment of her imagination. "Thank heavens you're safe. I can't imagine the ordeal you've been through and Aylesford didn't spare time for the details although it's plain to see he's quite taken with you."

"I love him." Scarlett hadn't intended to spill it out so bluntly, but then Julia had noticed the condition before Scarlett had allowed herself to admit it. "I love him and I don't know what to do." She attempted a valiant sniffle to quell the well of emotion rising up like an uncontrollable tide all too ready to overwhelm and consume her.

Julia reached into her pocket and produced a handkerchief embroidered with delicate ladybirds and daisies. Scarlett dabbed at her eyes but there didn't seem an end to her tears now that they had started. "I suppose I'm not as brave of heart as I've always believed."

"When it comes to love, none of us are." Julia soothed her hand over Scarlett's. "Not even your duke. He looked ready to tear down the world piece by piece in order to find you."

"It will lead him to scandal. His reputation is so important." Another sob interrupted. "I never meant for this to happen."

"Of course not. He knows that." Julia leaned back against the cushion, genuine sympathy in her eyes. "I would suspect it took him by surprise as well. But love has a way of uniting two people whether they plan it or not. It's what you do with those feelings that makes all the difference."

"I can't be his mistress."

Julia sat up again. "Has he asked?"

"Yes." Scarlett nodded, her tears slower now and she hemmed her lower lip to keep further weeping at bay. "But it isn't what I want. After my mother . . ."

"Surely you can't equate your mother's experiences with becoming the paramour of the Duke of Aylesford. You must know he would never mistreat you. Your life would change significantly."

"But his wouldn't, would it?"

"I don't understand. I know he cares for you." Julia's brow furrowed in confusion. "Deeply."

"He would still attend the opera and the theater, make social calls and dance through fancy ballrooms. He would eventually choose a wife and produce an heir, perhaps a whole family full of children." She grew quiet under the weight of saying the truth aloud. "He would see me when he was able. He would offer me what he could. It would always be the scraps. I've lived on scraps for so long, too long." Her voice was nothing more than a thready whisper now. "I have no right to lofty dreams. I wouldn't dare imagine my life as a duchess, but a respectable future with an agreeable tradesman is not so far-fetched. There's no cost to my dignity in a decision like that."

"I daresay a town house, gowns and full jewelry box is hardly considered scraps, but I understand. You know a completely different way of life." Julia leaned closer and hugged Scarlett's shoulders in a sign of support. "No matter what station your future husband holds, you deserve someone who can love you completely. You deserve every happiness, not just stolen moments and private kisses."

"Exactly." Scarlett nodded, her composure somewhat returned. "I just never expected it to hurt this much. To make the right decision."

"Love should bring joy, not pain."

"I'm more accustomed to pain." Scarlett folded the handkerchief neatly and placed it on the cushion beside her. "If only . . ."

"There's no sense thinking those thoughts." Julia's frown echoed how much she regretted stating the words.

As difficult as it was to hear, Scarlett knew it to be true. She needed to cut off her love for Ambrose with the efficiency of a guillotine's blade. She would say her goodbye and leave him to the life he was born to live. They'd shared tender moments, glorious intimacy and passion hotter than the flames in the hearth, but it was never meant to be and she'd exemplify every foolish female dream of whimsy to pretend their relationship would win out.

Julia clasped her hands, seemingly searching for the choicest words. "It would be a high expectation of any man to forsake everything he's been taught since the time he could comprehend the magnitude of his responsibility. I don't mean to imply you're not worth the cost. Your love merits any sacrifice. And let's not forget it wouldn't only be what he sacrificed in the face of society, but how they would treat you as well, Scarlett. Highborn ladies would give you the cut direct and make you the fodder of all their ugly gossip. If he came to resent that or if you simply could not abide the malicious whispers, it would eventually destroy your relationship."

"Ambrose despises gossip." She knew it to be true. "And I'm definitely not duchess material."

"You'd be a fine duchess." Julia's admiration shone through the words. "In fact, considering the way he looks at you with unabashed adoration in his eyes, I wouldn't be surprised if Aylesford didn't already consider it."

"We're twisting things around in an attempt to soften the blow, but please don't say things without reason just to make me feel better."

"I would do no such thing." Julia shook her head in denial. "I believe in matters of the heart everything is within reason. Lest we forget he's a duke and a fine one at that. He can do whatever he bloody likes and no one has the right to question him aside from the Prince Regent. I doubt England's self-consumed ruler is interested in your love affair."

"Aylesford never spoke of love."

"He's out combing the streets to find you," Julia answered. "That's a declaration in itself."

"No, that's duty." She gave a sad little nod. "Responsibility."

This conclusion put a finality to their discussion and they sat that way in silence a good long while. At some point a house-keeper entered and arranged a tea service on a nearby table, but neither Scarlett nor Julia moved to partake of it. The fire hissed and popped in wait. Time continued despite Scarlett's heart had stalled in her chest.

And then at last the front door swung open and with a wild wind that rustled the cards and invitations on the foyer sideboard, Ambrose entered, his voice a booming echo in the hall.

"Jamison! Is she here? Has Scarlett returned?"

He appeared in the doorframe, his hair tousled and clothing disheveled. Julia gasped as she rose from the seat and hurried across the room. Scarlett could only stare at him wide-eyed and watch as Julia rushed past Ambrose, granting them privacy without question. This conclusion finally snapped her into motion and she practically leapt from the cushions, across the room and into his arms.

"I feared—" She hadn't a chance to finish that sentence, his lips descending upon hers with unerring accuracy, neither one of them able to disregard the undeniable pull between them. It had always been there. It always would be.

His hold grew possessive and his kiss demanding, and she lost herself in the feeling. Too soon it would become a memory. Too soon she would struggle to remember the scent of his shaving lotion, the feel of his whiskers abrading her cheek, and the growly hum and vibration as he angled his head and began their kiss anew.

She didn't know how long they clung to each other. The household staff was clever enough not to interrupt. The ornate gilt clock on the mantelpiece was considerate not to chime. And when at last they broke apart, sharing each other's breath in an affirmation of life and love, she hesitated in pulling from his embrace.

But to wait any longer would make it all the harder. She had to find the right words and put everything back into place to restore the life he was meant to lead before she'd interrupted. Lord, but he was handsome. Most especially when the fierce, possessive look in his eyes made her heart turn over in her chest.

"I love you, Scarlett."

His declaration wasn't what she'd expected and she lost the words she meant to share. Now her heart thundered as if it was trying to break free of her chest, but steadfast reality was still ever present to shred the very same organ to ribbons.

CHAPTER 28

"Thank God you're safe. You're here." He drew a deep breath and attempted to find calm as he smoothed his palms up and down her arms. He heaved another breath composed of relief and gratitude. Scarlett stood before him seemingly unharmed. She hadn't perished in the fire or met with any untoward fate. She was here for him to cherish and love for the rest of their days. "I can't bear the thought of my duchess in danger."

"I can't be your duchess." The words were said softly. "I can't be what you require in a wife."

"I require your love and loyalty only." The liberation of all they'd experienced and the good fortune of the outcome coursed swiftly through his veins. He couldn't comprehend the gravity of her words. She loved him. Her eyes didn't lie. He knew that. She was in shock, nothing more.

"You have my love and loyalty already." She darted her gaze to his and then away again. "If only it were that easily done."

"It is." He smiled, wanting to reassure every hesitation in her heart. "You're fighting against the very thing you want most."

"I can't be your duchess." She shook her head vigorously. "What of your family?"

"It's just Martin and I," he quickly informed her.

"What of your brother's future?"

"What of it? Nothing you could ever do would tarnish the reputation to which he works so diligently to accomplish himself."

"After everything we've been through and experienced, tonight especially, you're just thinking with your heart." She stared at him, her eyes imploring him to listen.

And he was listening. To that point, nothing she said mattered at all if she meant to dissuade him. "Thinking with my heart is exactly what I should be doing." He brought his hand to the right side of his chest. His heart beat steadily with relief and love. *Thank God she was safe.*

"I still can't be your duchess, Ambrose." The sadness in her words pained him.

"Can't or won't?" Impatience that she would fight against what was always meant to be rankled him.

"Can't." She shrugged inelegantly, her expression a mixture of changing emotion. "I don't know how."

"You're a Maiden of Mayhem. You can conquer whatever you perceive as an obstacle." He reached for her but she stepped beyond his grasp. "You are the strongest, most resilient woman I've ever met."

"So, you see no problem with me continuing to aid the other Maidens in our dedication to right wrongs within London?"

Everything depended on his answer and the likelihood it would lead her further from an acceptance of his proposal, and yet he could never lie to her. "No. Once we are married that would come to an end. Honestly, after today, I didn't think you'd wish to be involved any longer. I know the kinship you've formed with the other women is important to you and that would not change, but your safety overrides any cause for vigilance. I can fight in Parliament for stronger protection in every working class after what has come to light. I can propose stronger enforcement of the laws that currently govern and support whatever concerns you may have. I'd already set several plans into action before this evening's events."

"And what of the many who ignore the law to fit their purpose or manipulate their position, as Felix did at Bow Street and Welles did as a peer?"

"While I can't control human nature or the choices individuals make, I can challenge any or all of the consequences and punishments from my governing seat in the House of Lords." He released a long-held breath. "My man of business has worked on a multiple of proposals. Change will come. Good work will be done."

She nodded and turned. "I don't know."

"I do." His words applied to all subjects, still she remained silent. He knew better than to persist. Something inside told him it would not yield the one word he desired to hear most of all and could only drive her further away if he continued to press her. "A room has already been prepared for you. Food and a hot bath await."

"Thank you."

She made to move around him to go out into the hall and he gently pulled her into his arms. "I almost lost you, Scarlett. I cannot bear the thought of any further danger befalling you. Look into my eyes."

She pulled back slightly and canted her head so she could see him clearly.

"Tell me what you're feeling."

"It's not about feeling. It's about thinking."

He wanted to shake her shoulders, to cause her to see how the reckless pursuit of crime could only lead her to further injury or worse. What would become of her if she encountered men intent on murder? What if she carried their babe? "I've been thinking my entire life, locked away performing my duties and caring for others, and now I'm ready to feel."

He pulled her against his chest and held her another minute, and then he loosened his hold and allowed her to leave. He couldn't force her to see reason. Nor could he force her to love him enough. It was her decision to make.

* * *

For the second time in a handful of days Scarlett sank into a decadent tub of scented hot water and rested her head against the rim, her eyes closed and muscles exhausted. What was she thinking? Becoming a duchess? Moving in polite society among the very same people who perpetuated poverty among her friends, who looked down their noses at anyone beneath their station?

And yet Ambrose had never viewed her in that regard. He certainly wasn't one for partaking of society's rigorous social schedule. And too, he loved her. He knew her, didn't judge her and accepted her despite her humble life and unconventional participation with the Maidens.

The Maidens. How would she explain that she'd gone ahead and done the very thing she'd said she'd never do? She'd fallen in love.

But no. Love wasn't a crime. They'd never vowed an alliance against falling in love. Julia has assured her, encouraged her, actually. And Phoebe and Diana would be equally as happy that Scarlett had found someone to share her life.

So, then, what was it? Why couldn't she accept his proposal? He loved her. She loved him with a strength and wealth of emotion she'd never experienced before. He spoke truthfully. She stood in her own way. Was she afraid of happiness? Security? Fearful to possess such a fragile and fleeting prize? She'd never before shown timidity or reservation. She fought against men twice her size and weight and ran headlong into danger to protect strangers. What was this fear to protect her own heart?

She sank deeper into the hot water with a forlorn sigh. For so long, everywhere she looked was chaos and confusion, most especially within her. Life seemed more complicated as each day passed. Could it be she didn't recognize the security of love now that she'd finally found it? Or more so the new role she would fill? Becoming a duchess when one possessed such commonplace beginnings would incite fear in anyone, wouldn't it?

And there it was, a truth so powerful she hadn't been able to confess it to Julia earlier. Only one thought invoked a greater emotion than her hesitancy to step into such fine slippers and that was to turn away from the love Ambrose offered and how she loved him in return.

Perhaps it was as he'd said, as simple as feeling, to cast away uncertainty and instead trust in love. They'd face the future together.

With that undeniable certainty all indecision melted away.

Ambrose heard Martin enter the hall before he had a chance to finish his brandy. Scarlett's brush with death and safe return still thrummed in his veins, yet until she accepted his proposal and he knew with certainty they'd share the rest of their days together he couldn't relax.

"All is as it should be here?" Martin joined him near the sideboard and helped himself to the liquor on the tray.

"Almost." Ambrose turned and paced to the hearth.

"Well, I bring news that should set your mind at ease." Martin dropped into a nearby chair and took a long sip from his glass. "Welles has fled London. Whatever you might have said to him, fear of prosecution, public humiliation or personal ruin, seems to have instigated his departure. Apparently, he was keeping company with a slip of a girl named Linie."

"Linie?" This snagged Ambrose's attention. "Scarlett's seamstress?"

"Yes, although I knew her as Daisy."

"Your friend from the brothel." Ambrose shook his head slowly as more pieces fell into place.

"More the fool am I." Martin cleared his throat. "Apparently, she worked from the inside to help persuade the girls to accept the opportunity offered to them by Welles. He masqueraded as Clive and wore the fancy ring all the girls went agog about. Although he wasn't the only one."

"Felix Howell, Bow Street operative."

"Exactly." Martin set his glass down. "Together Madam Violet, who was more than happy to look away for the right monetary compensation, and both Howell and Welles had established a tidy sex trade operation, convincing the working girls they could be high-paid mistresses kept in fancy town houses with all the trimmings. Once they agreed, they were quickly transported to places unfamiliar, disconnected from friends or family who could offer help and aid in their rescue. From then on they became trapped, and I suppose virtually served as sex slaves."

Ambrose shook his head, the unbelievable reality a disgrace to London and all the disgraceful participants. "What of Madam Violet now?"

"She's a slippery one. She's since cleaned house and to all those who might question her actions, she appears to be running a legitimate brothel, if you don't mind the irony of that statement. It would be near impossible to bring any substantial charges against her."

"And Howell?"

"Disappeared. He hasn't been heard from either, although some say he was last seen near the pier entering the fisherman's shack that burned into ashes."

"That leaves only one matter left incomplete." Ambrose set his glass down and folded his hands behind his back.

"Am I still in trouble?" Martin stood, his face a mask of skepticism.

"Not at all." Ambrose would have chuckled if his mind and heart didn't still labor over the woman installed in the guest room above.

"Scarlett." Martin stated the obvious.

"She won't have me."

"What?"

The two brothers stared at each other before Martin prodded for more.

"What will you do?"

Ambrose was quick to answer. "Whatever it takes."

It was much later when Ambrose knocked on the door to the chamber where Scarlett stayed. He didn't intend to bother her and thought perhaps she might seek him out, but when one hour had passed and then another, he knew he'd never sleep, never breathe easy again until he learned what she was thinking.

She answered his knock almost immediately and opened the door. He stepped over the threshold and fought against his immediate desire to pull her into his embrace.

"I wanted to say good night." He skimmed his gaze over her from head to toe. Dressed in a silky robe with only her small pink toes peeking out, she appeared a vision from his most recent daydream.

"I was about to seek you out for the same reason." She smiled and a wealth of warmth flooded his chest.

"I'm thankful you are safe." He made his way into the chamber and leaned one shoulder on the post of the large bed in the center.

"As I feel about you."

She approached him and he struggled not to pull her forward for a kiss, at war with better sense that told him not to pressure her further.

"I love you, Ambrose." She stopped within a pace of him. "But I won't impede your future."

"That will only happen if you force me to go forward without you." He shook his head and frowned. "I won't be able to hold a thought for wondering how I might have caused you not to leave."

"What will people say if you marry me, a commoner?" She untied the ribbons at her waist and her robe fell open. A sheer chemise was all that covered her skin now.

"It doesn't matter. People will always talk, whether it's about the somewhat reclusive duke who found true love in the most unlikely place or some more interesting scandal. Through history there are other peers, men and women who have put the matter of their heart first and who have chosen to do something out of character, and I fancy myself part of an elite group now because I understand the force of true love." He might have stopped there but he thought better to add a little levity into their conversation. "Besides, I'm Aylesford, a duke. I can do whatever I like in regard to my future and Scarlett, you have my heart completely."

Her eyes flashed to his, a bright streak of silver gray as they caught the candlelight beside the bed. Then she slipped into the shelter of his arms and raised her chin so their mouths nearly met.

"I love you, Ambrose."

"And I, you." His lips hovered over hers and their every breath mingled. "Now let's stop this tedious conversation. Will you marry me?"

His heart counted out an interminable beat, waiting, waiting for the one word he yearned to hear. Instead she brought their mouths together in a kiss that gave him her heart, full of joy and wonder. When they broke apart the slightest, she whispered against his lips.

"Yes, my love, I will be your wife and duchess."

Every second had been worth the wait and a burst of intense relief spread through his body like fireworks in the night sky, brilliant and jubilant.

Scarlett worked hard to stifle the smile playing at her lips as she entered Wycombe and Company the next morning. The Maidens had assembled at her request. She had news to share and while a new and unexpected nervousness produced a slight feeling of apprehension, her mind was at peace. She was confident her friends would respect her decision.

Excited greetings met her entrance and once the usual conversation was settled and the tea served, the four friends sat around the table, all eyes pinned to Scarlett as she was the one to ask for the meeting.

"As you already know, I've been through an ordeal and now"—she released a deep breath, the words on her tongue as unexpected as all recent events—"I'm to be a duchess."

"Oh, Scarlett." Julia was the first to react. "We all hoped so."

"We couldn't be happier for you." Phoebe beamed across the table.

"You'll make a fierce duchess." Diana's voice held a note of admiration. "I honestly didn't know if Aylesford would dare take on the challenge."

This remark evoked a round of laughter before Scarlett spoke again.

"It makes sense, you know." Her expression grew serious. "I can influence reform and lead by example. Ambrose values my opinions."

"He values your love," Diana added.

"He values *you*," Julia said just as quickly.

Scarlett grinned, her friends' reactions heartwarming and reassuring although she still had more to tell them. "I never believed I could feel this way, most especially about a lord, but I've learned so much through this experience, about myself and my capabilities."

Phoebe reached across the table and clasped Scarlett's hand. "We're thrilled for you. You deserve to be loved completely."

"I do. You're right. Although . . ." Scarlett looked at each of her friends, emotion welling within her. "It makes leaving our league no less difficult."

"We understand. I guessed as much." Julia nodded, the action matched by Phoebe and Diana. "But know that you're welcome here anytime."

"Thank you. This isn't the last you'll see of me." Scarlett rose from the table and hugged each of her friends. "I've no doubt you'll find a replacement. There are other audacious women out there even if they don't realize their own spirit yet."

"Future and fellow comrades with equal fortitude and a desire to make London a better place," Phoebe added.

"Exactly," Scarlett agreed. "I'm happy, ladies. Nothing ever felt this right before."

"Love changes things." Diana came to stand at her side. Phoebe and Julia followed.

"That's true for the most part but while I may become a duchess soon, I'll always be a Maiden of Mayhem at heart."

Two months later
July 10, 1817
House of Lords, Westminster

Aylesford took the floor in the House of Lords and waited for his fellow noblemen to yield the quiet. He was a respected speaker and contributed frequently to the laws and debates that kept Parliament a lively forum for initiative and reform. Unfortunately, the Disorderly Houses Act of 1751, which governed against brothels and other types of public nuisances, was an antiquated statute. He wondered how open-mindedly and progressively fellow peers would react to his suggestion the statute be revisited and updated. Surely the people of England were ripe for petitioning for change.

Nevertheless, the widespread sex trade provided entertainment for men of all social statuses, many who sat in Parliament along with him. Ambrose eyed Lord Calbert across the aisle, who shamelessly boasted of frequent erotic experiences outside his marriage. Calbert was middle-aged, wedded to an amiable noblewoman of good reputation who'd gifted him with a strong son and young daughter, and yet the gentleman chose to spend his money and time on women of easy virtue.

Much to London's dishonor, prostitution served as an economic necessity for these poor women, thereby bawdy houses were tolerated and excused more often than not, and often overlooked by Bow Street since the runners frequented the same establishments neighborhoods wanted ridden. With the House of Lords controlling the smaller constituencies and rotten boroughs where elected members were often chosen through corrupt practices of nepotism and coercion, the general population lost their voice for reform. It made what Scarlett and the other Maidens of Mayhem fought for all that more precious. That the four women would band together and attempt to change greater society when they engaged a complacent mass of nearly one and one half million Londoners, proved their altruism. Scarlett and her friends were remarkable and Aylesford remained in awe of her tenacious pursuit, in awe of her, in more ways than he could ever label. Still, he was thankful Scarlett had decided to leave the Maidens and help him initiate reform. She was the impetus toward so many subjects he had yet to learn about fully.

Like now standing on the floor before the peers with all this knowledge and emotion encompassing his ideas and effort. No doubt the fellow members of Parliament would assume he'd adopted religion, but he wouldn't let their ridicule or naysaying deter him. London needed to do better. England too. And he was primed to challenge the traditional and instigate change with Scarlett by his side.

That same day
July 10, 1817
Beneath Westminster Bridge

It was nearly daybreak and the air crackled with expectation. Some mornings began that way, with a glorious sunrise and a certain hum that could be anticipation or, better yet, opportunity. It was there. An unexplained energy, like a friction of life and good fortune colliding and beckoning anyone intuitive enough to answer the call.

Willie sensed it as soon as he opened his eyes under the paper-thin blanket he used for a covering beneath the culvert at the base of the London Bridge. He chased the rare feeling along the shoreline as he looked out at the dingy brown tide, the Thames its usual surly self, rank with the stench of rotten salmon and human waste overlaid with the fragrance of precious imports, sandalwood, hemp, ginger and tea. And he waited, waited for the river to call him to the right place, the tiny patch of sand and pebbles that would yield something special today.

When he'd followed the shore a length and reached his purpose, he glanced first to the water, knee-deep in the tide, his lips puckered in a quiet whistle to help tamp down his anticipation. The

surface was crammed side to side with tilt boats and square rig-
gers, their flags awave in the fluky winds strongest where he stood.

Yes, this was the right place. He didn't mind the smell of the
water or the slimy grime that coated his bare feet. He depended
on the treasures the river regurgitated to provide him and his sister with coin. Ever since his sister lost her job at the brothel, meals
had become scarce. Food was lean. But something told him today opportunity would visit. The air fairly crackled with promise and while he kept his eyes on the waves, he pushed his bare
feet through the mud in search of a valuable find. Something better than a brass button or broken pearl earbob. Not that either of
those wouldn't fetch a fine price, but today would be different. He
knew it as surely as he knew his own name.

He kept walking, only glancing up from his shadowy search
occasionally to appreciate the gift above, the sun rising to light
the morning sky and glitter across the waves in a glistening show
of encouragement. Someday he would have his own boat and sail
down the Thames. Someday he wouldn't have to worry about filling his belly or sleeping on the damp dirt beneath the bridge. He
was midway through these thoughts and almost as far downstream
as the fishing pier when his right foot settled upon something
small, hard and smooth.

An unexpected jolt of excitement gripped him. It could be any
number of worthless items. A rock, bit of shell or worn piece of
glass. Yet something told him to reach down quickly, before the
next wave broke against his shins and the undercurrent stole the
silt beneath his feet.

With the graceful sluice of a lightning strike he reached below
the waterline. His foot held the tiny treasure in place, his toes
curled tightly. With the agility of an eel sliding through shards of
broken glass, he dug beneath his foot and grasped the object. A
pulse of victory and hope undulated through him as his fingers
closed around the newfound item. It was hard, smooth and round,
just as he'd perceived. A hole ran through its center. His heart beat
harder. He knew with surety before he even opened his palm,

before he clenched his fingers tight around the prize, and he ran for the shore.

He looked left and right to secure no one watched and then he opened his small palm, shielding his fingers protectively. There a gold ring with a large ruby, encircled with glittering diamonds as brilliant as the reflection of sunlight on water, winked back at him. The price it would fetch was too large for Willie's imagination to conjure, but indeed his future was bright.

ACKNOWLEDGMENTS

My sincerest thanks to Esi Sogah, my brilliant and talented editor, who seamlessly combines incomparable knowledge and insight with unending encouragement and support. You will always have my gratitude. Thank you!

My deepest appreciation to the entire Kensington team, who incorporate skill, dedication and heart into everything they do. Your efforts bring my story to the hands of readers and I can never thank you enough.

And to all romance readers, thank you for keeping hope alive, sharing positivity and believing in happily ever afters.

Ready to make more mayhem?
Check out this sneak peek from the next installment
of the Maidens of Mayhem series
THE LADY LOVES DANGER
coming soon
from Anabelle Bryant
and
Zebra Books

Sebastian St. Allen eased into the damp corner until his shoulders brushed the soot-dusted bricks of the dilapidated tenement at his back. The night air was still, pungent with the familiar stink of raw sewerage and soiled dreams as if it too had given up hope. This was Seven Dials and any man with a shred of common sense wouldn't be found lurking in the streets after dark. An unfortunate soul could lose his life in a matter of minutes and no one would hear his desperate plea for mercy. Still, Sebastian remained, lost to the shadows in wait of a thief.

Not any thief, mind you. Not a taker of silks or gin. Nor contraband tobacco. This crime was one of reprehensible depravity. And now after weeks of following a whisper of information that yielded little more than stains to his fine leather boots, he waited again. The location and sketchy details that led him to this nameless roadway in the bowels of London came through an associate and while it had yet to prove its worth, Sebastian wasn't deterred. He'd nowhere in particular to spend his evening and he'd rather exhaust the possibility of interrupting the horrific exchange than second-guess his decision not to.

Pressing a palm to his waistband, he adjusted his pistol, additional reassurance to the blade he carried in each boot. He was an excellent shot and equally lethal with a knife, both skills learned as a means of survival, for while he now resided in a comfortable town house in a better part of London, that wasn't always his situation.

Hours crawled by and he shifted his stance, his steady focus keen to the squat tenement across the street. His mind dared him to exhume old memories and unpleasant thoughts best left buried in the abyss of the past. Surveillance forced a man to probe his own mind as each minute ticked by, a pitfall of too much solitude and not enough distraction.

Time dragged on until a barely discernible movement snared his attention and brought his focus to a recess of the building across the way. It was nothing more than a slant of gray against black but he sensed the action before he perceived the figure who'd caused it, a slight form in a long cloak with the hood drawn to conceal the face. *A woman*.

With unexpected convenience, the cloud cover dispersed and the waxing moon offered a murky shaft of light. Even with ample distance interrupting the dark thoroughfare, he knew the abilities and limitations of the physical body, gestures of human nature, and above all else, subtle yet graceful distinctions of the female form. Was this woman here to purchase what the thief brought to sell? It could only be. Not another soul haunted the streets. He muttered a black curse, unable to comprehend the abhorrent evil that drove a person to commit heinous crimes. He'd never accept desperation as a defense.

The approaching clop of horse hooves from the opposite direction divided his attention. Another beat and he spied the vehicle. Weeks of empty observation and wasted time finally crystalized into possibility. The nondescript carriage slowed at the curb and Sebastian angled his body to gain a better view of what he anticipated to be a swift transaction of contents for payment. The exchange must begin before he interfered. The slightest misstep would spark the thief into flight.

Being on foot, Sebastian couldn't follow the shabby conveyance far, but should someone emerge from the tenement and step forward to receive the goods, he'd be able to perpetrate a rescue, investigate further and possibly uncover the miscreants involved. He wasn't above pummeling men to gain the information he sought and he'd question any woman until she supplied the names needed.

The door of the carriage cracked open to reveal a struggle within the interior. With innate stealth, Sebastian moved undetected, at one with the black cast of the eaves above him. He waited, daring only to breathe. To make the slightest sound before the exchange unfolded held the potential to ruin everything. The silence grew louder. He shook off the unwelcome feeling of urgency and slipped his hand beneath his greatcoat to rest atop his pistol, all attention on the carriage door. From the corner of his eye, a blur of motion dissected his concentration for the second time. The cloaked woman stepped forward and he willed her to remain still. She could only mean to receive what was in that carriage and yet he needed to be sure of the circumstances before he acted.

The door widened fully now, its soft rap a lonely echo amid the eerie quiet. The wiry driver stepped down and accepted a writhing bundle, no bigger than a sack of flour. Sebastian's heart seized tight but he forced an exhale to jolt it back into rhythm, the suppressed emotion potent fuel for his anger. Fury shot a fiery rush through every muscle and vein.

"Oliver."

The woman's voice destroyed the silence with resounding alarm.

Havoc ensured right after.

With spry reflexes, the trafficker pivoted, tossed the bundle within the carriage and climbed the seat to slap the reins. Sebastian tore down the street in a futile race to catch the conveyance, the agony of what he'd lost almost too much to bear though rage flamed anew as he turned and started toward the cloaked stranger, motionless and alone on the pavement. Weeks of vigilant observation were ruined by her careless call and now she'd have hell to pay for it.

Delilah Ashbrook stood at the curb immobile, her thundering pulse a threat to coherent reason. Had she just located Oliver and lost him in the same moment? Had she destroyed her only chance at finding him? Fear took hold and paralyzed her reaction for the length of several heartbeats, but she rejected the suggestion of failure. She needed to be strong.

Blinking hard to summon fortitude, she opened her eyes and peered into the night. Her pulse hitched another notch. The broad stranger who'd emerged from nowhere, invisible one minute and in pursuit of the carriage the next, had now turned his attention on her. She couldn't be caught.

Spinning on her heels, she aimed for the darkest alley, heedless of the danger ahead as she fled the danger behind. He gained ground easily, the resounding echo of his boots as they struck the slick stones not unlike the hectic beat of her heart. What did he want with her? Had he watched the carriage in wait of purchasing the child within? What kind of man stole children? Trafficked them to others to be used for illicit purpose? Her stomach rebelled and she wrapped an arm around her middle sickened by anyone who'd perpetuate such an unforgivable crime. A cramp gripped her side. She wasn't accustomed to running for very long. *Running at all.* Never mind she wore layers of skirts and a heavy cloak. She dragged in a painful breath. Cursed corset. She couldn't get air into her lungs fast enough. Her throat burned but she pushed on.

The alley she'd chosen was narrow, the space between the brick-lined walls barely twice the width of her shoulders. Perhaps the stranger wouldn't fit. He appeared a hulking presence, tall and threatening, as he loomed closer. She reached the end and stalled, taking the next turn at a slower pace, the cramp insistent now. This passage widened and promised multiple escape routes. She could still hear his approach despite her breathing was loud in her ears. He'd managed to keep her in sight though she'd done her best to cling to the shadows, pivot between streets and dart around corners.

In a panic she turned left and aimed at another dim alcove. How long would the stranger pursue her? What did he want? A barking dog sounded an ominous alarm as she passed and it wasn't until she reached the end that she realized her mistake. Here another threatening form emerged from the darkness. A vagrant whose face was not nearly as discernible as his odor, though she perceived enough to know he meant her no kindness. Gripping the small dagger kept in her pocket, she pulled it out and clasped it with both hands in front of her. The short blade glinted in the moonlight as she retreated with a tentative step, unsure of what he would do but refusing to turn and allow him an advantage. Still, it was all for naught. He snatched the edge of her cloak, reeled her in and belted his arm around her ribs to render her helpless. The stench of his clothing and foul breath caused an involuntary retch.

"It's my lucky night." His left hand covered her breast and squeezed while his right remained locked around her middle. "And now it's your lucky night too."

Terror caused her mind to blank. She still held the dagger but it was useless in her body's position and a scream would be lost to the night. She struggled to think calmly, to react before he violated her further. He jerked backward, reversed their positions and trapped her body against the wall, crushing her to the grease-covered bricks with suffocating pressure as his legs bracketed hers. Desperation tied a knot in her stomach and she dropped the knife lest she impale herself. She was powerless but she wouldn't succumb. She needed to survive for Oliver's sake. She was the only chance he had.

The vagrant shifted his weight and the pressure of his jagged fingernails bit through her sleeve as he yanked her sideways to push up her skirts. She twisted in vain and he scoffed low and ugly against her neck. With horror she realized he'd released her breast to work at the button on his breeches. With immediate rebellion, she fought against the arm that held her captive.

And then, in the next instant, she was free.

The vertiginous force in which she was released left her breathless and disoriented. She steadied herself, one palm flattened on the raw brick biting into her palm before her senses discerned the dull thud of fist meeting flesh.

It was over before she comprehended it completely. The forbidding stranger who'd pursued her through Seven Dials now rescued her instead. The brim of his cap masked his face in darkness though the moon at his back lent his broad shoulders a burnished glow. She darted her eyes to the crumpled form on the cobbles and backed up farther before she spoke.

"Thank you." The words seemed inadequate. Her pulse still sprinted an erratic pace and her hands trembled.

"I am, if nothing else, an excellent rat catcher." His voice emerged from the shadows, the words spoken matter-of-factly to reveal little as to whether he was friend or enemy. "Are you unharmed?"

"Yes." She breathed deeply as she laced her fingers together in an attempt to calm. "You saved me."

"Momentarily."

His voice was smooth. Refined. She dared believe she had nothing to fear. And yet when he didn't continue, ill-ease consumed her. The way he waited, fierce and uncompromising, did nothing to reassure she hadn't traded one type of peril for another. She took a moment to straighten her bodice, tug at her skirts and retrieve her fallen dagger.

Still wary, she stood with the knife in hand and he coughed abruptly.

"Are you going to slice an apple?" He moved closer and a shaft of light illuminated his profile. His features looked as hard as his rigid stance. What she could see of his expression remained intense and inscrutable.

"It's protection."

He leaned down and withdrew a long slender blade from his right boot. "This is protection. That is an eating utensil."

She didn't reply, her eyes glued to his knife in wait of what he would do next. Had he saved her from the vagrant's assault so he might perpetrate his own debauchery? But no, he replaced the knife and straightened. He didn't move otherwise and his position held her captive.

"I've waited weeks for that exchange with the carriage and you ruined it with one careless word." His voice, low and lethal, sparked warning across her skin like static electricity.

"I—" She couldn't explain the true reason she was here in Seven Dials, courting her own death while attempting to save Oliver's life. But perhaps if she understood why he'd come to await the carriage, if she discovered the information he possessed, it would assist in her search. Could it be he wasn't the type of man she initially perceived? She could only distinguish his outline in the intermittent light, but while his dark clothing might cause him to blend seamlessly into the night, there was no denying his presence. He was a man of power. He likely knew influential people. She'd grasp onto any lingering hope if it assisted in Oliver's return.

She pocketed her knife and waited. He'd positioned himself in a way that disallowed her escape and she had little choice but to hear what he had to say.

His gaze coasted over her from the top of her hood to the tips of her boots and it was as if he held her motionless with nothing more than the command of his existence. A tremor that had nothing to do with the chill night air coursed through her.

But he was just a man.

A man who had saved her from an abhorrent attacker.

Dare she believe he meant her no harm? She struggled to understand his indecipherable expression.

"I owe you my thanks, Mr. . . ." She hesitated, unsure how to proceed.

"St. Allen."

"Yes." She breathed deeply. "Thank you, Mr. St.—"

"Just St. Allen."

"All right." She took a small step closer.

"And you owe me more than gratitude." He delivered this information with some semblance of a grin as his teeth flashed white in the darkness. "I saved you so that I can interrogate you."

"Interrogate me?" Her voice rushed out in objection.

"Exactly." He waved his hand as if the gesture explained everything he hadn't.

Connect with Us

Visit us online at
KensingtonBooks.com
to read more from your favorite authors, see books
by series, view reading group guides, and more.

for sneak peeks, chances to win books and prize packs,
and to share your thoughts with other readers.

facebook.com/kensingtonpublishing
twitter.com/kensingtonbooks

Tell us what you think!

To share your thoughts, submit a review,
or sign up for our eNewsletters, please visit:
KensingtonBooks.com/TellUs.